I'M DYING HERE

Damien Broderick met up with Rory Barnes (who'd learned to walk and talk in a tribal mud hut in Northern Rhodesia) more than 40 years ago at Australia's Monash University. They shared various student houses with a motley crew of would-be writers who did what students did in the '60s: got pissed, screwed around, smoked some pot, engaged in a small amount of semi-violent protest and wrote a lot of essays. Broderick sold some stories and books and eventually got a PhD, Barnes did some teaching then wandered around Southeast Asia and the Middle East. Since 1983, they have co-authored five novels. Barnes lives with his wife Annie and two sons in Adelaide, South Australia. Broderick shares several houses with his American wife Barbara in Melbourne, Victoria, and San Antonio and Lockhart, Texas. They are both far more law-abiding than their raffish hero, to their regret.

I'M DYING HERE

A Comedy of Bad Manners

Damien Broderick
and Rory Barnes

POINTBLANK

Set in Bembo

POINT*BLANK* is an imprint of Wildside Press
www.pointblankpress.com
www.wildsidepress.com

Series editor JT Lindroos

For more information contact Wildside Press

ISBN 0-8095-7316-4

To Pam Sargent and George Zebrowski —D.B.
and to Wainwright's ghost —R.B.

I was running a nice little earner called *Feng Shui Solutions* when my past caught up with me. I'd hung my shingle on an ornate free-standing Victorian mortgage, not mine, in Parkville—close enough to the university for academic respectability and not so close to the zoo that the lion stink annoyed the clients. The cast iron door knocker knocked. I wasn't expecting a client so I'd left off my Knights of Bushido kimono, but I was fucked if I was going to climb out of my jeans just to open the door.

"Mr. Purdue?"

My caller had seen better days, but she'd kept herself trim. I suspected twice weekly workouts at the gym, which is as much as I can be bothered with myself these days, and twice-yearly dry-outs at the fat farm.

"At your service."

"Sharon Lesser. I have an appointment for eight thirty?"

I blinked. Something troubled me but I couldn't put my finger on it. Then again I've had a few blows to the head in my time. "I believe that's for tomorrow." One of the drawbacks of doing your own secretarial. "But come in, Mrs. Lesser."

"Call me Share. No, definitely this evening, yesterday was my bridge night and that's been Thursday for two years."

I helped her off with her fur. It was real, minimal entry wound, no exit. I hung the coat myself. The upside of doing such menial tasks is no nosy secretary, no secretarial wages either. We went into the Seminar Room, and I was pleased to see that Sharon Lesser was not intimidated by my bulk. Some women are. I don't know, some of them say they like a bit of brawn to go with the deeply sensitive gaze and readiness to listen but plenty shy away.

A decade and a half earlier I'd have been dismissed with a curt glance: the angular Vegan-diet poet type that only rangy Vegan-diet women and cooing butterballs favor. Eighteen months in a boutique prison outside Seattle had made a man of me: ten hours daily of weights work and my heaped handful of vitamins. Anyone can get heroin and blow in jail, it's the common currency, but steroids and HGH are at a premium. It made me shudder, sometimes, recalling what I'd had to pay for my supply. But beefy crims are less choosy than good looking women. Supply never outstripped demand. After a year I was able to set my own terms, and when they offered me parole for the final six months I carefully beat the shit out of my original supplier and remained where I wanted to be, full gym facilities and three good fattening meals a day, without the fat.

Share avoided the jumbo House of Orient beanbags, settled herself into the big Franco Cozzo *faux* leather armchair and regarded me with satisfaction, I was what she wanted. My clients are gullible fuckwits, obviously, but Vinnie would have looked this one over and muttered from the corner of his toothless mouth, "Well-stocked hope chest her Mum left her." But then Vinnie's a seventy five year old alky, and I have no idea what he's talking about most of the time.

"I've been reading in *New Idea* about this *feng shui*," she said.

I raised one hand, smiled with capped teeth. "That's *fong shway*, Share."

She wasn't flustered. "Oh, is that how you say it?"

She crossed her legs. Share was on the wrong side of forty and the gym was battling the crème caramels, but I appreciated the result. Something noisy happened in the street, like a pallet of bricks being dropped from the second floor. Share leaned forward and started to say something else when the front door, visible through the arch of the Seminar Room, slowly opened. The blood drained from my face, seeking refuge from terrible things. The door was triply-dead bolted with a fail-safed electronic controller, fitted into a sturdy frame. Nobody else had the key code.

The door bent open in the middle, like a soufflé folding down with a sigh when you open the oven too soon. I grabbed Sharon Lesser and shoved her under the big desk at the far end of the Seminar Room. She squealed and then I jumped across the room looking this way and that. I knew there wasn't a gun conveniently in the sideboard, I'm not totally stupid, it was the phone I was after. Once upon a time phones stayed where they were, anchored to the wall. The door stopped buckling, caught on the bolts at top and bottom. I could see one corner of the shiny steel bullbar of a Mack truck peeking around the edge. I found my cellphone, stabbed three letters. It started ringing. I slammed the phone against my ear.

"Jesus, what? I'm busy."

"It's Purdue, you fuckwit," I yelled. "What bullshit is this?"

"For Christ's sake, are you still *in* there? Get the fuck out right now, Purdue."

"Bugger off, Mauricio, it's only Thursday you cretin, I've got a customer with me. Client."

"Friday, Purdue. I got carefully laid plans, mate. Ready or not." Mauricio gunned the Mack's motor, the door screeched and buckled some more. The door would hold, I was sure of that. The steel frame would hold too. But the frame was set into bricks and mortar—bricks and mortar from the century before last.

"You'll wake the neighbors," I yelled into the phone.

"Do something!" Share screamed from under the desk.

A section of plaster above the door broke away from the wall and crashed into the room. The dust billowed up like farm soil in the Big El Nino Drought. Bricks cascaded down on either side of the frame. The ceiling was starting to go.

Thank Christ for the inner-city outhouse!

In the century before last, when the bricks and mortar now rapidly disintegrating around us were troweled expertly into place by skilled artisans, even the elegant homes of the colony's robber barons were a bit light on for amenities. You could have all the cut-glass chandeliers you wanted hanging from the ceilings, the crystals bending the candlelight to softly illuminate the starched collars and deep cleavages arranged around the mahogany dining table, but the privy was still out the back. And it wasn't connected to anything as sophisticated as a sewer. When the bucket was full, the night soil carter trundled his horse and dray down the purpose-built cobbled lane and did what his title demanded: carted night soil. Which means that in this more refined and sewered century, the elegant piles of Parkville all have excellent rear access. Good for a quick getaway. The real estate agents don't make a song and dance about it, but it's a selling point, especially for punters in my line of work.

My solid steel door-and-frame unit burst free of the surrounding walls with an unholy crash and shattered the jarrah floorboards of the hall. The Mack backed up a few meters and Mauricio planted his foot, the crazed fuck. The truck surged through the gap, taking out Share's fur on the Queen Anne hall stand. The elephant's foot umbrella tidy disappeared under a Dunlop High Rider. My rented hall was wide, wider than a Mack truck, but it narrowed once you got past the arched entrance to the Seminar Room. The truck hit the bottle-neck hard. The oak staircase to the right twisted and snapped. The repro Von Gerhard fell off the wall, glass splintering and skewering the paper. I didn't stop to watch any more, I raced over to the desk, hauled Share out by her ankles and dragged her upright. She was screaming fit to burst, but there wasn't much panic in her voice, it was all anger, distilled fury.

"That was fucking *sable*, you arsehole."

"Not my fault," I yelled.

"The prick in the truck! I got that fucking thing in Paris France. Champs E fucking lysees. Five hundred thousand francs. Pure albino sable."

"Rabbit," I said.

Her reply was drowned by the howl of the engine as Mauricio backed up for the *coup de grace*.

"Come on, for Christ's sake," I yelled. "We're outta here."

I dragged her towards the French doors that opened onto the courtyard. Of course they were shut, locked and secured by automatic solenoids. A shock wave from the *coup de grace* twisted them free. I gave the central strut the boot and we were through. Clouds of dust followed us like mustard gas billowing across the Somme. Broken glass and bricks started to rain down fairly heavily. As we ran, a pot plant took a direct hit. *Poinsettia mysteriosa*, I'd never liked it.

I got Share into the garage and bundled her over the passenger side into the Cobra. Luckily the top was down and we didn't have to play ladies and gents with the doors. I bounded into the driver's seat and grabbed the remote for the roller door into the lane.

"Night soil forever," I shouted at Share over the noise of a major collapse in the main house.

"Start the bloody car you idiot."

I did. The turbo kicked in with a growl that would teach the Zoo's farting lions a thing or two. But we had to wait interminable seconds as the roller door slowly dragged itself off the floor. When the gap into the lane was almost high enough I gave Share her orders.

"Keep your head down," I yelled.

Mauricio bounded into the garage, took a flying leap straight over the Cobra's spoiler and into the luggage compartment behind the seats. I winced, thinking of the buttery leather jacket folded there.

"This is a coupe, you arsehole," I shouted. "No room for three. And watch the jacket."

"Drive, Purdue," Mauricio yelled.

"Jesus Christ, he's got a gun," Share shouted.

"Of course he's got a gun, nutters like him are always waving guns," I said and put the pedal to the metal. The Cobra shot into the lane. I fishtailed it round to the north and tested the shockers on the cobbles.

"Smooth as a baby's," I said.

"Drive to a police station," Share said insistently.

"Do a circuit, Purdue," Mauricio said, gesticulating with the gun over my shoulder. "Up Sydney Road, down Victoria Street, hang a lefty onto Melville and back to Royal Parade. That'll give the cops enough time to arrive and set up shop. Who's the tart?"

"Sharon Lesser, meet Mauricio Cimino, my landlord."

"G'day Sharon," Mauricio said.

"She's called Share," I said. "Put the fucking heater away. And take that thing off your head. You're making a spectacle of yourself. You ought to be ashamed."

Mauricio did as he was told, throwing the balaclava onto the tram tracks in Royal Parade and wriggling down into the luggage compartment, pulling his overalls off in a complicated series of maneuvers that bumped the front seats. We ground to a halt at a set of lights in Sydney Road. I turned round and had a good look at Mauricio. He was wearing a cashmere business suit, striped shirt with French cuffs and expensive opal cuff-links. Beside me

Share started a search for the Cobra's door handle, but the lights changed and we were away.

"Just what are you pricks playing at?" Share asked in a tone not to be trifled with.

"Fang Shooy," Mauricio said.

"It's *fong shway*," I said. "I keep telling you."

"This is some sort of *joke*?"

"The alignment was all wrong," Mauricio told her calmly. "Wrong ghosts kept coming down the hallway."

"What crap is this?"

"Like Purdue says, *feng shui*," he told her airily. "You've got to line up the hallway with the cosmic force fields, otherwise the daemons and ghouls and all those inhorse... inhorse..."

"Inauspicious," I said.

"Yeah, all those inauspicious omens put the mockers on things."

She nodded at him over her shoulder. "Ah. You were realigning the house. With a truck."

"Reckon."

"You *demolished* it."

"Fuck." Mauricio grinned, I could see him in the mirror. "I'll have to start from scratch."

For a while we drove in silence. Autumn evening was falling fast, although with the greenhouse effect it still felt like late summer. I flicked the Cobra's lights on. A delightful shepherd's sky hung over Tullamarine and the tram wires were etched against it like cosmic force fields. There was a lesson to be had in the wires, but I couldn't quite put it into words. I sensed that the mood of quiet contemplation that had settled on the Cobra's occupants required nothing as crass as speech to give it meaning.

When we rejoined Royal Parade, Share finally said, "I take it that house was heritage-listed?"

"Governor LaTrobe once kept a mistress there," I said.

She nodded. "So the Council wouldn't even permit you to build a dog kennel in the backyard, let alone knock the whole place down and build..." She paused, trying to imagine the atrocity we must have planned. "Fifty-seven brick venereal units."

"Eighteen units," Mauricio said, offended. "Top of the range. Master bedroom with en suite sauna and walk-in robes. En suites for the other two bedrooms. Studio/study with sun roof. Security entrances standard. All fittings stainless steel or owners' choice if bought off of the plan. Which saves on stamp duty, which isn't getting any less pricey these days, you mark my words."

"Good Christ. Criminal vandalism!"

"Inner city resurgence. Breathing life into urban decay."

"Decay? Parkville?" She knew her real estate, did Share, as had everyone who'd prospered in Melbourne in the days of rampant financial lunacy and negative gearing. You might get more per square meter in patrician Toorak, but Parkville was still there near the top of the chart as a den of restorers and gold chip heritage bricks & mortar.

"Structurally unsound, the way it is now." My former landlord tutted at the public risk he'd just averted. "A menace to passersby. Rise from the flames of destruction like a fee nix. That's progress, Share."

We were approaching the wrecked household, but the whole street was blocked by police cars, fire trucks, television crews. More flashing lights than sequins on a stripper's bra. A uniformed constable tried to divert us, but I brandished my driver's license complete with *bona fide* address.

"I live here, officer."

"Shit, mate," the cop said, taking in the number. "It's your house. Be prepared for a shock." He waved the Cobra up onto the footpath, where we left it standing with its emergency lights flashing, adding its twenty cents' worth of glitter to the festivities. We proceeded on foot. The driving license got the three of us through two lines of tape with Do Not Cross written in endless sequence. Outside the caved-in front fence and gate a detective sergeant I knew of old was talking to some guys in hard hats. He turned, recognized me.

"Who the hell are you?" Detective Rebeiro said.

"Occupier," I said. "This is the landlord."

"Fuckinjesus H. Christ," Mauricio screamed, "what cunt's done this to me fuckin property there's a fuckin *Mack* parked in the hall fuckin truckies they're all on *pills* you know no fuckin sleep for forty-eight we're talking *fifty-six hours straight* this cunt probably started in Brisbane and got lost south of Wang and thought he was parking the family wagon in the carport in fuckin *Perth* these guys are so off their faces I take it the cunt's dead?"

"There's no one in there," Rebeiro said.

"Fuckin truck driving itself?"

"Wonders never cease," the cop said.

"You hungry?" I asked Share. A grinding noise told me the whole front of the mansion wanted to lie down for the night. Half the old places in the street had been turned into moderately upscale offices, used only during the day and for some occasional skulking at night, but those occupied by accountants on the rise and abortionists on the decline were flooded with light from open doors. Half a dozen people stood on the footpath, or nervously in doorways.

"Are you mad? I couldn't eat if I was starving." That didn't make much sense to me, and perhaps not even to her, because she added, "What I need's a stiff drink. Oh, and you can write me out a check for the sable."

She took a deep breath for some more complaint, and I liked the effect.

"You can be sure my insurers will have the matter in hand on Monday morning," I said reassuringly. "I'd offer you a double malt, but unfortunately the drinks cabinet has half the staircase on it." Something rumbled, and more crashings sounded inside. A pasty faced local from two doors up bared his teeth in the flashing blue light, unable to decide whether to go back inside his own place and hope for the best or run for his life. "Let's retrieve Mauricio and get a bite to eat. I'll stand you a drink."

"You *are* mad." She peered this way and that. "Where the hell did I leave my car?"

"Probably on the far side of the Mack." The huge truck's arse stuck out into the street. She stalked away. I called, "Look, calm down, okay? Stick with us, we'll go for a drink to steady your nerves, then I'll bring you back to your car, okay?"

Mauricio had abandoned his conversation with the cop and was now staring straight into the bright lights of a television crew.

"The vicious animal that done this has to be hunted down and

prosecuted to the full vigor of the law and they'd better throw
away the key before the dog ruins any more priceless Australian
icons like my property here. It is typical of the gutless wonders of
today's modern criminal class that he runs away from the scene of
the crime and doesn't face the music like a man."

"Was there anyone inside, Mr. Cimino?"

"Only my tenant, and he's a harmless Fang Suet Master who
doesn't have an enemy in the world he's a man of peace and tran-
quility it's part of his philosophy."

I took Share by the elbow. "Come on, we'll leave Mauricio to
it. There's nothing for us to do here. We can come back for your
car."

For a second it looked as if Share was going to march straight
up to the cop with a view to helping him with his enquiries. With
bad grace, she allowed herself to be escorted back under the two
strands of tape. Silently she opened the Cobra's passenger door
and slumped into the seat.

I had just bumped the car over the gutter and completed a three
point turn when Mauricio slammed into the back compartment
of the Cobra. "They won't wait for daylight, they've got some
heavy haulage tow truck coming," he said, face theatrically black
with rage in case any of the cops were watching, tone creamy with
satisfaction. "You won't be sleeping there tonight, Purdue. I hope
you've made arrangements."

I turned my head, muttered directly into his ear, "Shut up, for
fuck's sake." He ferreted under the back of my seat, fished out
his gun from under my leather jacket and casually disappeared it
under his suit coat. "Christ," I said with a certain bitterness, "that
was thoughtful of you."

"Well, I couldn't very well cart the thing around in front of the
cops, could I? C'mon, what are you hanging around for? I could
eat a horse."

"He could probably arrange that for you," Share said wither-
ingly. I thought, If only she knew.

The cop let me through, and I drove back into Royal Parade,
headed north. "No, they still don't serve horsemeat to humans in
Melbourne," I said. "Raw fish, yes. Anyone fancy sushi? Sashimi?
With a bowl or two of hot saki? Just what you need to soothe the
nerves after your house has been demolished by a raving lunatic."

"You're going the wrong way," Share said. "The best Japanese is in East Melbourne, Albert Street, opposite the Fitzroy Gardens."

"That's wall to wall surgeons' consulting rooms," Mauricio said.

"They have to eat too," she said. "The *Nippon Tuck* got four stars in the *Age Guide*."

"I have a better idea," I told her. The Cobra hummed up Sydney Road between a lumbering green tram and more four wheel drives than you could shake a yuppie at. People still buying SUVs, amazing. Something had happened to Brunswick lately. I shook my head sadly, and took a left into a bumpy alleyway between a closed-down book store and a classy new fish shop that looked like they'd style your hair while they grilled your batter-free piece of fish. "Have you ever eaten at the Alasya?" I asked Share.

"What, is that place still open? When I was a student nurse."

"Noisy, but the food is good and Mauricio won't be tempted to shoot anyone in such a public place."

He punched me sharply in the back of the head for that, so it was a good thing I'd found the rear of the shop I was looking for and parked the Cobra next to a huge and moderately smelly industrial-grade Dumpster bin.

"We can walk from here," I said.

I pulled my jacket on for form's sake and nipped in to buy several reasonable bottles from a pub that had improved its game markedly since Share was a student. At the eatery, the guy carving hot spitting gyros nodded me upstairs to the private room. They serve you fast at the Alasya. Mauricio undid the top button of his pants and tucked in, shoveling flat bread into plates of pastel dips and chewing it up with black oily olives, lamb chops, sliced lamb, lamb kidney, minced lamb and some other foodstuffs derived from the sheep family. Even Share got into the spirit of the thing after a couple of glasses of rather attractive Delatite 1998 unoaked chardonnay. I stuck to red, and it stuck to me, taking away the stiffness in my neck and shoulders and with it my desire to beat Mauricio into a pulp. Most of it.

"That was a really fucking stupid thing to pull, Mauricio."

"Purdue, you're a loser, you know that? Can't tell one bloody

day from the next," he confided to Share. "What kind of businessman is that?"

"I'm not a businessman, you fucking thug," I told him with
dignity. "I'm a *feng shui* master. I prefer to be addressed as *Sensei*
Purdue."

I stumbled a little as we went back down the alley from light-
smeared Sydney Road, so I put my arm around Share's shoulders
to make certain she was okay. Whistling, Mauricio stopped behind us, and I heard a zip unzip and a moment later a cascade of
piss against a brick wall. It made my own bladder ache. When we
turned into the loading area behind the store where Vinnie lived
upstairs, someone was out cold in the driver's seat of the Cobra.

Share touched my arm. I leaned over and shook a naked shoulder poking out of an ancient dinner jacket with its arms torn out.

"Wha? Mumph?"

"Time to go beddy-byes, Animal."

Share whispered, "I don't think you should—"

Animal convulsed, and was out of the seat like a scary jack-in-
the-box doing its surprise. I looked down into a face that hadn't
seen the sun in about three years, eyes black with something
so thick you'd expect the lids to stay gummed up after a single
blink, and with more metal stuck through skin than you'd see in
a fragged lieutenant in an Iraq tent. Sodium light from a pole high
over the alley gleamed revoltingly from a mostly shaven scalp.
One hand stuck out in my direction, quick as a flash, while the
other beckoned demandingly. I shrugged and pulled out my wallet,
placed a crisp new fifty in the outstretched hand. Share snorted,
probably wondering if I'd succumbed either to a stand over job or
a particularly sleazy invitation to a quickie. The banknote stayed
where I put it. Before it could blow away I sighed and deposited
another hundred.

"Come to tuck me in, then, daddy?" Animal said in a sulky
voice. She gave Share an inscrutable glance.

Feet clattered: crazy Mauricio approached. Animal gave me a
big kiss, then turned away and climbed the steps to the back of
the shop.

"Hey, sweetheart darling," Mauricio shouted. "I wish we'd

known you were home, you could have eaten with us, Anna-belle."

My daughter had the door open to Vinnie's cave by then, and was through it, banging it shut. "Not hungry. Come on, I'll drive you back to your car."

The heavy haulage tow truck arrived. The hapless Mack had been dragged into the street and half the front of the heritage-protected mansion had come with it. The roof on the top floor had caved in. I pulled up a safe distance away, and Share was off like a filly. You could have heard the shriek in Flemington.

"Mother*fucker*!"

Mauricio had caught a cab home to Fitzroy, so he was well out of it. Wearily, I bolted the driving wheel again and followed her past the behemoth. Reversing it out of the front of the house, they'd managed to run the back wheels up the hood of the Audi and through the windscreen.

Share was shaking, white faced, clutching herself with clenched fists. I suppose she was cold, too, without her fur. Autumn in Melbourne is delightful, but even with El Nino and greenhouse it can cool down shockingly fast at night. I thought of lending her my jacket, but that would have involved getting nearer than I planned just at the moment. Gingerly, I held out my cellphone.

"You could call your husband, have him pick you up?"

"He's in K.L. this week, don't you listen to *anything*?"

Oh yeah, that had been somewhere after the second bottle of red.

"Well, a cab. I'll call you a cab, Share." I poked around in my jacket pocket, looking from her crushed car to my dismantled home. "I haven't even got anywhere to sleep, you should think yourself lucky, Share."

This time the shriek woke the elephants, or maybe one just hap-pened to trumpet in sympathy. It was unearthly. She came at me with nails extended, and I had to hold her forearms or I'd have looked worse in the morning than Animal. Enraged words were pouring from her mouth. I suspected that her inner harmonies were not all they might be, not at that moment.

"I'll see you in court, Purdue," she sobbed, pulling herself free, stumbling away from me. "Every penny you own, and then some. I'll have you in jail for this, you and your thuggish friend Cimino. You'll hear from my solicitor on Monday morning. I could have you arrested for carrying weapons and, and felonious intent to scam your insurers. No, keep away from me."

"Share, I was just going to offer you my jacket. You must be freezing."

"Stay away." People were peering from behind curtains. What an entertaining night this must have been for these burghers.

"Let me drive you home, Share."

"You're drunk, you lunatic. Just piss off."

I sighed heavily. We looked at each in silence for a while. Finally, I said, "So I suppose a fuck's completely out of the question?"

It took a couple of moments. I suspected the top of her head was about to blow off, but then, thank god, she started to laugh. She leaned against a lamp post, and I smiled back at her as the makeup ran down her cheeks.

"Oh Jesus," she said, then. "Okay. Drive me to Balwyn, Purdue, then we'll see."

And that was it for me. I slept like a bloated pig.

Breakfast at Share's was basic: black coffee and some sort of rusk. The rusk was only a marginal improvement on the proverbial branding iron, and the coffee did little to soothe the hangover—I'm a hair-of-the-dog man, myself. I said so to Share, who looked terrible. She seemed unreasonably upset, but then Sharon Lesser was evidently a woman living on the far edge of the edge.

"We drank the dog last night, Purdue. Hair and all."

The empty vodka bottle abandoned on the kitchen floor seemed to bear this out. I took a pull of the coffee. It tasted like tin.

"Okay, Purdue," she said from the other side of the kitchen table, visibly pulling herself together, "about the consultation."

"The consultation." I wanted to lay my head down on the table.

"You seem a bit slow," Share said. "The words are a bit slow coming."

"My reactions are always a trifle torpid in the morning," I said. "I'm not a morning person." My dreams had been black and curdled. I'd half woken needing a piss, convinced I'd heard

Mauricio's Mack truck slamming through a wall. No, that had been earlier. My house was gone, as planned, but sooner than planned. Oh Christ, the stupid fuck could have killed me. And I didn't know where Share's bathroom was, so I'd rolled over and gone again into the murky dark.

"Be that as it may, there's still the matter of the consultation. I'm your client. I came to see you last night, remember? You know, you were running this *feng shui* Consulting outfit. You had a really nice office suite in the downstairs part of this really nice heritage-listed gaff in really really nice Parkville. Is it all coming back to you? Let's get on with it, shall we?"

"Now?" I said in dull amazement. "You want a *feng shui* consultation at this hour in the morning?"

"Stop fart-arsing around, Mr. Purdue. Do your stuff."

"If you insist, Share." I squared my shoulders despite the pain. "What needs to be understood about *feng shui* is that the words mean 'wind' and 'water'. These two primal elements represent the space between heaven and Earth. In this space, which is our dwelling place, the mighty force known as 'chi' eddies and swirls with all the wild grace of wind and water. But for all its grace and power, water can grow stagnant, it can become trapped..."

"It can become putrid, can't it, Purdue? Fouled with pollutants, dead rats, old condoms, plastic bottles, oil slicks, cryptospiridium, *e. coli* by the bucket load..."

"You seem to have grasped the concept admirably," I said. The tinny coffee was all gone, and the chi with it, leaving something foul and brackish in the bottom of the cup. I reached for the pot and poured some more, shuddering slightly. "It is the *feng shui* consultant's job to identify those malformed spaces where the mighty force of chi is trapped like the stagnant water to which we have alluded..." I trailed off. I was too old for this sort of thing, I decided. This time yesterday I'd thought of myself as a young fellow in the prime of life. Bang. Bang. And the house came tumbling down.

"What about Yin and Yang, Purdue?"

"I was coming to that, Share. The concepts Yin and Yang are very important to the practice of *feng shui*. They are the light and the dark in constant opposition. You don't have any orange juice, do you? I hesitate to say so, but your coffee is appalling. Mineral water would do at a pinch. I'm a bit dehydrated."

"Plenty of water in the tap. You've got to balance the buggers, haven't you?"

"What buggers?"

"The Yin and Yang, you're not brain-damaged by any chance?"

I stood, made water flow into a tall glass. Chi sparkled in a beam of sunlight, or it might have been a film of detergent.

"It is indeed necessary to achieve a harmonious accommodation between the forces of Yin and the forces of Yang—"

"—in order to enhance not only one's physical surroundings but also one's life, career and interpersonal relationships... that's right, isn't it, Purdue?"

"You appear to know almost as much as I do, Share. I see you've had occasion to consult a *feng shui* master before."

"I've read the same bloody website, Purdue."

"The role of the internet in spreading the good word about *feng shui* cannot be overestimated. However, a word of warning: full mastery of the insights of this ancient art can be obtained only by many years of study and contemplation at the feet of an enlightened master. The temptation to use a little learning gleaned from the internet—"

"Without paying huge amounts to a charlatan like you."

"—should be avoided at all costs."

"Sugar, Purdue. Can you tell me something about its Yin and Yang?"

I was getting whiplash. Maybe I'd nodded off for a couple of seconds, the way you do when you are majorly jetlagged, but I hadn't been out of the country for years. "What?"

"That white stuff, the sort you don't snort up your nose. You put it in tea."

I shook my head sadly. I suspected her tea would be as awful as her coffee. "*Feng shui* has little to say about sugar, Share. Tea in China is traditionally drunk without the addition of either milk or sugar."

"But the average race horse in Australia is no respecter of tradition and takes its sugar neat."

Oh. Oh fuck. I felt sicker, all of a sudden. "Just what is this all about, Mrs. Lesser?" Had we or hadn't we? I honesty couldn't remember. Our clothes had been all over the bedroom floor. But I'm notoriously untidy when I'm pissed, it didn't necessarily signify a night of wild passionate screwing.

"I think you are a man of parts, Purdue. I think it is possible to consult you about a lot more things than this *feng shui* crap. Or do I mean horseshit?"

"I think it might be a good idea if you said what was on your mind, Share."

"The stewards were very interested in Canned Fish."

Yes, correct weight. For about half a minute I just looked at Share and she returned my gaze. She was a good looking woman, all things considered, although she looked terribly strained. Just how far *had* I managed to get with her? Were we known unto each other? We'd certainly woken up in the same bed. I couldn't remember a fucking thing, literally. Dreams of my house falling about my ears, that was all.

"Canned Fish," Share said, just in case I'd missed it.

"It's a bit early in the morning for canned fish, darling. Kippers, perhaps."

"No it's not."

"Well you tell me," I said. "Just what do you know about Canned Fish?"

"That the nag suddenly developed a massive turn of speed in the 3.30 at Flemo a couple of years back. A few very select punters did rather well out of it. Your good self included."

"Jesus, this is history, Share. We're talking about a bygone era."

"We're talking about pet food. About three quarters of a tonne of pet food."

"Poor old Canned," I said. "He broke a leg a year later. He was a little battler, but there was nothing we could do. The bullet was a kindness."

"Cut the crap. About the 3.30 at Flemo. Before the nag got turned into Cat-O-Meat."

"Just who *are* you, Share?"

"I'm someone who wants to know about tanking a horse up with sugar. That's what you used, isn't it? Just sugar. Nothing detectable by sophisticated methodology. No fancy drugs, no steroids, no growth hormones. Just the old CSR table sugar." CSR was Colonial Sugar Refinery, the Australian byword for white sugar since my parents' childhoods, and their parents. I wondered for a moment if the company had changed its name to Postcolonial. "The poor animal went hyperactive, it had to run like stink to burn up the sugar."

I looked out the large window at the large grassy back garden. Tall native trees blocked out the neighbors. "All horses like sugar lumps," I said. "You want to hold your hand very flat, though. Just let the lump sit on the palm of your hand. Don't curl your fingers or you'll get nipped."

She regarded me with scorn. "My understanding is that the horse had half a sack of sugar in it. I don't think it ate that off some guy's hand."

"All right," I said. Her hair was wild and uncombed, a look I approved of, and I still couldn't remember, but it would have been a good idea. "I'll tell you. You get a jug and you put some water in it. Then you put some sugar in the water and stir it with a stick."

"And the horse drinks it?"

"No. You get a plastic tube, a funnel and the bottom half of a hypodermic. You connect them all up and jam the hypodermic into a vein in the nag's neck. Blood spurts out through the needle and into the tube, so you've got to raise the tube to a height greater than the animal's heart can pump the blood." The roof of my mouth felt dry, all the wine and vodka presumably. "Are you sure you don't want to take notes? I could help you draw a diagram."

"I think I can remember all this, Purdue."

"So you need a chair. It's very important to have the chair ready before you start. Otherwise blood goes everywhere. You stand on the chair and hold the tube with the funnel above your head with one hand and pour the sugar solution from the jug with the other. Gravity does the rest. The solution pushes the blood back into the horse and then trickles in after it."

"Shit, really, you just pour the stuff straight into the bloodstream, no digestion necessary."

"That's about right," I said. "You want to know this why?"

"We might have forgotten the chair." She got to her feet, stepped into the pantry, came out with a half-height aluminum stepladder she lifted easily in one hand. "I assume this'd do the trick."

"Who's 'we'?"

"You and me, Mr. Purdue. After I've made a phonecall or two

to line up the equipment, we're going for a little drive into the country."

"No need to be formal, Share," I said. "Call me Tom."

I blame my name for leading me into a life of crime. What I told Share was true, as far as it went, but it didn't go all the way, not by a long chalk. My mad parents were flower children years before Rupert Murdoch and his yellow press mates ever heard of the term. With a handful of their arty mates, they raised us kids in a pile of dirty mud brick mansions and hovels out Eltham way, miles north of Melbourne, still the edge of the scrub when I was a boy. Other artist colonies had the same idea, but my mob was the weirdest of the lot. From the beginning none of the men had shaved, and none of the women either, and this had started before Women's Lib or third stage feminism had ever been heard of. These hirsute seekers after truth wove their own cloth, milked their own scrawny goats, and taught us in a kind of Steiner curriculum designed by Martin Kundalini Richardson, king of the loonies, a sort of unsuccessful mix of L. Ron Hubbard, George Adamski and ancient aboriginal myths as interpreted on the back of a Corn Flakes' packet.

You wouldn't credit the extent of the brain-damaging crap they shoveled down our gullets. Transforming into bandicoots by the light of the full moon. A tunnel reached from the depths of Ayers Rock to the lair of the Hidden Masters in Tibet. "Ayers Rock" is what we whites used to call Uluru, that big slab of red stone in the middle of the Australian continent that the aborigines revere. The navel of the universe, we were taught. Joe Bannister and I used to snigger and wonder if the arse of the world would fall off if you got a really big fucking Phillips head and unscrewed it. That earned us gentle reprimands and extra hours churning up the slurry for the mud bricks. I didn't mind that one bit, although it could get cold sloshing in the wet; it was better than learning the sixteen portals of the reptile mutants who secretly ran the world. The Queen of England and the rest of the royal family were among their number. In fact, they and certain other leading Jewish dynasties were the world's leading reptile invaders. I swallowed it all until I was about fourteen, when I was already a bad kid, and then one day I woke up and looked around me at the real world and started shaking my head. I suppose I can't complain; it gave me a rich line of bullshit for my future careers.

None of this is what turned me to crime, not directly. That happened when I was twelve and three badly dressed State education department heavies, one male and two females, visited our classroom and sent in a report that eventually reached the Minister. "Damned jackbooted busybodies!" thundered Kundalini Richardson, but it was too late, we were pinched. I spent the next six years at Eltham High, going through culture shock roughly equivalent to a Stone Age Papuan being hijacked and put to work for Amway.

"Children, we have three new students joining us for class today. Stand up, boys. I'll ask you each to tell us your name, then sit down and open your geography book at page 121, the Principal Imports of Peru. You there, son."

I jumped up breezily, grinned around at the class. The other kids had been nervous, scared even. I'm the extroverted type, I knew I was in for heaps of fun.

"Recherché," I said loudly.

Ears pricked up. A ripple of manic joy passed across the classroom, but I was too dumb to understand what it was that had happened.

"I beg your pardon?"

"I'm Recherché," I said, "and this here is my cousin Con, that's short for Contrapuntal, and this bloke's—"

The ripple had became a haze of muttering. Some residue of survival instinct made me stumble into silence. The teacher was a burly youth with hair parted firmly on the left, some hapless bonded victim of the Education Department fated by his contract to penal servitude in the sticks, or near enough. He stepped forward and his fists clenched.

"Are you taking the piss, son? You having a lend of me?"

I blinked at him. "Eh?"

"I asked for your name. Just tell us your name." He consulted a list. "If he's Con, you'd be Tom, is that right?"

Triumphant glances were being exchanged across the rows of desks, and a soggy spitball hit me behind the ear. I flinched, rubbed at it, stared around. A fat kid with boils stared at me with hatred. I looked back at the teacher.

"My name is Recherché Doubting Thomas Purdue," I said carefully. "Sometimes Outsiders just call me Tom..." But the room was in uproar. That set the tone for the next few years. One day I'm going to borrow Mauricio's gun and drive out to Eltham and blow fucking Martin Kundalini Richardson's noble Alzheimerish head right off his fucking shoulders.

Share stowed the step ladder in the back of the Cobra, which somehow I'd parked in the brick carport at the side without smashing it. The ladder didn't fold up as neatly as Mauricio. It stuck straight into the air like some mediaeval torture rack. There was no way we could carry the thing and put the canopy up. I didn't really feel like uncocooned driving. But there again, maybe the wind in my face would be good for the hangover. Share looked at me with undisguised mistrust.

"Sure you are up to driving?"

"No," I said.

"Give me the keys."

I handed them over meekly.

For a while Share drove in silence. She was heading East. I fumbled in the glove box and found a pair of shades and put them on. They cut down the glare a bit, but did nothing for the headache. I decided to take my mind off my condition with some polite conversation.

"So what line of work are you in, Share," I said. Jesus, I must have quizzed her on all this last night over ten kinds of lamb.

"Christ, Tom, you've got a memory like a sieve. Alzheimer's already? Or did they smack you around the head a bit too much in prison?"

Fuck, she knew that as well. "Disgraceful, I know. I put it down to the vodka."

She shot me a tired look, reconciled to my inadequacies. "Investment advice. Risk assessment. Risk management. Financial services. Import/export. That sort of thing."

"Sounds interesting," I said, and my eyes drifted away to the passing street life.

"Somebody's got to do it."

"Big firm?"

"Big enough. Just me."

"A one woman outfit?"

"Exactly."

"Saving on the secretarial side of things. I do it myself."

"Christ no, I've got secretaries. Two of them."

"A three woman outfit, then."

"I don't think Wozza and Muttonhead would like to hear that."

"Wozza?" I said. "Wozza O'Toole? Muttonhead Lamb?"

"Those are my men."

"They're your *secretaries*?"

"You got problems with that?"

"I... um... I had occasion to meet Mr. O'Toole once."

"Yeah, he told me: Remand yard, Pentridge, 1993."

Pentridge. Good god, that brought back memories, and a hundred years of scuttlebutt traded by old crims. The great gray terrible walls, topped with barbed wire, guard towers with guns at each corner. Jika-Jika, the dreadful hell hole for the worst of men. Gardens where bodies were buried in shallow graves, they said. The place had been closed for years. And now some hungry bastards had reopened it as a district of expensive homes. A veritable walled and gated community, Pentridge Village, not five miles from Vinnie's shop. Lovely view of the Coburg Lake, now they'd removed the razor wire. Fuck, nothing was beyond parody in this day and age.

"Why are you smiling? Fond memories of your cell in Pentridge?"

"No. Thinking of Wozza as a secretary, that'd make anyone smile. Bloke couldn't write his name. Couldn't add two and two."

Share shrugged. "The education system had totally failed him. He was a lost cause from day one at kindergarten."

"So, how come...?"

"You've got to do something inside, you should know that. Might as well do a bit of Adult Literacy. Get yourself a cushy billet in the prison library, read a few books. Matriculate. Enroll in a TAFE. Get yourself a degree. It impresses the bejesus out of the parole board."

"A *degree*? Wozza?"

"Bachelor of Information Technology."

"Fuck me, all I did in Seattle was lift weights."

"Wozza won't talk down to you, Tom. He's an egalitarian sort—wears his distinction lightly."

"What about Muttonhead?" I said. "You're not going to tell me Muttonhead is now a doctor of semiotics."

"No, Mutton's more your action type."

"Standover man?" Mutt was about three feet tall.

"Don't be unkind. Somebody's got to hold the ladder."

"What ladder?"

"The one behind your head."

"Mutton's going to be at the track?"

"Wozza too. We do these sorts of things as a team."

"Look," I said. "Just what sort of ham-hocked nag do you have on the card?"

Share Lesser gave me a bland look. "Who's talking about horses?"

"I thought we were going to some country race meeting."

"After a fashion, but it's private. And the sheikh's not interested in horses."

"What sheikh?"

"Abdul bin Sahal al Din."

I was getting fed up. "I think you'd better explain things, Share. This is starting to look like false pretenses. This is starting to look like kidnapping, and in my own car at that."

"All will be revealed, Tom. And I wouldn't fuss about the car after what your oaf did to mine last night."

I looked sideways at Share. She was driving with considerable aplomb—that's the only word to describe it. If there was an opening in the traffic, she'd switched lanes and taken advantage almost before the guy in the other lane blinked. Quite often the guy in the other lane registered his displeasure with his horn. Share ignored them all. I did too. I decided against pursuing the matter of the race meeting. Just go with the flow. Even if the flow took us straight into the dubious company of Wozza O'Toole and Muttonhead Lamb.

Share was right. I'd met Wozza and Mutton years ago in Pentridge. We'd all been on remand. Me on a charge of grievous bodily harm against my father-in-law, and the other two on a bog-standard bank hold-up: stockings, sawn-offs, plastic shopping bag for the contents of the till, hot wired getaway car and a wheelman who drove straight through a set of red lights and was sideswiped by a mob of hoons in a lowered Customline. The hoons piled out of the wreck brimming with righteous road rage, and were settling to the task of beating the shit out of Wozza, Mutton and the hapless wheelman when they discovered the plastic bag. By the time the cops arrived the hoons had done a runner with the proceeds, leaving the other three to begin their life behind bars with nothing in the kitty. I'd hired a Queen's Counsel by the name of Muldoon who charged like a tax collector and drank with the vice squad. Despite my prior record in the USA, the case against me proved very arguable, the terrible strain of the circumstances, your honor, and the police evidence curiously muted. I left court a free man without a stain on my character and never saw my in-laws again. Wozza and co. were on legal aid. They got eight years each with remissions.

Share was pointing the Cobra straight at the Dandenongs. I knew of no race course in this direction, but I said nothing. The traffic thinned. As the Cobra picked up speed, the wind began to howl in the rungs of the ladder. Civilized discourse was now impossible anyway. The Cobra comes into its own on a hill climb and Share exercised it to its full potential on the roads that dipped and twisted through the greenery of the Dandenongs. By the time she suddenly left the road, shot down an unmarked track between towering rows of mountain ash and swung round onto a gravel drive in front of a mansion, I had no idea where we were. Share didn't stop but continued past the mansion and over a cattle grid. Finally she ground to a halt outside a row of fake half-timber stables, painted black and white like a Christmas card.

"Where are we?"

"Shangri-La," she said.

"I can believe it."

We left the car and entered the stables. They were gloomy and

empty of horseflesh. The only inhabitants were two guys in overalls sitting on a feed bin drinking tea from a thermos. Well, it
might have been tea.

"Purdue, you old bastard. Long time no see, fella!"

"G'day, Wozza," I said.

"Looking fit, Purdue, me old mate, looking bloody fit."

"Not that fit," I said.

"You could go a few rounds these days, don't tell me you
couldn't."

Wozza bounded from the feed bin and playfully danced up to
me, sparring with his fists. His fingers still carried prison tats.
Written across the knuckles of both hands was a crude invitation
to sex—one letter per knuckle. I hadn't run across the guy for
years, but he hadn't changed much, you still wouldn't trust him as
far as you could kick him. I sidestepped Wozza and made my way
to the feed bin. Mutton, on the other hand, *had* changed. Someone
had cut or bitten his nose off.

"G'day, Mutton," I said, extending my hand and trying to look
at his face without surprise. He was a shrimp of a man, hardly
bigger than a twelve year old, too small to be a jockey which had
been the disappointment of his life.

Mutton shook my hand without leaving the feed bin. His greeting was indistinct. The nose job hadn't done much for his diction.
I turned back to Wozza.

"Share tells me you're into Information Technology these
days."

"It's the future," Wozza said. "Information is power. Simple as
that."

"I wouldn't mind a bit of information about what we're doing
here," I said. "Pleasant though these surroundings are, and however delightful the company."

"We're expediting things," Share said. "Speeding them up."

"What things?"

"Come and take a squizz, Purdue, me old china," Wozza said.
"Come and take a decko."

Wozza and Share turned and walked out of the stables, I followed and behind me I could hear Muttonhead lumbering his way
off the feed bin. We followed a well-worn track through the forest
for a few hundred meters. The track ended at a gate and beyond

the gate was a small paddock. It was well hidden, entirely surrounded by trees. With a slight shock I realized that the field was
completely free of marijuana plants. Something moved against the
trees at the other end of the field. I leaned against the gate and
studied the shape, the slightly rocking motion of the dappled pale
brown against the grays and green of the forest.

"Bloody hell," I said.

"Ship of the desert," Wozza said.

I stared in disbelief at the animal. It's not the sort of thing you ex-
pect to stumble over in a Victorian paddock, not outside a circus.
I wouldn't have been more surprised if it had been an elephant.
"We're not going to try and dope that thing," I said.

"Nile Fever," Share said. "She's fast, but could be faster."

"Why the buggeration do you want a fast camel?"

"They race them in Saudi and the United Arab Emirates," Share
said. "It's big time. Very big money indeed."

"Forgive the observation," I said, "but we are not in Saudi.
Saudi is a very long way from here. So too was Dubai last time I
consulted my atlas."

"Jeez, I hope your passport's up to date," Wozza said. "Hasn't
been impounded by the police or nothing."

"Get knotted," I said.

"Just kidding," Wozza said.

I looked at Mutton's face. "Don't tell me the camel bit your
schnozz off?"

The Mutt expressed disappointment in me. "Nile's as gentle as
a baby!"

"The sheikh is dropping in for a road test at eleven o'clock,"
Share said. "By then we want Nile Fever at her tip top best."

"In the pink of condition," Wozza said. "The mistress of the
track. Nile Fever, Queen of the Desert. Export quality DNA."

"You want the animal full of sugar," I said.

"Right in one," Share said. "Correct weight."

Behind me Muttonhead said something I didn't catch, but
Wozza said, "Yeah, right, Mutton, no worries."

"This sheikh guy is buying Australian camels with a view to racing them in the Middle East?" I said. How would you get them out

of the country? Not the sort of thing you could smuggle in your underpants. DNA, Woz had said. Did they want the sperm? Ova, I corrected myself. Could you get viable, transportable ova out of a camel? Or even fertilized embryos?

"Best in the world," Wozza was saying with every evidence of national pride. "Free of disease. Guaranteed syphilis-free, which is hard to find anywhere else. Go like the clappers. Your average OPEC billionaire pays top dollar. But the beast's gotta perform. No three legged numbers in Jeddah, mate."

I looked at my companions in prospective crime and didn't especially relish the odds. I was beginning to regard Share as lethal. It seemed prudent to show willing. "What you've got to understand," I said with all the authority I could muster, "is that the beast—be it horse, camel or anteater—starts to metabolize the sugar as soon as it's... er... supplied. It can't store it, not even in its hump. If that animal over there is to be up to speed at eleven o'clock, we shouldn't give it anything until half past ten at the earliest. Quarter-to would be better still."

And, I thought, let's hope the fucking sheikh arrives sooner than expected.

Prime racing bloodstock can be skittish, nervy before the jump. You can almost see the adrenaline seething in their arteries, which stand out pulsing on their necks like living ropes. Canned Fish, though, had been tranquil; doping the poor bugger presented few difficulties. The gelding usually took a relaxed view of the sport of kings. He was phlegmatic to fault. That's what made an injection of pure sugar work on him like a charm, like Seven League Boots.

Camels, they looked likely to be a different story again.

I regarded Nile Fever with a blend of disapproval and sheer fright. The old Canned Fish had been fourteen hands high. This evil-eyed brute was twenty at the shoulder, taller than the top of my head, and her single camelhair coat-colored hump rose over me like a low hill of hairy sand. It wasn't that big, the hump. I'd always imagined them looking like mountain tops. She met my eye with a rolling, yellowish orb of her own, and her lips peeled back. Teeth like slabs of rock. Coral-red palate that reminded me of one of the gaudier caskets in Ben Crosby's undertakers' showroom in Sydney Road. Breath like an open sewer. I coughed, and started taking in the rank air through my mouth instead.

Someone's going to have to climb up a ladder, I told myself, and whack a bag of Colonial Sugar Refinery's finest into this brute. Not me, I swore. Nile Fever shuffled on her great padded feet, banging me with one roughly callused knee. The vow was pointless. I knew better, of course. Muggins would get stuck with the job. Again.

"Is it Indian or African?" I asked. Two big fat toes per hoof, spread out in the grass. Not the sort of hoof you could nail an iron shoe to.

"That's elephants," Wozza told me in a scornful tone. "What's happened to you, Tombo, 'roids ruined your brain?"

"She's an Arabian camel," Share told me, looking up with satisfaction at the beast, "bred from the finest feral herds of desert Australia."

"A brumby!"

"You could put it that way. Hybrid vigor, Darwin at his best. Trounce those effete Saudi dancers."

Maybe so. It was a good selling line, anyway. I reached up and patted the animal's back.

"Don't mares have a decent sized hump?"

"Cow," Wozza said. "It's 'cow', not 'mare'."

"Fuck," I said, "whatever. I don't want to marry it. I don't even want to buy it."

"Just give her some sugar," Mutton said with a snigger.

"Arabic or Bactrian," Share shared with me.

"Eh?" But it came back to me instantly, then, from Eltham high school, along with a blast of memory, stale banana skins in the hot playground sun, dried white bread sandwiches with Vegemite from the tuck shop, milk that had gone off. "Yeah, right. One hump or two."

"As the actress said to the bishop," Mutton said.

"Nile Fever is a young 'un", Share told me, ignoring him pointedly. "Look at these lean legs, what a beauty. We're keeping her on a strict diet, you wouldn't want her overweight."

I'd heard that camels hissed and spat, but apart from the evil eye Nile Fever was behaving herself like a lady of breeding. I looked at my watch. Getting on for 10:30, the moment of truth.

"Time to saddle up," Wozza told his mate, checking his own watch.

"Right you are." We led the camel back to the stables, took her in under cover. This wasn't the sort of thing you wanted some keen-eyed passer-by to witness. Skipping happily like a kid, Muttonhead disappeared into a side room while I dragged the ladder over from the Cobra. He emerged after a while with the strangest apparatus I'd ever seen outside a bondage brothel, two X-shaped pieces of beautifully grained timber connected by bars. He'd changed out of overalls into somewhat tatty silks in pink and gold, and wore yellow-tinted goggles and what Animal would have called a skid lid in place of the traditional jockey's cap. Without his nose, he looked like some kind of alien from a horse-drawn UFO.

"Come on, sweetie," he called up to the beast, "come to pop-pa." Strike me pink, the brute lowered herself groaning to her knees, joints flung out sideways like a hairy Transformer toy half-way between robot and Humvee, or maybe a collapsed K-Mart sun chair. Mutt strapped the harness in place, one X in front of the small hump, the other behind. Now I saw that he had a comfort-ably padded seat at the back, right over Nile's tail. He gentled the animal with soft words, patting her nose, then ran a thin thread through the nostril peg. He settled himself in the saddle.

"Good Christ," I said, "is that all you've got in the way of reins?"

"It's the wrists," he assured me. "A horse, you can pull him up with a jerk. This little beaut, she reads a man's mind."

"Just as well," I said. "That thread would snap the moment you put any pressure on it."

"No need to. Nile Fever and me, we're like that." He raised a hand with two ugly thick-knuckled fingers crossed.

"Let's get a move on," Share said, taking charge. "They'll be here any minute. Can we run the sugar in while she's down on her knees like this?"

Safer than teetering on the top of a kitchen ladder, I thought, but Wozza was shaking his head.

"Break a leg if she took fright," he said. He gave me a hard look. "Wouldn't want another Canned Fish on our hands, and before the race has even been run."

I said nothing, I was sick of explaining that it hadn't been my fault. Wozza brought the ladder over. The animal groaned and bawled to its feet at Mutton's instruction, shuffling suspiciously as it saw me dig into the bag Woz had supplied.

"What you do," I told Wozza, "is—"

"Not me, mate, I'm scared of heights."

I looked at Share, holding out the instruments of acceleration.

"In these clothes?" She was pulling a beautifully patterned silk scarf over her head. "Get real, Purdue. I have to talk turkey with the Sheikh."

It just seemed easier, suddenly, to get it over and done with. Without another word I mixed the sugar in a bowl with a couple of liters of warm water from the thermos Wozza handed me, poured it into a glass drip container that might have been stolen from a hospital ward.

"Hold her steady, for fuck's sake, Muttonhead," I said.

"Apples," he said, and crooned to the beast. I thought I heard him saying something like *Ata Allah*. God Almighty, the world's gone mad when old Mutt starts babbling in Arabic. I wondered if he'd converted to Islam. Surely not, there had to be some sort of limit.

I climbed the ladder cautiously, clung to the rough fur, feeling for the arteries in the neck. Nile Fever didn't feel feverish, she felt cool. She swung her head to inspect me, nearly knocking me off the steps. Little ears that seemed to be lined with fur. Made sense, keeps the blowing sand out. Big doe eyes, with sexy lashes. I caught myself gazing into them. Something—Oh. Double sets of eyelashes in each eye, thick and curly as a supermodel's. Who would have thought. I gave her a wink, and sank the needle deep into her neck.

Nile Fever flinched but then settled down chewing the cud. At least I think that's what she was doing. I didn't enquire. I stood on the ladder and poured the dissolved sugar into the funnel. In truth, pouring sugar into an animal can become a bit tedious, a bit boring. The solution goes in slowly through the hypodermic and you've got to keep topping the level up in the tube. Your arms get tired. In hospitals they have those steel pole things with hooks for the plastic bag: drip stands I think they're called. Nurses have better things to do than play at being human skyhooks. I tried to distract myself by inventing a snappy one liner about it being harder to get sugar through the eye of the needle than a camel into heaven. The formula escaped me and anyway I didn't think Mutton had the necessary cultural referents.

I said to Share, "You sure this sheikh snoozer knows the way here?"

"Doubt it," she said.

"For Christ's sake," I said. "What if he gets lost?"

"His chauffeur will know the way. You don't think he drives himself, do you?"

"Buggered if I know," I said. "What sort of ride has he got?"

"I don't know. A Roller, something like that."

I could feel the sugar starting to take effect. I took the needle out, disconnected it from the plastic tubing. You wouldn't want a needle-stick injury from a camel, God knows what you might contract.

"Get rid of this, would you, Woz?" He took the bloody needle from me, left me the tubing, and with his usual furtive manner emptied the needle into a small plastic bottle, which he wrapped up in a sheet torn from his newspaper. Worried about infection himself, fair enough. He went over to the camel. Mutton leaned down in the saddle, and they put their heads together and murmured. Mutt placed something carefully in one pocket, maybe a rabbit's foot for luck. I noticed then that Nile's cud chewing was becoming more determined, a trifle manic, the tempo was increasing.

"Come on, gentlemen, enough farting about."

We walked her back to the paddock. She was starting to shift her weight around on her feet as she swayed beside us. Keen for a canter.

The air began to vibrate like a sewing machine on speed.

The chopper came in low over the trees. You'd think the pilot was doing an evade the way he swung the crate around, tilting it. I looked for the police markings—sorry to disappoint, officers, no funny plants growing here, just a routine veterinary procedure on an ordinary, everyday camel. But the chopper was a private machine and it was about to land.

"The fucking sheikh," Share shouted above the noise. The

downdraft from the landing chopper hurled dust and grass and all manner of crap at us. Nile Fever took off like a shot, Mutton clinging on for dear life. The animal wanted out, but it was a galloper not a jumper, it wasn't going to attempt the fence, although the brute slammed against it once or twice, knocking a post free of the ground and leaving a bright red streak of blood from the small open wound in its neck. Within a minute it had done a complete circuit of the paddock, rolling and bucking like a ship at sea. As the noise from the chopper abated I could hear Mutton yelling at the beast. His precise words were unclear, but their intent wasn't: Mutton was trying to rein the beast in with no reins at his disposal other than foul words. Plainly, the single string had snapped instantly. Nothing connected the rider to the animal's head. Mutton was a steerage passenger on a ship of fools of the desert.

The noise from the chopper died. The sheikh emerged. You could tell he was a sheikh by his clobber: head dress, djellaba, the works. He was accompanied by a small man in a standard jockey outfit. The pilot stayed in the machine, talking into his headset. On the perimeter of the paddock Nile Fever was starting her fourth or fifth circuit. Mutton still uttered the occasional indistinct curse but the main sound now was the monotonous drumming of well padded hooves.

"My dear Sharon," the sheikh said. "How nice to see you again." American accent. I suspected Harvard or Princeton, something Ivy League.

"My dear sheikh," Sharon said, "the pleasure is all mine."

The pair of them shook hands like old friends. Abdul bin Sahal al Din seemed quite at ease in the company of western women with bare faces. And at least Share didn't call him your royal highness. I realized I was still holding the plastic sugar-water tube. I shook the geezer's mitt, transferring the plastic tube to my left hand to do so. There was a lot of gold wrapped round the sheikh's fingers. He nodded at the tube in a genial way and said, "Drenching?"

"Sodden," I said. I had no idea what he was talking about.

"Beats giving them an enema," he said. "Ever tried that with a camel?"

I shook my head, shuddering slightly.

"You wouldn't want to, doctor."

We all stood and watched the thundering beast.

"She's fast," the sheikh said and turned back to me. "Will she go the distance?"

"Depends on the distance," I said. The sheikh seemed to think I was some sort of expert, presumably a vet.

"Fifteen kilometers," the sheikh said.

I turned away and coughed convulsively. After a moment, I told him, "No problem."

The little jockey guy started talking very fast in Arabic.

"Amed is worried that your rider is not in control," the sheikh said.

"Well, he isn't," I said. "He's got no reins."

"Reins are unnecessary. The relationship between the camel and its rider is one of psychic communion. It is traditional that all a rider needs is the thinnest strand of silk. The true rider knows his mount's mind and vice versa."

"I think you'll find Mutton is a bit light on when it comes to psychic communion type skills," I said.

"No matter," the sheikh told me in a tranquil tone. "It is the animal we are interested in. She obviously has the temperament of a stayer."

That, indeed, was all too clear. The sugar was working wonders. I had visions of Nile Fever running flat out for another hour and then falling down dead. There'd be no stopping her. Mutton was useless, but you could hardly blame him, stuck up the arse end of the brute with no control mechanism save his own powers of telepathy. Amed began carrying on in Arabic again, a fraught edge to his complaint. I looked at the sheikh. The sheikh looked at the thundering duo and then at me.

"What is your rider doing now?"

"He's not mine," I said. "He's Share's. Her secretary."

"But what's he doing?"

Certainly it was a good question. We stood together and watched as Mutton lay down flat on the animal's back—or as flat as the hump would allow him. His right hand was clamped firmly to the lower bar of the saddle. He appeared to be doing something with his left hand, but it was impossible to see what since the left side of the charging camel was permanently out of the line of sight.

Mutton sat sharply upright. In his hand he brandished the other wooden bar. The little guy, Amed, swore.

The sheikh said, "Good grief!"

Mutton raised the bar, holding it with two hands, and brought it down with a mighty crack on the top of Nile Fever's head. The camel faltered, began to collapse like a slow wave at Bondi beach, rolled over in a cloud of dust. Mutton was thrown free. The camel scrambled to her feet, bellowing like a zoo, galloped off. Without a rider to cramp her style she picked up a turn of speed. The fool of a thing ran in every possible direction, swerving and jinking. Wild eyes rolled in her head, crazed, deranged, stunned; there was no purpose in her madness. The chopper pilot revved up his engine, and who could blame him. As the noise level rose Nile Fever sensed her opponent and charged straight at the roaring machine. The gale of dust and twigs failed to stem the charge and Nile reached the chopper as it lifted. Blades flashed above her head. The machine swayed. Nile went for the open door, missed, got her head through the gap between the skids and the body of the chopper.

"Jesus, it's like a bloody Honda ad!" Wozza was agog. "Oh what a feeling!"

For a moment beast and machine remained locked in a violent, roaring tug of war, dust hurtling away from the conflict like a meteorite shower. If Nile Fever had been centrally placed, things might have been stable, but she wasn't, she was off to one side. The machine tilted wildly. A rotor hit the dirt. The machine crashed in an explosion of flying bits of metal. We all ducked, covering our faces with our arms.

Everything was silent, with the silence that rings in your ears. A crazed roar, then, and Nile Fever was hurtling away from the wreck. Blood flowed from the lengthened gash in her neck, but otherwise she appeared full of beans. This time she wasn't content with a stampede around the perimeter. She charged the gate, smashed it open, vanished in the direction of the house called Shangri La.

The pilot climbed slowly from the pile of twisted metal. He was covered in blood and one arm hung down, apparently useless. After a moment he flexed it, but his mouth said some terrible words. I decided against running forward to help him. He didn't look too friendly and there was a strong smell of aviation fuel in the air. Slowly he walked towards us, a hightech zombie. His face was dead white. From the far side of the paddock Mutton was also starting his walk. Unlike the pilot he was limping badly and he still carried the piece of wood with which he had belabored the camel. I saw blood leaking into his silks.

"I suppose there's no chance of snifter," I said.

"Shut up," Share said.

But the sheikh silently produced a silver hip flask from his robes and handed it to me. "Double malt," he said.

The fuel exploded. The air was thick with sound. The shambling pilot was silhouetted against the flames. A black cloud billowed and made for the heavens. The whisky was as smooth as milk and I realized that my headache had completely cleared. I was feeling quite chipper.

I sat in the back of my own Cobra as Sharon Lesser drove me and our fabulously wealthy guest back to Melbourne. Let her talk to the bugger, it was her mess. Over my shoulder I saw the chopper pilot waiting beside his ruined vehicle for the Air Traffic Authority inspectorate to arrive in their own helicopter. Silk-clad Amed looked crestfallen and faintly comical beside him. Wozza had taken the Mutt haring off in their van to the nearest hospital. Nobody seemed especially concerned about retrieving Nile Fever.

"She might come back in her own time," the sheikh said confidently. "This is not a landscape where a dromedary might feel at home." He turned aside and spoke for a time, in Arabic I assume, into an extraordinary thing, made of gold and diamond with black onyx and probably the ivory tusk of an extinct species of whale, the size of a postage stamp. He slipped it away and told Share, "I have arranged for someone to recover the creature." I didn't think that news would thrill her, especially if they ran a test on the maddened animal's blood. Then again, by the time anyone caught up with Nile Fever she'd probably have metabolized all her spare calories.

Overhead, a Channel 9 TV crew raced in their own chopper toward the devastation now well behind us. Two cop cars roared by. I wondered what sort of beat-up we'd see on the news. War on Terror reaches Melbourne Town? Surely not, too much money tied up in the man in the burnoose, too many oil wells in the hot Mideastern desert, too many delicate trade sensibilities quivering in Canberra. Share was apologizing again, and Abdul bin Sahal al Din waving her regrets aside, blaming it all on the unsophistication of the local breed and his pilot's carelessness. I wasn't too sure which local breed he had in mind but had dark suspicions. A phone rang, and each of us pawed at a pocket or purse. It was mine. I looked at the caller ID.

"I hope you've got somewhere decent for me to sleep tonight, you prick," I said.

"She wouldn't come across, eh." Mauricio was worldly wise but sympathetic. "Those Eastern suburbs bitches, fuck like ferrets until they turn 22, then it's all tennis, swimming and bridge parties."

I leaned over and tapped Share on the shoulder. She shot me an irritated glance in the rear vision mirror. "Can't you entertain yourself for a few more minutes, Dr. Purdue? The sheikh and I are making dinner plans."

"I thought you might be," I said. "Count me in. I'm ravenous. I could eat a camel."

"Shut up. You're a disgrace to your profession."

Hmm. So the cover story continued its cover. Mauricio was nattering on tinnily as I put the phone back to my ear.

"—complete collapse, sorry about your paintings but the insurance will cover at least half the—"

"The paintings were crap from a Kings Cross pavement dauber," I said. "Fifty thou should cover it. Where are you putting me up? We're headed for the Regent, should I put it on your tab?"

"The Regent motel in Regent, maybe." He gave a coarse guffaw. "Who's we? I thought you said you didn't get a bang out of her?"

"I said nothing of the kind," I told him with dignity. "We is me and Share and the Sheikh Abdul bin Sahal al Din, of Saudi Arabia a prince."

The two in the bucket seats had fallen silent. I could hear them listening.

"Don't shit me, Thomas. Listen, the reason I'm calling—"

"I was hoping we'd get to that before we roll up the drive to the Regent. I'm thinking a nice corner suite on the fifteenth floor."

"Dream on. Vinnie was trying to find you."

"He's got my phone number." But Vinnie was too old, too mired in the 20th century, too technologically challenged to understand the uses of cellphones. He paid extra to keep a landline on his desk with an ancient handset. It saddened me to think of the jail time I'd served for a modest evasion of an absurd sumptuary law when the telcoms pocketed billions on endless upgrades. Small beer, granted, compared to the pocket money of the geezer in the passenger seat, but still, it gave a man pause. "What's Vinnie want, Mauricio?"

"Annabelle's got herself into trouble."

"What!" Animal's been a dyke since she was fifteen years old. How the hell could she be "in trouble"? Yes, obviously she could get pregnant of her own free will, gritting her teeth as she did it with a living male, or more likely wielding a turkey baster charged with the stuff of life from some guaranteed HIV-free gay pal, if any, but it wasn't the sort of thing a girl like my daughter stumbled into by accident. Oh fuck. I felt suddenly sick in my guts. Had one of the bent sons of bitches that lurk in the dark dank places she hangs out in got her zonked on roofies and sunk the pork sword? Rage and anxiety fought it out inside my soul, while my body banged about furiously in the back of the Cobra. "I'll kill any motherfucker who got my little girl up the—"

"Not that sort of trouble, you nitwit. She wants you to—" The connection fell out as we hummed between outer and inner city cell boundaries. I smacked the small stupid thing and the hinged portion with the microphone fell off in my lap.

"Will you *goddamn settle down in back?*"

"Pull over, Share."

She put her foot on the accelerator. "Don't be ridiculous."

"This is *my fucking car.* Pull over and let me drive."

"I'll do no such thing. You're an angry man, Dr. Purdue, and I can understand your anxiety, my firm will certainly be prosecuting you to the full extent of the law for the misfeasance your veterinarian malpractice has wrought in respect of our prime racing camel Nile Fever, and I cannot too strongly advise you—"

The sheikh gave me a manly grimace from behind the edge of his burnoose and handed me his own elegant phone. It looked like a shrunken iPhone. But there was no display.

"Speak to it," the sheikh said. "Speak carefully, like myself it understands English but not always Australian."

"I seem to have come out without my Filofax. How do I get directory assistance?"

"Just ask the program, it is quite capable," the sheikh said. He didn't have the look of a man who spent much time talking with directory assistance, or looking up the telephone directory either.

"Get me Vincent F.X. Mannix," I said.

"Vincent F.X. Mannix, 35a Wilson Lane, Brunswick, Victoria, Australia?" the phone said in a soft female American accent.

"That's the old goat," I said.

"Please answer 'Yes' or 'No'."

"It's bloody him, all right?"

"Please answer 'Yes' or 'No'."

"Yes. Fucking *yes*. Christ."

"Hold the line, please."

"Fuck off," I said, "There is no line, this is a mobile."

"Hold the line, please."

"Who's this cretin I'm speaking to?"

"A telco AI pod," the sheikh said. "In Bangalore."

"Good God, no wonder it sounds like something out of a Stephen King movie."

"That's Bangor, Maine, you oaf," Share told me, eyes on the road. "Bangalore is in India."

"The new computational center of the free world," the sheikh said. There was pride in his voice, as if it was all his doing. For all I knew maybe it was. Free world, that was a laugh. I recalled a current affairs special on TV, a sickening little program about fifteen schoolgirls getting burned to death in Mecca. The righteous religious police fucks outside wouldn't unlock the doors for them, because they weren't wearing their scarves. I really hate watching TV.

"I have to talk to *India* to get a connection to Brunswick?"

"It's a global village," the sheikh said.

The phone purred like a cat with cream. After a few seconds Vinnie's voice said, "Yup?"

Before I could answer, the smooth, female American voice said, "Go ahead, please. Have a nice day."

"Who the fuck's that?" Vinnie said.

"It's an Internet site in India pretending to be a country switch-board operator in 1920," I said. "Nostalgia chic. The shock of the old. Ignore it, Vinnie."

"Tom? Just where are you, in bloody America or bloody India?"

"Halfway back from the Dandenongs, mate. Our camel's done a bunk." Wait a moment, Vinnie didn't know about Nile Fever.

"Quit bullshitting me. Animal's in trouble."

"So Mauricio said."

"Well, what are you going to do about it, Tom? She needs you, she's your daughter."

"What sort of trouble are we talking about?"

"Girl trouble."

"Period cramps? Tell her to talk to her quack."

"One of her friends..."

"...her *lesbian mates*."

"Yeah, one of them. Could be dead, Tom."

"You don't die of period pains," I said.

"A lot you know," Share said from the front seat.

"Shut up, this is private. You can die of PMT, I'll give you that, especially if you're the bloke in the picture."

"Animal wouldn't say," Vinnie told me. "Just said she needed you."

"Okay, Pops," I said. "I'll drop round and see her."

"You do that, Tom. She's a good girl at heart. You should try to be a bit more of a father. Take an interest."

"See you, mate."

I exhaled slowly and relaxed as much as I could in the nar-row confines of the luggage compartment. No bun in the oven for Animal after all, unlikely as that had seemed. The delights of grandparenthood receded. A good thing too, I was far too young to be a granddad, I still had the best part of my life ahead of me. I handed the slender phone back reluctantly to the sheikh, wonder-ing how he'd react to a request for a loan. Not just of the phone. I was skint. With my *feng shui* headquarters now reduced to rubble, my chances of earning anything in the near future seemed slight. The monthly repayment on the Cobra was a month overdue as it was. The Easy Finance man had already been round, making easy threats. It occurred to me that it might be time to relinquish the vehicle completely, go a bit Gandhian in the material possessions stakes.

I told Share, "Drop me in Brunswick, will you? Same place as last night. You can keep the car for the moment. Use it until the Audi's back on the road."

"The Audi, Purdue, is worth its weight in scrap metal and you know it. The only 'road' it'll ever get back on is the road to oblivion."

"Yeah, well, anyway, hang onto the Cobra for the time being."

"I might just do that."

Too right. Let the fucking sheikh pay the mortgage.

I don't often visit Animal. The notice on the door at the top of the stairs—*Well Cut Your Balls Off*—is a powerful disincentive to paternal contact. This time things were different. She needed me, and a father always wants to be needed. Plus I needed a place to stay. Animal and a shifting population of girlfriends live above Vinnie's shop. Vinnie himself lives two streets away with an old crone called Mrs. Murphy who is the Czar of all the Russias' great great grand-daughter when she is not being a reincarnation of Cleopatra. As she once pointed out to me when I questioned the apparent contradiction, there is no reason why Cleopatra couldn't have been reincarnated as the Czar's great great grand-daughter. It seemed quite proper, actually. Maintain the bloodlines down the ages.

I waved a hand at the departing Cobra, wondering if I'd ever see it again, and entered Vinnie's shop. Vinnie prides himself on running a ships' chandlers with pawn broking facilities. What he actually sells is stuff that has fallen off the back of a truck. I pushed the door open and listened with pleasure to the *ting*. There's nothing electronic about Vinnie's door's *ting*. Opening the door compresses a powerful spring, then trips a hammer that slams into a ship's bell. The bell in question belonged to the S.S. Windermear which sank off Portsea with the loss of all hands in 1897. Vinnie himself looted it from the wreck in 1951. On the back wall of the shop a picture hangs of Vinnie all dressed up in his 1950s diving gear. It's been a long time since Vinnie last went swimming.

"That you, Tom?" Vinnie looked up from the form guide.

"You can see it's me," I said.

"You're standing in the light."

"You're blind."

"I'm not as young as I was."

"Never a truer word," I said. Actually he looked quite chipper, for an ancient wreck of a man.

"Didja see your house on telly last night?"

"No," I said. "I never watch television. I prefer the opera and the company of heart-breaking women."

"I could get you a nice little set. Friends' price, of course."

"You're not my friend, Vinnie," I said. "You're Animal's pretend grandfather. The preferential price still applies, though, I hope." Annabelle actually still had two sets of grandparents, Patty's mother and father and mine, but Patty's parents hated me with a passion and I loathed mine and everything to do with them. She once told a little friend that Vinnie was her fairy grandfather, which caused his eyes to narrow before he gave a gruff laugh and tousled her hair fondly. She might have been the only person ever to mistake Vin for a fairy.

"You see all sorts of interesting stuff, you should try it," Vinnie assured me. He keeps a small set behind the counter. It's never switched off and the sound is never above a whisper. God knows what the deaf old coot actually gets from it. "Take this morning," he said. "One of those helicopters collided with a camel."

"It's worse than the *National Enquirer*," I said. "You'd believe anything."

"The camel escaped from captivity and seems to have collided with a bus filled with nuns. A write-off, the bus, they say, nobody badly hurt thank heavens. The poor animal was just running down the road, maddened by terror." His voice became sepulchral, and his eye uncanny. "When the authorities arrived it had been *mutilated*. UFOs, Mrs. Murphy says. It's not for me to say, of course, there were no camels on board ship." He returned to the form guide. "I believe *you* mentioned a camel."

"Talking of Animals—"

"You'd better go up and see her. Trouble in the family."

Vinnie might regard all his borrowed grand-daughter's lesbian mates as family, I'm not so sure I do. But then Vinnie probably regards the Czar of all the Russias as family. A mob of dykes would just be chicken feed under that sort of family tree. I opened the flap in the counter and made my way to the back of the shop. Apparently Vinnie had got in a job lot of Belgian camembert—six months past the use-by date and smelling of it. Gagging gently, I held my breath and climbed the stairs to the door with the welcoming message, knocked, entered without waiting.

Heavy curtains completely blacked out the living room, if you could call it that. A red candle burned on a low table. The air was heavy with incense, luckily.

"Christ, Dad. Shut the door," Animal said. "You're letting the dark out." I did as I was told. "Sit down, Dad. Make yourself at home."

It took me a few seconds to locate a chair in the darkness. And another few seconds, luckily before I sat on it, to identify the cushion as a cat. I picked up the cat and sat down. The cat began to purr on my lap.

"Fuckin traitor," a voice which wasn't Animal's said from the same corner of the room as my Goth daughter. "Some fuckin attack cat you are, Sappho."

My night vision was coming into play. Animal lay full length on a disintegrating couch, her head on the other woman's lap.

"Who's your friend?"

"This is Grime Grrl. Grime, meet my dad."

"G'day, Mr. Animal," Grime Grrl said.

"My name's Tom."

"Whatever."

During a slight pause in the conversation, I stroked Sappho the cat. Sappho's purrs began to sound like gravel in a cement mixer. The candle light glinted on the metal in Grime Grrl's face. It didn't appear that I was about to be offered tea and biscuits.

"So about this missing grrl," I said.

"We want you to find her," Animal said. "You being a private eye and all that."

"*Feng shui* consultant," I said.

"Jesus, Dad, I thought you were a private eye."

"That was years ago," I said. "I lost my license, if you'll remember. You're really not permitted to have one when you've been in prison. They get quite tetchy."

"No, can't remember that," Animal said. "*Years ago* is a bit of a blur, actually." I got the impression that Animal thought this was a good thing; anybody who could remember years ago was in big trouble. "Anyway," she said, "we want you to find Cookie."

"This Cookie is a missing suspected possibly deceased person?" I said. "You don't actually have a corpus delicti to show me?"

"There you go, Dad, you can still do it. Deceased person. Corpus de Licketty. Fuckin ace."

I felt tired. "So tell me about this Cookie," I said. "Full name. Address. Physical description. Last known whereabouts. Reasons for suspecting foul play."

"She's Grime's sister. She lives here. Only she doesn't exactly live here now if she's dead." It was banter, but there was a choke in her resolutely Goth throat.

"How do you know?"

"Well, it's obvious, Sherlock. She isn't here."

"Real homebody is she?"

"Was, maybe," Grime said in her flat, depressed voice.

"Or maybe she just went out for a bite to eat."

"We cast the runes. They say she's no longer on this plane."

Sappho choked, convulsed neatly, put a wet hairball in my lap and jumped off. I knew just how she felt.

"The captain and crew have all left this plane," I said. "I blame the air traffic controller's strike."

"What?"

"Or maybe the luggage handlers." I found an old snotty Kleenex in my pocket, captured the hairball, went looking for the trash bin. It was neatly under the sink, where you'd expect it to be anywhere else than here. I ran cold water over my fingers. I don't know, I've become fastidious living in Parkville.

"He's a sarcastic bastard," Grime Grrl told my daughter.

"Cookie's a bit overweight," Animal said. "She doesn't like going out in public. She's shy."

"I need a bit more evidence than a handful of runes," I said. I blame myself, for her twelfth birthday I gave her a box of Druid's Scrying Stones, With Solomon's Key to All Mysteries. She'd been a pretty thing in a pink party dress and gawky coltish limbs. Animal never went through the tomboy phase. Dolls and lippy in front of the mirror and pretty sparkly thread wound around her hair one day, industrial machinery protruding from her face the next, that's what it seemed like. Of course I hadn't been around a lot.

"We read her blog. Some prick was stalking her."

I sat down again, and allowed Sappho to return. How many hairballs can one cat hide? "I have no idea what the fuck you're talking about, Grime. What's a blog, and how can you stalk someone who never leaves the house?"

"Web log," Grime Grrl said. She gave me a dark, wondering look in the darkness. "On her site?"

"Cyberstalking," my daughter said. Her hands were shaking a little, and she delved in her layers of black and purple. The light of her match went off in my adapted eyes like a flare. She lit a second cigarette from the first, handed it to Grime. The stink of the fumes filled the room, and I was wheezing instantly. I thank God every day that I gave up smoking when I was 15. From the age of 12 I smoked a packet a day. It was my first taste of crime, and crime tasted tasty after the first few days of gasping and retching, and besides it was wholesomely vegan, no animal products at all in your average ciggie. They used to have these vending machines in public places that disgorged packets of 20 when you pushed in a handful of coins and kicked the thing a few times. Hard to credit in these politically correct days. In the lobby at the movies, in the pub when you went in the Ladies Lounge with your Mum, at the cop shop and church probably. Me and my mates quickly learned the dozen best ways to tickle the stupid things. A galvanized washer on a string was a good one. They weighed about the same as a coin. You'd feed the washer down the slot, wait for the click, yank it back, drop it again until it threw up its nicotine hairball. Or you could just boot the machine to bits, but that made a racket and people tended to chase you down the street.

I opened a black-painted window. It groaned, and the two women shrieked. Smoke eddied in the stream of light, I wondered for a moment if their vampire flesh had caught fire.

"It's one or the other," I said, waving at the polluted air in front of my face. "I know it's banal of me, Animal, but those filthy things kill you."

Wrong approach. A man would do better frightening a Goth with news that cigarettes give you a hearty appetite and a summery suntan.

"I know it's anal of you, Dad, but I really don't give a shit about your obsession with health and *feng shui*." She put out her smoke with a bad grace, got up and shut the window again. Grime's fag glowed in the dimness for a moment, then she crushed hers out as well. The stink lingered. A disbarred doctor in the joint told me it's a kind of phobic allergy you get once you give up the cancer sticks. It's a physiological defense to keep you out of harm's way, makes the temptation too disgusting. I dunno, never seems to stop junkies, they're always puking their guts out after a hit, seems to be part of the joy of the thing.

"Watching your Mum die of cancer might have something to do with it," I said.

"Yeah, well, everyone's got to die. It's part of the balance." She's surlier now than she was when she wore dresses and clomped around in her mother's shoes.

"Maybe that's what happened to Cookie," I said, getting to my feet again. "Can I use your crapper?"

"There's one downstairs that Vinnie uses. Are you coming back?" Animal looked a bit anxious, there in the darkness.

"Yeah, hang on."

I went down the outside steps, had a whiz in a loo that hadn't been cleaned for a while, a bit out of character with the neat sink and trash bin upstairs. I decided they just didn't want me messing up their bathroom, or even being in there with my heinous testosterone emanations. God knows what kinds of abominable underwear was draped over the shower rail, I was probably well out of it. I went back through Vinnie's shop to Sydney Road and bought some ham rolls with tomato and non-Camembert cheese from Ivy's Cafe, currently being run by a pair of middle-aged Cambodians.

"Thanks, Chhom," I said, folding a copy of *The Age* as I paid her. "Look, give me three black coffees to go, okay? Make that three black and one with milk and two sugars."

"Mother Hen in the fourth at Randwick," Chhom said.

"Five to one," I said, nodding. "I hear Brute Force is good for a canter up in Brisbane."

"I'll put a dollar on for you, Mr. Purdue. No charge."

It was an arrangement we had, a tip or two for snacks. I carried the booty back to the shop, evading a Number 19 tram and the hoonish van tailgating it.

"Fuckers," I said to Vinnie. "No courtesy. You take milk don't you."

"Two sugars. Thanks, Tom. Mother Hen's been scratched."

"Damn."

When I got back to the den of the night, the women were stretched out just where they'd been ten minutes earlier, but some dreadful racket was coming from about fifteen speakers scattered around the room. I could see why the vicars call it Satanic music. I gave my daughter a pained look, and handed over two of the coffees. Grime took hers with an ill grace, but waved a thing in her hand and the noise dropped a few decibels.

"I can make a few calls," I said. "Won't promise anything."

"Okay."

"Well, where's your phone?" Sappho had disappeared, I suppose her musical taste agreed with mine. I'd seen a phone line running along the top of the door, but it didn't seem to end in anything you could hold a conversation over.

"We got cut off for non-payment. Use your mobile, you're as clueless as Vinnie."

"I can't." I fished the remains out of my pocket. "Never buy technology from the Philippines." I tried to push the two pieces together, but it was completely pointless, they might as well have come from totally different phones. Maybe they had.

"Give me a look, Tom," Grime Grrl said. She stayed where she was on the couch, fat arm extended, fingers loosely open.

"I'm telling you, it's broken."

Her arm stayed where it was. I sighed and crossed the room, gave her the buggered phone. She held the parts close to her eyes, wiggled them, pulled a long dangerous metal pin out of her hair, jabbed twice rather crossly at the mouthpiece, put the pin back in her hair, jiggled the bits, handed me the healed phone. It was like a miracle from Lourdes.

"Grime's doing a masters in Electrical Engineering at RMIT," Animal told me with offhand pride.

I was punching numbers. "Hoping for a job with the privatized Telstra, are we?"

"I'm the sound wonk for Bleeding Anus," Grime said.

"Melbourne City Morgue," said a nasal voice in my ear.

I couldn't believe it, still couldn't. Like seeing the lame walk.

"Can you hear me?"

"Hold the line a moment," the voice said.

"Good Christ." I said. "They're all doing it."

When Jake came back he told me that no young defunct over-weight women lay at that moment on his slab. He could offer me a Vietnamese hoon stabbed to death outside King's in King St at three a.m., and a rather bloated elderly woman fished from the Coburg Lake.

"Thanks, pal."

"Mother Hen's scratched," he told me gloomily.

"Someone must have talked," I said, and clicked the phone shut. Jesus, half of fucking Melbourne must have talked.

"Show me this web site thing," I told Animal.

The picture on the 19 inch flat screen was not unflattering. If a man's tastes ran to the pleasantly plump and necrophiliac, with dead-black dyed hair and up-thrust boobs like Vampirella's, he could do a lot worse than Cookie.

"I thought you said she was fat."

"That's when she was 16. Hang on, where's the one you got at the bar mitzvah."

"Fuck, don't show him that," Grime shouted, "Cookie will kill you."

"I thought Cookie had done a bunk," I said. "I need to know what she looks like now, not what she looked like in her fashion shoot. Urk."

Like a whale in black satin. Like a small orca with legs like hams. Like an orca porker. Cookie liked her tuck, you could tell. But she didn't like the camera. From her furious expression, I had the feeling Cookie might have chased her sister with a carving knife, if the poor thing was able to heave herself out of her chair.

"How the hell did you get her wheelchair up and down these stairs?" I said.

"I told you, she didn't get out much."

"So when did you last see her?"

"I dunno," Animal said. "A few days ago."

"How many days?"

"Some."

"Come on, think, Animal."

"Look, I don't count the days, right? I'm not a 24/7 freak. I work to more elemental rhythms."

"What rhythms are those?"

"The phases of the moon. The tug of my own menstrual tides."

"So how many moons ago did you last see Cookie?"

"Look, she was meant to show up in court yesterday. And she didn't front. So some arsehole from the court—called himself a sheriff—came looking for her."

"Bloody sheriff," Grime said. "Keep them doggies rolling, rawhide."

"We told him she didn't live here, of course," Animal said. "We told him she'd gone to New Guinea. That got rid of him."

"And had she?" I said. "Gone to New Guinea?"

"Christ, no. She was in her room. Only she wasn't."

"You went looking for Cookie in her room? To tell her about the sheriff?"

"Yep."

"And she wasn't there?"

"Nope."

"And how long before that had you actually seen her?"

"Dad, quit with the third degree, right? We hadn't seen her for some time."

"So why do you think she could be dead? Maybe she's just moved out. Couldn't stand you two, or something."

"There was a note."

"Not a suicide note?"

"I dunno. It was a note."

"Do you have it? Are you actually in possession of the note?"

"Of course we bloody do," Animal said.

"Of course we bloody are," Grime Grrl said.

"Well, could I see it, please?"

"Try not to sound so aggressive, Dad."

"Annabelle, I'm meant to be helping you. You are meant to be engaging my services as an investigator. A certain element of co-operation might—"

"Yeah, yeah, and don't call me Annabelle." Animal shifted her head slightly to allow Grime Grrl to get off the couch. Grime Grrl didn't move. "Do us a favor, Grimes. Get Dad the note."

"You had it last," Grime said.

"It's in Cookie's room. On the mantelpiece."

Grime Grrl spoke to me: "It's in Cookie's room. On the mantelpiece."

I had half a mind to walk out on the pair of them. But Animal is my daughter and, if the truth be known, I'm in debt to her for certain favors rendered in the not too distant past. So I did like a proper investigator: I asked which was Cookie's room and made my way to the scene of the crime. If crime it was.

Cookie's room was high-tech. It was surprisingly neat and well lit by ordinary daylight; for a moment I stood and blinked in the glare. There was a huge bed, a wardrobe and two tables. The tables were piled high with computers and their peripherals. I didn't recognize any of the brand names. Cookie obviously worked with gear that was a cut above that found in the average suburban *feng shui* consultancy. I turned my attention to the mantelpiece. A collection of sea shells and dried flowers stood sentinel beside a single sheet of A4 torn off at the end. The paper was covered with letters cut out of magazines. The note read:

by the TiME U read this I ShalL B
GoNe .Yr s iN SisterHood cookIe ,

I found it a bit hard to take the thing seriously. It looked like no suicide note I'd ever seen. It looked like a joke. I left the joke where it was and sat down at one of Cookie's computers. I dislike computers, but I do know how to use them, a bit. It took about five minutes for the machines to defeat me completely. Everywhere I went I was confronted with demands for passwords, curt pronouncements that access was denied. I managed to open one document and thought for a moment I was getting somewhere, but the page was covered in numbers arranged in lots of six. I'm no code buster, I couldn't even make the msn messenger virtual phone work, the headset stayed dead as a doornail. Under the counter was a large contraption on slithery rails. I drew it out. Laser printer, electronic gray tail running back into the bowels of the computer. A pile of paper in the output chute. I took them out and looked at them with the keen insight of a disbarred private investigator. I switched off both machines then and made my way back to the darkened living room. Animal and Grime hadn't moved.

"Did you read the note?" Animal said.

"Every word of it."

"So, there you are, she's dead."

"I doubt it," I said. Like a magician, I showed them several sheets of paper like Cookie's death note. Each was made from individual letters torn from papers and magazines, scanned, printed on a high-quality printer.

hELP! i aM dr.Morris GOLDfiNKle ! said one.

The diNGo TOOk my baBy! said another.

by The TimE u see This, my body wiIl Be aToN By croKS! warned a third.

"Regard the small print at the bottom of each sheet," I said with quiet modesty. I was proud of my detection. In the smallest font known to man, each page said www.deathjoke.com.

"Aw right," Grime said. "Yeah, we saw them in *Suicide Girl*. I suppose she must have printed them off the website."

This gave me a measure of confidence that Cookie was not sleeping with the fishes, but I still wondered how she'd got out of her room. The whale was not likely to be nimble on her feet. Someone she'd met on line?

"Tell me—what did she do in there with all that computing gear?"

"Made enemies," Grime said.

"How?" I said.

"Cookie was the scourge of cyberspace. There are some real arseholes out there, posting all sorts of crap about women. And Cookie was onto them."

"How," I said.

"I dunno. Do you know, Animal?"

"She squeezed their balls," Animal said.

"In cyberspace?" I said.

"It's what's called a *metaphor*, Dad. Cookie hacked into their computers and did things to them that could be regarded as analogous to squeezing their owners' balls in a vice. You could call it an objective correlative. Get it?"

"I'm glad we sent you to that expensive school," I said.

"It was a dump," Animal said.

"But she's not so limber in the real world. Climbing up and down the stairs, say. She's..." You weren't supposed to say *crippled*. "She's, like, *differently mobile*, right?"

Our conversation paused. It idled, motor humming. You could have gained the impression that it had been switched off, or sent to bed without its supper. In most other situations this would have been embarrassing, have led to uneasy coughing and head scratching and, sooner or later, a forced bit of dialogue. But I know Animal and her friends well enough—they go silent on a regular basis. There's nothing strained about it. I allowed myself to think my own thoughts. (a) I had little doubt that this Cookie girl had just done a runner, even if she was in a wheelchair or needed crutches or just had to pause for breath and a bite to eat every few steps. The joke note was too ridiculous to be taken seriously. We might as well be concerned about the dingo taking Cookie's baby. (b) I was in dire need of somewhere to stay, somewhere where an energetic police force wouldn't come knocking to ask questions about the re-alignment of my previous abode, the death and mysterious mutilation of Nile Fever (and what the hell was up with *that*?), or associated criminal damage done to a helicopter. (c) It was true that I did owe my daughter for some small services rendered.

I said, "Look, I'll see what I can do about finding Cookie for you. But I need somewhere to stay. Cookie's room will do fine. When I find its tenant I'll move out."

"Jeezus H!" Grime yelled. "That's against the rules. This is a respectable house. No men!"

"Rules were meant to be broken," I said. "Go on, Grime, be a rebel."

"*You* tell him, Animal. It's bad enough having him sitting here in broad daylight. Now he wants to sleep in poor Cookie's bed. Tell him to sod off, Animal."

"He's my dad," Animal said.

"Fucking patriarch! They're the worst—"

"Tell me," I said, changing the subject, "what exactly was Cookie meant to be doing in court?"

"Fucking *men*," Grime raged on, ignoring me. I was used to that from Animal. "Always sticking their bits and parts in where they're not wanted. If this guy whacks off all over Cookie's new satin—"

"Hey, he's my *dad*, Grime."

I was startled and, I have to admit, rather pleased to find that Animal had her limits. My squeamish Goth kid.

"The nuclear family... Christ, what a fucking bourgeois institution. More rape goes on in—"

"Hey, listen, Dad," Animal said, raising her head from Grime's lap. "Me and Grime Grrl have got some talking to do. How about you go out and do a bit of investigating. Ask a few questions. You can sleep here tonight."

"Then I'm *not*," Grime said. My phone rang. I flicked it open, and the mouthpiece section fell off again. "Jesusmaryandjoseph," cried Grime Grrl, "*now* what have you done to it?"

I held the two segments out to her, shaking my head, making it clear that her self esteem as an electronic artisan was at stake. The part with the ringer in it was still ringing. She snatched them from me, jammed them back together.

"What?" she said into the phone. Her eyes widened. "Share! What are you doing calling this number?"

"Share?" I said. I reached for the phone. Grime leaned away from me. Bits of metal in her face clattered against the plastic.

"Yeah, this is his phone. No, they took ours away two weeks ago, the pricks. Non-payment of rent, have you ever heard such shit? Information wants to be free! Telstra and Optus and the unions are all conspir—Sorry, what? Oh, all right." She held the phone out, not looking at me.

"*Feng Shui Solutions,*" I said. The mouthpiece stayed where it was, for a wonder. "I take it I have the pleasure of addressing Mrs. Sharon Lesser of Balwyn?"

"G'day, Purdue," Share's voice said. "I see your phone's working again. Stick your daughter on, will you?"

"And the top of the morning to you, too, Share. Why didn't you just get Grime Grrl to pass it over directly to Animal? I mean, yes, it's my phone and my phone number, and I pay the monthly bill which is more than these slack layabouts can manage with their own connection to the world although I see that it hasn't stopped them hooking their bloody high-end computers up to a premium optical fiber feed—"

"That's Cookie's," Animal said, eavesdropping. "For her job, obviously."

"I thought you said she had trouble leaving the house? What job?"

"Pay attention you nitwit," Share said. "I'll be there in five minutes. I have a little present for you, by the way, so you might as well stick around. Now let me speak to Animal."

"You didn't even know her last night."

"What are you talking about?"

"You thought she was a hooker. The very idea offended your prim Balwyn sensibilities."

The phone was silent for a moment. I thought I heard a sigh. "She was sulking. Tom, would you stop fart-arsing around and *fucking put Annabelle on the fucking line.*"

"There *is* no line," I said feebly, and handed it over. Animal tucked it between her shoulder and her jaw and sloped off to Cookie's room, shutting the door behind her with a bang.

After a bit more silence I coughed and said to the recumbent if not dead Grime, "You know her, then?"

"Well, shit, obviously. Me and Cookie."

"Uh huh. And is Cookie also a—"

"A muff diver? A carpet eater? A canyon yodeler? A butch man-hating ball-lopping dyke? None of your beeswax."

I wondered if Share hadn't been entirely frank with me. A few tumblers were tumbling into place.

"Animal told Share about the sugar? Me and Canned Fish?"

Grime Grrl looked at me. Our companionable silence extended itself for a bit.

"Hmm. You were telling me about Cookie's source of income?"

"Well, Vinnie, for starters."

I felt the hairs rise on the back of my neck, and the juices in my guts curdle. That *was* disgusting. Vinnie? He was a hundred if he was a day. Well, seventy-five. Surely his balls had shriveled up by now. The man was meant to be devoted to commerce and the sacred memory of the sea.

"What?" I said. "Vinnie what?"

"She runs his investment web site. Ran, maybe." A slow tear leaked down Grime's face, taking some pale makeup with it. "She coulda done a real suicide, how can we tell?"

Animal's laughter rang through the door. A moment later she opened it and came back, clicking the phone shut. As she did so, the mike part fell off and clattered on the hard flooring. I ignored it.

"My father-in-law is running an SP shop by phone?" I asked in amazement. "In this day and age where one can find a Tabaret on every corner or place your bets by touchphone from the privacy and comfort of your own home?"

"Running a what?"

"Starting price bookie. Strictly illegal. Untaxed. Pursued by the State government and its licensed gambling minions with the full vigor and malice of the law."

"All over the world," Animal told me. "Peer-to-peer." Grime was back fiddling with the phone, snuffling in her grief but wielding her hair pin like a top neurosurgeon. "Lotto syndicates. Track meets. Football games across the planet. Digital two-up. Horse races in eighty-nine nations."

"Camel races," I said.

"Yeah, that too," Animal said.

I got to my feet and went to the cupboard looking for something to drink. I found a fifth of Scotch, two-thirds empty. One seven and a halfth of Scotch. You get quite nimble at mental arithmetic, being a runner for an SP bookie like Vin when you're a teenager. I whipped the top off and glugged down a good quarter of it. A thirtieth of Scotch down the hatch. It burned satisfactorily. I heard my Cobra pulling in to the parking space below, there's something distinctive about those American sports models, something that sounds like all the money you've shoveled into the endlessly open cash register of the one authorized maintenance garage in the Southern Hemisphere and certainly you wouldn't wish to risk going anywhere else and violating your warranty. Sharon Lesser's boot heels clipped their way up the steps, so I went to the door and opened it. Light cruelly penetrated the darkness, and I saw what Vinnie had meant about not being able to see who it was.

"Don't stand there gawking, man, the game's afoot and we have urgent business elsewhere." She kicked the door shut, walked past me as one does the doorman in the Ruritanian outfit standing at the entrance to the Regent. Sharon embraced Animal with a degree of warmth, obviously they *did* know each other. Grime Grrl at least looked at her without scowling, and showed her cheek for a peck. "The sheikh was well satisfied with his purchase," she told my daughter. "Here's a little something for you good grrls." An envelope went from her handbag to Animal's sleeve like a needle passing through the eye of a camel. Before I had time to protest, she found its twin and handed it to me. The paper that the envelope was hand-crafted from smelled of the attar of roses or something in that neighborhood, and contained ten hundred dollar bills.

"And this is for *feng shui* services rendered?"

"Your aid this morning netted you five thousand dollars," she said. Even as I opened my mouth in outrage, she said, "Of which I have naturally retained four thousand to cover the damage to my Audi. You can appeal to your thuggish mate Mauricio for a rebate."

"He went for it," Animal was explaining to Grime. "Bought the consignment."

"Racing camels," I said, to show everyone I could read between the lines. "From the western desert. Even now being prepared and pampered for their flight into Egypt."

"Not exactly. And into Saudi, actually," Share said.

"Or would be, if the bloody creatures existed outside of your fevered imagination."

"There are cynics among us," Share said to Animal. She gave her a kiss which looked surprisingly motherly and went to the door, tossing me my keys. "It's a little more complicated than that, Mr. Purdue. You can drive," she said.

"Hang on," Grime Grrl called from the couch. Her tone was plaintive. "He's solving a case. He's finding Cookie for us."

"Cookie's not here?" Share spun on her heel. In the dimness, her face seemed to grow paler but it was hard to be sure. I was finding almost everything hard to be sure about, however.

"She left a note," I said. "'BY tHE TiME U rEad tHiS i ShaLL B GONE'."

"Oh shit," Share said. She shook her head. "Poor Jonquil. She's such an unhappy child. But we don't have time for her tantrums right now. Toot sweet, Purdue."

I generally try to stay one klick under the speed limit in town, which is not hard to manage in Sydney Road. The Cobra hums along country roads like a dream of fluid dynamics, more cat than snake, but grinds and gargles and groans in the stop-start nightmare that the Coburg end of Sydney Road has become. What with clearways alternating with parking for shoppers, and the great green and yellow or madly Leunig-daubed behemoths of trams scratching along their tracks in the middle of the road like Victorian aunties out for a stroll, a man was lucky to get better than jogging speed. You'd see insouciant bike riders skim by, zip through the lights, leave you stuck behind the tram as one little old lady made her painful descent to the street. Don't get me wrong, I love Melbourne's trams. In the holiday break between school and uni I worked for six weeks as a conductor, wearing their daggy, baggy government issue brown uniform and cap, and a happier time I can't recall. Dinging the bell for stops, stuffing the cardboard backing of a block of sold tickets behind the cardboard advertisements placed at eye level for the many poor buggers who stood swaying, crammed together, hoping for a seat. That was before the State government got all twenty-first century and threw out the conductors, replacing the friendly and helpful connies with clunky machines everyone hated and nobody bought tickets from. It was a people's passive resistance strike, Gandhi would have been proud of us.

The tram line terminated at Baker's Road, and the pace picked up.

"Where now?"

"Just keep going," Share told me.

"Christ, we'll be on the Hume Highway in a minute."

"Not for long. Take a left at the first lights after Boundary Road." She was dabbing at her eyes. An emotional woman.

"Jonquil Lesser," I said, "is your daughter."

She gave an angry bark of laughter. "Break it down, Purdue. How the hell old do you think I am?"

"A gentleman never says."

"Well not that fucking old. Cookie is my husband's child."

"I very much doubt that she's dead," I said.

"Of course she isn't, you idiot. Girls fall out. She probably felt cooped up there in that place."

Maybe so, but how had she got out, in her condition? And why leave her computer and other tools of her dubious trade? I watched her and the road. "You don't get on."

Share shot me a glance, shrugged. "She's difficult. How did you know?"

"Well, you didn't put your head into her room with a cheery hello from the visiting stepmother."

"She's taken a set against me, doesn't like me in there. Ruby's nearly as bad. God knows why. The trophy wife syndrome I suppose. I've asked Annabelle but she just clams up."

"Animal and clams are as one." I thought I should leave it at that for the moment. Really, what the hell did I know? Somehow I didn't like the husband doing his mysterious business in K.L. and I'd never even met the man. Hard to track the logic of it all, although some connections were becoming clear. Part of me was very angry indeed at Annabelle. But I couldn't say that I was displeased to have made the acquaintance of her friend's stepmother. Crazy bitch though she was.

For a wonder the lights were green. I turned smartly through the great wide gates of Fawkner Crematorium & Memorial Park and round the fountain, patiently following Share's instructions. The road was candy striped with parallel paint lines in many merry hues, like a hospital floor, the better to guide the dead to their destinations, some peeling off to the right, some to the left, some forging straight on.

"Not only is the end nigh," I said, "it's conveniently color coded."

A stifled snort implied that I was forgiven.

"Seventh Avenue," she told me.

We had to wait as a funereal cavalcade passed, headlights burning sullenly in afternoon daylight. In the long dark gray limo behind the hearse, a wife or mistress wailed behind smoky glass. Several vehicles back, four hearty real estate agents or used car salesmen howled as the driver, beefy red face creased with hilarity, reached the punch line of his joke. We crossed Merlynston Creek.

Never flush with water at the best of times in these greenhouse El Nino days, it looked parched and cracked. I parked on asphalt outside a blandly tasteful interfaith chapel. Share put on a broad-brimmed hat with a handy obscuring veil.

"Who's being buried? Or is it roasted?"

"Walk with me," Share said, taking my arm. "Let us reason together."

A cemetery is perhaps the finest place to meet when skullduggery is on your mind. You wander respectfully among the headstones, speaking softly, heads close, consoling one another. Family members might meet by accident, bearing floral tributes or simply dropping in to commune with the spirit of the deceased. We passed a few clumps of strangers standing tranquilly beside plots, or perhaps hatching them. Sharon Lesser knew her way around the place. We stopped under a tall Australian native tree, and waited there for the man meditating with his back to us at a nearby grave.

"Who's the mourner?"

"Surely you know him."

I shrugged, although there was something familiar about the man.

"Everyone should know Culpepper," Share said.

Christ, so it was. "Really," I said in a flat voice. The underworlds and overworlds of Melbourne are variegated and many, despite the regular outbreaks of internecine murder in the streets. I'd only known Mutton and Wozza by chance, really, and never met Culpepper, which was not remotely surprising. Not that he was the chairman of the Stock Exchange, but he moved in those circles, although you never saw his picture in the social pages or heard his name on TV.

"He expedites things," Share explained, as if to a moron.

I gave her a cryptic look. I was getting a bit jack of Share's woman-of-mystery act. Two can play at that game. "What things?"

"For heaven's sake, man," she said, impatient with me in her turn. "He expedites whatever you want expedited."

Maybe that was about as much as she knew about the man. It wasn't that I knew a whole hell of a lot more, but international gambling figured near the top of the list. Maybe he knew the sheikh. Bound to. I decided to ignore her. A couple of lorikeets in the tree above our heads were carrying on like pork chops, shouting and screeching at each other, hanging upside down by their claws, ripping at the gum nuts like vandals. I studied their behavior for a minute or two. The mourner stood beside us. Incongruously, he held in one hand by its sturdy plastic handle a white polyurethane cooler—an Esky. So he liked to sip a beer during his meditations on mortality, drawn from the chill embrace of a twenty-first century CFC-free Australian icon.

"A certain animal vitality," he said in a plummy English accent, head tilted, regarding the chortling birds.

"They're not what you'd call funereal," I said. "Not your classic birds of ill omen."

He was rueful. "The avian kingdom is no respecter of human *gravitas.*"

Share introduced us. We shook hands. Felix Culpepper was very well dressed in a hound's-tooth suit with impeccably pressed shirt and Melbourne club tie. I especially admired the crisp lines of his collar. I can never get that right with my iron.

"Ever been inside a mausoleum, Thomas?" the Culpepper said.

"Nope."

He made the slightest motion with his head.

Share and I followed his back along a twisting path through the gravestones, cutting across the rectilinear roadways and paths. The cemetery mimicked Melbourne's ethnic map. From an area of headstones each of which carried an enamel image of the deceased and hearty recommendations in Italian to the Almighty, we arrived at a more waspish, moneyed suburb of the dead: from Brunswick to Toorak in one bound, you might say, except that these days the Toorak dead rarely took the long trip north and across the Yarra River. Still, some of these graves were old and expensive and palatial. Some more palatial than others. We stopped beside a scaled down version of a Roman villa. A marble Botticelli angel brooded on the roof. Culpepper placed the Esky between his feet, unlocked a gate in the wrought iron fence, strode the three long steps it took him to arrive at the villa's door and unlocked that as well. The door was steel, equipped with one Yale lock and two padlocks.

"Should keep the stiffs from going AWOL," I said. No one

laughed, not even me.

"After you," Culpepper told us.

I took a look around at the daylight. Suddenly the open cemetery seemed a very cheery place: lorikeets, trees, fellow human beings. I followed Share into the mausoleum. Culpepper closed the door. I thought for a moment that he was intent on locking us in. No. In the total darkness, I could hear him fiddling with something; at least he had followed us inside.

"How about you leave the door open."

"Better that I don't," Culpepper said in the dark. A flashlight in his hand came on. We stood in a square room of marble. Shoved against one wall was an open casket, extra large, its lid propped beside it. Light gleamed briefly from the rich lining. My pulse accelerated. He couldn't fit both of us into it, surely? A flight of steps led down into the earth. "The dead have little call for electricity," he added. "In some respects these places are distressingly primitive, but they have their unique virtues. Let us proceed to the underworld."

The flashlight beam pointed down the steps. Culpepper left the Esky in the upper crypt, beside the coffin, descended, turned to direct the beam back in our direction. Share followed, stepping carefully. I did the same, and I wasn't even wearing high heels. We halted before another steel door. This one might have graced a bank vault. Culpepper turned the knob right and left in a swift series of maneuvers, far too fast for me to memorize the combination. He spun the well-oiled wheel and the door opened soundlessly. It was ten centimeters thick and padded on the inside.

"About fucking time," a voice said from inside.

"I've bought your stepmother to see you, dear," Culpepper said, entering the crypt. If that's what it was. It might have been a World War Two bunker, except that we'd never had to fight the Germans and Italians on our own soil. Well, the Italians, once they started immigrating after peace was declared, and then we called them reffoes and beat them up in the school playground. So my father told me, anyway.

"Share? Is that you?"

"Christ, Culpepper," Share exploded. "You didn't tell me you had *Jonquil* in here, you bastard. I thought we were here to discuss camel genetics!"

"One can't be too careful on the telephone."

I took it all in fast, as the flashlight beam swung across the chamber. The crypt held a wall of small headstones. Apparently Culpeppers from the time of the First Fleet were interred here. Cookie was slouched, all tonne and a half of her, on a sagging camp bed. She hadn't been sweeping the floor, but then she didn't have a broom and pan. A handful of burnt-out candle stubs and a box of matches lay scattered on the floor, amid the remains of several fast food cartons. It occurred to me that I had solved the mystery of Cookie's disappearance, or at least of her reappearance, with surprising ease. Risen from the grave. The Goth grrls should be impressed. Maybe, I thought, I should go back to being a private eye.

"What are you doing with my step-daughter in here, Felix?"

"Ms. Lesser is helping us with our enquiries."

A police phrase, doubly sardonic under the circumstances. I said, "What enquiries?" My nose wrinkled. Nasty smell, like stale piss. In a crypt? I wondered how long the poor grrl had been trapped down here. More than a day, if Animal's guess was right.

Radiance flashed into my face, away again. I blinked.

"Into certain curious anomalies that have appeared recently in my family's trust accounts."

"What fucking accounts?" Share was indignant. "Jonquil has only been helping out an old friend with his SP—"

"Quite so. Accounts associated with the racing industry." Clearly, Culpepper had attended Timbertop school, perhaps with Prince Charles as his fellow student, and he wanted us to hear it in his calm, modulated tones. "And other... associated activities."

Cookie shouted, "These arseholes have been rigging the camel export trade for the past ten years. Every poor sucker who ever wanted to get rich quick is into camel breeding, you must know that, Sharon. Buy Australian camels, guaranteed syphilis-free, blah blah blah. Win millions of OPEC dollars by owning half a hind leg of a prize racing camel in Jeddah blah blah blah. These goons and their Saudi mates have been taking everyone to the bloody cleaners—"

"It's a legitimate investment opportunity, Cookie." Share sounded defensive, suddenly sensitive about her own association with the camel trade.

"Pigshit it's legitimate. Some of those bloody ships of the desert are owned five thousand percent. Others don't even exist."

"Oh dear, what have you got yourself into now, Cookie?"

Her step-daughter snorted, but said nothing. After a reflective moment, Culpepper's mellow tones informed us that Ms. Lesser had been using her not inconsiderable computer skills to hack into certain accounts and databases held here and overseas with a view to relieving the account holders of certain points of a percentage of their wealth, a supposedly undetectable method widely advertised in so many blockbuster movies that nowadays even Steven Seagal would refuse to—

"Jesus," Share said to her recumbent, reeking step-daughter. "Your prick of a father raised you with more sense than that."

"Frankly," Culpepper continued, "we admire Ms. Lesser's skill and acumen—"

"I can't *stand* men, you idiot!"

"Droll, Ms. Lesser, very droll."

"We'll fucking do you for kidnapping and wrongful imprisonment—"

"In which event we would be obliged to 'do *you*' for fraud, larceny, invasion of privacy and sundry computer related malfeasances."

Culpepper was surely armed, more than I could say for myself. Even if I overpowered the toad without being shot, how were we going to get Cookie out of here? There wasn't a wheelchair within coo-ee. The maimed dead leave theirs at the hospital bedside. If she hadn't been differently mobile, she might well have propelled herself through the air and killed him with her raw bulk. Poor girl, all she had for weaponry was her tongue.

"Sod off, hairy legs," she said.

Plucky, I thought, but not really the fatal thrust.

Culpepper's imperturbable voice went on: "Jonquil, we admire your cyber skills. We would far prefer you to be with us than against us."

"You offering me a fucking *job*? After *snatching* me?"

"Gainful employment might be in the offing."

"I wouldn't work for you motherfu—"

"And speaking of mothers," he said sharply, "perhaps your stepmother and her friend might like to chat with you about your prospects. I shall take a turn around the necropolis." Culpepper handed the flashlight to Share and made his way up to ground level without its aid; obviously he knew his way around the place. The door closed with an inaudible shock of air that hummed in my ears. I broke a minute's silence in the crypt by asking, "How did he get you out of Animal's place, Cookie?"

She was silent for another long minute, and I suppose she was blushing furiously. Or biting her lip. "I got conned. Net sex's all I've ever been... good for."

Christ, I thought. Poor woman.

"Male or female?" I asked.

"None of your beeswax," said Grime Grrl's younger sister.

"I'm not prying, Cookie. I'm trying to find out—"

"They said they wanted to meet up in RL," she said. RL? Real life? "I told them I couldn't get around easily. They said they'd come and get me. So I left the door open and made sure Animal and Grime were out."

"You foolish child," Share said. "Sorry," she added immediately, "that wasn't a helpful thing to say."

"No it bloody wasn't. Anyway, here I am. No net sex, just two fucking male bruisers lugging me down to a hearse and your friend Culpepper sneering at me. Now he wants me to fucking *work* for him. *Christ,* I need to take a dump."

Another silence.

Eventually I said, "Anybody have any idea why *I'm* here?"

"Felix asked me to bring you," Share said.

"Felix." I let his name sit there like a turd on the doorstep. "Why would he want you to do that?"

"I imagine he also wants to offer you a job."

"I wouldn't work for those mother—"

"You've got no more choice than Cookie here. He could do you for sundry malfeasances as well."

"I've got to have a shit," Cookie said. "I've been holding it all day."

"What malfeasances?"

"I'm serious," Cookie said desperately. "I had to piss in those McDonalds' cartons. I spilled some of it."

"Obviously we can't do anything about that, Jonquil, but you have our sympathy. Well, just for starters, there was the little incident with Nile Fever this morning. It might be argued in a court of law that attempting to defraud a prospective buyer by artificially increasing a camel's running speed—"

"It was a mad idea anyway. You can't fool a wily old sheikh of the desert by just bunging some sugar into a poor beast's neck, Share. And now the creature's dead and it was all for nothing." Dead and mutilated by *X Files* aliens, I wanted to say. Anything to get a mordant laugh out of this writhing mess. Suddenly I didn't feel at all like laughing. "That was *Culpepper's* idea? He put you up to it?" I felt stupid. That whole stunt had been some sort of entrapment caper? Not aimed at me, certainly, I was smaller fry than they'd bother with.

"Not Culpepper." Share sounded affronted.

"Good Christ, the *sheikh* was in on it?"

The room filled with a horrible smell, and I saw Cookie's shadow fall back against the wall. I hoped it was just a ripe take-out fart and not loss of her bowel control.

"Really, don't be a cretin. Let the scales drop from your eyes, Purdue. Think technology. Think 21ˢᵗ century. Be thankful that you've fallen amongst friends."

"Amongst scumbags," Cookie said.

I still had no idea what she was talking about, unless it really was fertile ova from the hyped-up animal. In which case the sugar wouldn't be an issue, just a device to give the beast an Extreme Makeover for ten minutes. So there'd never been any plan to export it or smuggle it out in a padded shipping container fitted with camel chow and a water supply, and run it in Jeddah. I wondered exactly what kind of mutilation had been performed. Weren't the aliens supposed to carve out the anus and the sexual organs? But that was just the *National Enquirer,* surely.

"Mind you," Share mused, "the helicopter was unscripted."

I shook my head in the darkness, giving it all up as a bad job. We had more urgent problems. Getting out of durance vile, for starters.

"Suppose Cookie and I accept Culpepper's deal," I said. Whatever the fuck it was. "Then what?"

"'Accept', bullshit. Speak for yourself," Cookie told me, but she was just enjoying a sulk. I had the strong impression that she knew the score as well as I did. The pair of us would sign on in the camel corps whether we liked it or not.

"If you don't get me out of this fucking hell hole right now," Cookie shrieked at Share, "I'll put rat poison in your Harvey Wallbanger."

I took the flashlight from Share's hand, flashed it high and low. No other exit, unless it was concealed. I shook my head. "This joint's got lousy *feng shui*," I said. "No wonder all the inmates are dead."

My phone rang. I opened it very carefully, handing the flashlight back. The signal was patchy. Marble, six feet at least of good dry earth, solid steel to put a bounce in it.

"—and pick me up at the Moreland Arms. Or has the bint still got your Cobra?"

"Mauricio, you're breaking up," I said.

There was some garble. "—reaking up? You've only just met."

"I'm locked in a vault," I said.

"You're in a bank? The banks are shut at this hour of a Satur—"

"A crypt. A mausoleum."

"Ah, that'd be the Culpepper place in Fawkner."

"Good god," I said. "Can you come and get us out, seeing you're so familiar with the location, location."

Some more cryptic garble, suitably enough I suppose, and then he was saying, "—in for a lube. Look, I'll get a fuckin cab, but those buggers have to report what they see to the cops, you know."

"Bring Chook with you."

"Give me that." Share took the phone out of my hand as I started to return it to my pocket. "Why the hell didn't you *say* you had a cell—" The mouthpiece fell off it. Cursing, she bent to retrieve it and so did I, flashlight bobbing, and my heel crushed it into the marble.

"You knew I had one. You just called me, for Christ's sake. Where's yours, anyway?"

"I left it in the car, you smug prick."

After a rather long, dismal, somewhat acrimonious time, light opened above our heads. The heavy vault door swung outward like a slo-mo shot of Mohammed Ali's fist fired into Frazier's chest. Culpepper stood at the top of the stairs with a portable fluoro. He stepped aside to allow two thugs in undertaker black to descend ahead of him. Lit from above and below, their broken noses and crooked brows, not to mention the muscle heaving under their suit jackets, detracted a bit from the general Tobin Bros undertaker look.

"G'day, Bulldozer," I said.

He squinted in the gloom. "G'day, Tom. You know China?"

"Only by repute, mate. You were robbed in the eleventh round."

Dozer shook his head sadly. "Fuckin ref. On the take, mate."

"It's criminal," I said.

"Get the young woman back upstairs," Felix Culpepper said. "You two wait down here for a moment, I have a proposal that you'll wish to hear."

Share was saying quite a lot at the top of her voice, but nobody was interested. Cookie added some commentary, and lashed out with her beefy arms when China bent to hoist her bulk off the sagging camp bed. I admired the expert way he pinned her limbs and avoided her snapping jaws.

"Ward nurse," I said, speculating.

"Ten years at Fairfield Psychiatric," he said, breathing hard. "Criminally insane." It wasn't clear whether that meant his charges or his cause of dismissal. Dozer had her thick legs. They crabbed up the stairs as she shouted her fury. "Sorry, love," China said, and tapped her on the side of the head with the wall. In the silence, I realized that Share had stopped yelling. She stood with her back to the entombed Culpeppers, teeth bared, flashlight raised over her head ready to be used as a club. She looked a little like a really riled Statue of Liberty.

"You're taking her out in the coffin," I said.

"Less conspicuous, I think you'll agree," Felix Culpepper said.

"She needs to go to the toilet, you bastard. You can't leave her in a closed casket."

"Only for a short while. Your associate's step-daughter remains of some interest to us, but we mean her no harm if she cooperates. She'll be accorded all the conveniences as soon as—" His phone rang. Frowning, he put it to his ear, murmuring. I thought of rushing him, but what was the point. I hadn't gone around armed since my short stint as a PI, and there was no way Share and I would get past the two gorillas. "Oh, very well," Culpepper said in vexation. "I'm waiting for the limo, I'll collect you once it arrives and we can discuss matters further on the way to the airport." He clicked it shut. "Change of plans. Up the steps, if you please."

"You wouldn't like us to tidy the place up first?"

Culpepper wasn't listening to me; he had his eyes warily on Sharon Lesser, who seemed on the verge of cracking up and flinging herself at him with the flashlight, something stepmotherly and fairly pointless. I took the flashlight from her.

"Come on, Share. The prick won't hurt her unless we get him really angry."

From the sounds upstairs, they seemed to be having some trouble fitting the orca into her casket. Felix Culpepper edged up the steps ahead of us, stood aside to let us through the vault door, fell down suddenly and dropped his fluoro. It rolled across the marble floor, throwing crazy patches of light. Both the gorillas were sitting beside the casket, looking dazed. I bundled the reeling undertaker muscle down the steps, and swung the vault door shut behind them both. Mauricio's brothers stood nervously at the nearly-closed front steel door to the mausoleum, fingering their heavy knouts. The room stank. Poor unconscious Cookie had shat herself.

"G'day Chook," I said. "Dago, Woggo."

"Tom." There was a definite lack of cordiality in their voices, they deplored the way I had led their brother astray, not to mention their sister. Mauricio, their ancient mother told me tearfully whenever I got dragged around for a meal with his extended clan, had been meant for the priesthood, as his sister had been intended for the nunnery. Fat fucking chance in either case. It grieved her that her son had fallen among villains. The brothers set about their task without enthusiasm.

"Can't we have a bit of bloody light?"

"Sorry boys," I said, "if we open the front door every Tom, Dick and Harry—"

"Well, Tom's already in here," said Woggo, the wit of the pair. Their sister Juliet, of course, outshone them both like a lighthouse.

Dago reached up behind him in the gloom and flipped a switch. Soft light suffused the entrance to the crypt from recessed lamps. Dago was the Einstein of the pair.

"Well bugger me," Share said, and sank the tip of her shoe into the groaning member of the Melbourne Club lying in a heap next to the coffin. "Psychological warfare, Felix, is that it? Keep the poor sods in the dark and off balance?" Her toe clipped his jaw, and she nearly lost her own balance.

Woggo was in cantankerous mood. "I'm not moving her until she's had a bloody good wash. Someone should take to her with a hose." He must have seen Share's sharp glance. "That's not what I mean. Wash her down, you know. She's on the nose."

"Shut the fuck up," said Share, and I added: "Gentleman, this poor child has been treated very badly. Show a bit of respect for her suffering."

"—fuckin Lebos," Mauricio was muttering.

"No, Sunshine, this was the establishment's work." Share crouched beside her step-daughter, feeling her skull. No blood, nothing broken. She averted her face, nostrils pinched. "C'mon, Tom, help me out with her. These oafs are too—"

Dago lifted Sharon aside with one effortless, biceps-bulging move, bent, had the young torpid whale under the arms. His brother took the feet. They had her out of the casket in two shakes of a lamb's tail.

"Put this cunt in," Share said, kicking Culpepper again to make certain they knew which cunt she had in mind. "And close the lid."

The lights were now on down in the vault, too, presumably. It was satisfying to know they'd go off when we left. I could hear a dull thudding from below, quite faintly actually. You had to be listening. "We should take Felix the fixer with us," I said.

"We will. In the casket. Let him breathe the fumes for a few minutes."

Mauricio and I got him in, cinched the top shut, heaved the casket to the door. The brothers were stumbling amid clumpy, untended grass to the back of their dirt encrusted white van. It looked as if they'd just got back from a six month outback safari, kangaroo shooting. I doubted it. Urban cowboys, these two. Three, counting Mauricio, the most urban of the lot. It was in their genes. Their ancestors had loitered, malice aforethought, with the bawds and pickpockets on the Spanish Stairs in Rome for centuries, or some equivalent den of iniquity in Sicily. I was never very good at geography in school. They swung the orca into the back, returned to help us with the casket. I was sitting on it, looking at the gleaming black vehicle. Of course it was a hearse. A hearse is a hearse, of course, of course, I found myself thinking absurdly, dazed by confusion and anger. On a venture, I went back inside the crypt and brought Culpepper's Esky out with me, popped it on top of the coffin.

"Give the lads your address, Share," I said. "I'd rather not have my daughter involved in this."

"What about fuckface here?" She couldn't keep her feet away from him, the toe whacked a silver cross on the grained casket. Some vandal had punched a handful of holes in the side and top, not very large holes but it ruined the melancholy *Six Feet Under* shine of the thing.

"He's provided us with luxury transport," I said. "C'mon, fellas, put your backs into it and we'll have him laid to rest in a flash."

Chook locked him in comprehensively, tossed the casket key to me. Culpepper, may he rest in peace, slid neatly into the prepared undertaker coffin-grappling apparatus in the back of the hearse. I thought the synthetic white of the Esky spoiled the line and gravity of the thing, and brought it around to the front with me. It wasn't very heavy. Culpepper might have drunk his fill already and put the empties inside, in an ecologically responsible way. I hopped in behind the wheel, Esky between my heels. Smoked glass is a wonder of science, it looks perfectly clear from inside. Sharon Lesser took the passenger seat and watched me, waiting for the penny to drop.

"Fuck. We locked the keys in the vault with the heavies."

"I'm sure you have ways and means," she said. "A career criminal like yourself."

"These things get blown out of proportion," I said. I got out and caught Mauricio and the boys as they backed on to the narrow cemetery road. Dago grumbled, followed me back to the hearse, took something out of his pocket protector and had the machine hotwired and purring in less than 30 seconds.

"I know how," I told Sharon, who was laughing quietly. "I do.

But why exert oneself when there's specialist help at hand?"

Culpepper, awakened in darkness and stench and enjoying it no more than we had, began banging. Given the lavish upholstery of his casket's lining, I was surprised we could hear anything even with the airholes Culpepper's cronies had thoughtfully punched to spare Cookie from suffocation

"Get some music on the radio," I said.

Share found something liturgical on a CD. I drove toward the gate to the Hume. The banging grew louder. A gardener glanced our way.

"Something noisy," I said, "Here, Gold FM should do the trick." I punched the radio through to the Boss howling out the news that he was Born in the USA and feeling a bit betrayed about it, all things considered. That seemed apt enough to me so I turned the stereo up full bore. They had a very nice sound system, full surround boom boxes in the back. Burials by day, shaggin wagon by night? I found myself hemmed in at the roundabout. A cortege was headed for the crematorium, headlights burning. Faces turned, eyes swiveling, at the racket. I didn't care, I'd lost all sense, the madness of the last days had frizzled my reality principle.

"Fuck this," I said after the third car, and cut into the stream of mourners. The vehicle ahead picked up speed, following its colored code line, or perhaps the arse of the car ahead. Culpepper made noises. I turned, reached with a long left arm, banged on the top of the coffin.

Beyond the gates, the Hume looked chockablock. Sharon punched off the rock station and accidentally hit a race call instead. "—Bandersnatch neck and neck at the turn," the high, frantic, nasal voice was calling, "it's sensational, Loose Lips has stumbled, the gelding's taken a tumble, and here comes Brute Force, the long shot is stretching out now, by a nose, Brute Force at fifty to one has—"

"You little bloody beauty!" I said. "Free lunches at Ivy's for the rest of the year. *Shut the fuck up back there!*"

A discreet toot from the car behind. Distracted, I surged too far, missed the exit, found the hearse carried in a large curve once more around the memorial fountain that ran with water like a pair of flying saucers lifting from the ocean's bowl. All it needed was Cathy Freeman in her pristine white "We come to your planet in

peace" starship suit and it would have been a re-run of the rising
Mother Ship from the close of the Sydney Olympics, that time it
got stuck. Flicking my own headlights on, I turned right in time,
went out the gate, turned left. Sharon doubled up in laughter.
She hit the radio button again, went back to Gold. Roy Orbison
informed us at the top of his resonant, mournful voice that love
hurts, burns you like a stove. Burns you like a crematorium, I
thought.

"What are you braying about?" I said, eyes on the traffic.

"Check the mirror," she said.

We had a tail, like a comet. Headlights burning, drivers teary
with sorrow, the cortege had followed us back into the highway. I
saw my chance, accelerated into the passing lane. In the back, the
coffin bumped. I thought I heard a throttled scream.

The urban sprawl began to thin out. Flight paths, car factories
and frozen chicken warehouses lay ahead.

"You do realize we're pointed north?"

"Go north, the rush is on," I said.

"What?"

"It's a line from a song," I said. "Some ditty of my youth."

"Where are you taking us, Purdue. Sydney?"

"The romance of the open road," I said. "The hypnotic drumming of the tires. The world is our oyster bar."

"We're in a stolen hearse and we've got a live body in the coffin."

"Ah, yes. Midshipman Culpepper. Our messmate on this voyage
of discovery."

"Shut up, Purdue. What are we going to do with him?"

"I thought we might have a bit of a chat with him."

"What? You want me to shout at him through the air holes?
Don't be absurd."

"He's got a phone, Share. Sooner or later he's going to tumble to
that annoying little fact. Got yours?"

"No, damn it, it's in the Cobra's glove box."

"Mine came to grief back at the crypt. We'll just have to find a
public phone. Assuming they haven't all been recycled."

We were approaching the turn-off to Coolaroo. I flicked the

indicators and took to the exit ramp at Barry Rd with a fine turn of speed. Broady to our left, Coolers to our right, the road to Beveridge and points north abandoned.

"Ned was born not far from here," I said. "Another twenty-five klicks or so."

"Ned who?"

"The bushranger. You know, in the armor and interesting iron head dress?"

"Ned Kelly wasn't a bushranger, he was a freedom fighter."

"Good god, you *have* been talking to Animal."

"Anyway, look what happened to him, murdered by the law."

"Such is life," I told her.

I managed to park the hearse in the main street, directly in front of a telephone booth which was directly in front of an Adults Only shop. A customer bearing a plastic bag emerged from the shop, looked at the hearse, sniggered and scuttled off down the street.

"Probably thinks we're sales reps," I said. "Purveyors of ghoulish fetishes."

"Get on with it, Purdue."

A phone muttered a solemn tune of church bells, heavily muffled, and it wasn't from the one outside.

"Got Culpepper's number?" Through the air holes, I could faintly hear him babbling on his cell phone.

Without a word Share produced a credit card sized address book from her handbag, pulled a minute pencil from the spine of the book, transcribed Culpepper's mobile number onto the back of an envelope. I had the feeling she was keen that I didn't get my hands on the book itself. I took the envelope and made my way to the phone booth. Share stayed put.

Culpepper's number was engaged. The prick was still having a bit of a yarn with some friendly soul. The Call Waiting beeps kicked in.

"Culpepper."

I couldn't help it. I disguised my voice a trifle. "Ah, Mr. Culpepper, this is Roderick from Fit as a Fiddle. Mr. Culpepper, I won't take up much of your time. You have been chosen to receive a free introductory offer of one week's yes that's six days' free introductory workout at Fit as a Fiddle's all new anaerobic lifestyle studio. Tone up those pecs!"

"I have no time for this sort of—"

"Time is what we offer! In today's modern world life can become pretty stressful. But science proves that just half an hour a day yes that's thirty minutes a day pumping iron at Fit as a Fiddle can increase your lifespan by eight years and three months. Wouldn't you like to live an extra eight and one quarter years, Mr. Culpepper, sir?"

"Purdue!"

"Pardon?"

"That's you, isn't it, Purdue?"

"My name is Brian William Roderick the third."

"You listen to me, Purdue. Unless I am released immediately—"

"Fat chance."

"Unless I am released immediately I say—"

"I heard you the first time."

"You don't know what you are playing at, Purdue. Even if some ill were to befall me, even if I were to *die* as a result of your games, my associates would track you down. You should remain in absolutely no doubt about that. You would be very well advised to release me immediately, Purdue. Immediately."

I watched the dollars and cents tick over in the pay phone's little window. Culpepper's mobile was eating my phone card. And I was less than five meters from the coffin. I reckoned the card would expire in a few moments.

"Okay, Culpepper. What's the deal?"

"Just let me out."

"This job you are going to offer me. Rates of pay, Culpepper. Bonuses. Fringe benefits. Perks of office. We need to talk turkey. This is enterprise bargaining."

"I'm striking no bargains until I'm released."

"You're not in a position to talk tough, Culpepper."

But Culpepper was in no position to talk to me at all, or me to him. The phone had gone dead. I went back to the hearse limo and sat in the driver's seat.

"Well?" Share said.

"Culpepper has a fine appreciation of his current predicament," I said. "But I think he will behave like a gentleman if allowed a little exercise."

"You're thinking of letting him *out?*"

"What else do you suggest? We could dump the coffin some-where, but—"

"Yeah, okay," Share said. "Let's go somewhere a bit more se-cluded..."

"I think not," I said. "I'd be happier if there were people around. The sod might be armed."

I dug into my pocket for the casket key, climbed into the back of the hearse and beat a hearty little drum riff on the lid with the handle. Culpepper cursed and kicked. He seemed to be in good spirits. After I had turned the lock at the top end I looked up. Night was falling and the Coolaroo street lights were coming on. Three kids stood on the pavement looking with undisguised delight at the scene inside the hearse. I ignored them. They approached and pressed their faces against the glass. From the front seat Share shouted at them, "Go on, bugger off! Have some respect for the dead."

The kids ignored her, pushing against each other and giggling. Two were girls with bare midriffs and dyed hair. The other was a young lout eating a hot dog. The girl with the purple hair knocked on the window. "Hey, Mister," she yelled. "Got the wrong body in the coffin?"

I ignored her. Her friend said something about bodysnatchers. The first one knocked on the window again and yelled. "Are you a medical student?"

Share opened the passenger door and climbed out. She started to remonstrate with the kids—a mistake, they were keen for a bit of argy bargy. I unlocked the lid on the other side, then one near the foot, only fitfully listening to the sounds off. More people had arrived: when I looked up half a dozen faces were pressed to the glass, a couple of them adult: habitués of the Adults Only store if their poxy skin and leery grins were anything to go by. A car with blue and white checkerboard on the side and red and blue lights on the roof either side of the siren ground to a halt on the other side of the hearse. I heard a door snick open and shut, then the driver's door of the hearse was flung wide. Cool air blew in. Just behind the back of my neck a gruff cop's voice said, "What are you playing at?" The remaining lock was torn from the coffin with a screech and a splintering of wood as Culpepper loosened the top near his face, managed to get his knees up and applied his brogues to the underside of the lid. The stench was immediate.

"Get out of there!" the cop yelled. "Who the fuck are you?"

"Ah, officer, good evening to you," Culpepper said, climbing out of the coffin. Three or four of the watching kids cheered and screamed like fans at a grunge concert.

"Step outside the car, the pair of youse," the cop said.

"Certainly officer," Culpepper said in his immaculate tones. "Everything can be explained."

"It had better be," the cop said. "Where are the flowers? There should be wreathes."

"The crypt," I said in a clear, carrying voice, catching Culpepper's eye. He paused, tightened his lips. We had each other over separate barrels. If he fingered us for meat wagon theft and body snatching (his), we pinned abduction, kidnapping (hers), false imprisonment and reckless endangerment on him. I dug out my wallet and found a card, pressed it on the cop.

"R. D. Thomas Purdue at your service, constable," I said. My mind slipped into free-wheeling scam merchant mode, and words flowed from some strange dark inner crypt and out through my lips without any intervening effort. "Of Feng Shui Multi-Media, a division of Hector Crawford Productions."

"Hector Crawford's dead," the cop said, looking at the card, turning it over. "That was years ago. The whole D-24 squad went to the funeral."

"His spirit lives on."

"Detective Sergeant Smigrodzki sang 'Danny Boy'."

"We'll be using that very moving and appropriate song in our sound track."

Culpepper had been wiping traces of human feces from his jacket with a monogrammed handkerchief. Shuddering, he flung it into the back of the hearse, and held out his hand to the cop.

"Allow me to introduce myself, officer. I'm—"

"Count Dracula," Share said. She's quick, that girl.

The cop stared in bafflement from one to the other, back to me. "Don't try to take the fucking piss, Mac."

I goggled with delight. "He recognizes you, Mack!" I clapped Culpepper on the back. "You said nobody would, but I assured you your fans are legion!"

"What?"

"As you guessed, this is the great movie idol of the 1950s, Mack Truck, here in our sunburnt country to make a major motion picture about Count Dracula, *The Count Down-Under*. You must be a fan of his masterpiece, *Love at First Bite*."

"That was George Hamilton," Share said. "Mr. Truck starred in *Going Down for the Count*."

"What kinda fuckin bullshit name is 'Mack Truck'?" the cop asked in outrage.

I leaned in confidence toward him. "A screen name, but please don't let it go any further. His birth name was Brian William Roderick III, but the mavens of Hollywood deemed it inappropriate for the marquee."

"Well maybe so, I've never heard of the bugger, but *what the fuck is he doing covered in shit in a coffin in the back of a fuckin hearse in the main street of Coolaroo?*"

"Not real shit, officer." I drew back, offended at the implied lack of professionalism. "That's a substance known to the wizards in the special effects trade as Shit-Hot. Same consistency and odor as real feces, comes in a can."

"I saw the prick climbing out of a coffin!"

"Our rehearsal," Share said. Culpepper's phone rang. He took it from his pocket, I took it from his hand.

"Now, now, Mack, this is exactly what brought you undone the last time." I told the cop, "His attention span isn't what it was in the glory days. He lost his role in support of Russell Crowe when he answered his cell phone during the gladiator scene." I tucked the phone in my own pocket. Culpepper stared in apoplexy. "You never get over it, though," I said. "It calls you back. The raw grease, the smell of the crowd."

"But what's the bugger doing rehearsing on the public thoroughfare at this hour of the day?"

Share gave him a seductive giggle. "Re-*hearsing*, eh? That's very clever, constable."

It went right over his head. I coughed, and added: "Mack is starring in a remake of *The Cat and the Crypt*. Based on the beloved poem by Edgar Allen Poe. You might recall it from *Sesame Street*."

"Yeah," said Share. "Who could forget those opening lines: "The cat crept into the crypt, crapped, and crept out.""

"Are you saying we're on TV right now? Where are the lights and cameras?"

"Concealed." I gestured thrice, swinging my arm wide like a real estate auctioneer plucking bids off the wall, an illegal practice these days but still not unknown to the profession. "Not TV, constable, digital motion picture cameras. Marvelous what they can do these days with miniaturization."

The cop squared his shoulders. You could tell he wanted to favor his best side, but didn't know which camera to address. "You should have a permit."

"The office has done all that, let me provide you with the documentat—"

"Well, I'm going to have to ask you to move along. Sorry if that interrupts your filming, but a thing like this could cause an accident. Look at all these children here. One of them runs on to the busy street—"

Coolaroo was not looking terribly busy to me, aside from our own commotion.

"Absolutely, I see what you mean. Thoughtless of us." I took out Culpepper's phone, pressed a random button, murmured, "Camera teams Two and Five, pull out, break down the set. We'll meet in the Green Room at twenty hundred hours for a full debriefing."

The cop went back to his patrol Ford Falcon Forté, revved his engine a couple of times, watching us. A young mother in a veil was calling an inquisitive child who had clambered into the open back of the hearse: "Car *mee* yuh."

"Agile enough of you both," Culpepper muttered. He looked sideways as the woman repeated her call. "What on earth language is that creature speaking?"

"Australian," Share said. She got back inside the hearse, shut her door. I opened it again, ushered Culpepper in beside her. Share drew away from the stink.

"An Aboriginal tongue, eh? She doesn't look dark enough."

"Australian English, you eastern suburbs prat. She said 'Come here'." I slammed the door hard, but he withdraw his hand in time to save his fingers. "Cheerio, kids," I called, and gave the assembled company a big wave. "Watch for us on Channel 10."

A few of them cheered, one smart aleck jeered. We drew away,

I returned to the Hume and its endless stream of traffic, while the cop tailgated us until he got sick of the sport and roared past, hot on the tail of a FedEx truck with attitude.

Culpepper was eying the Esky. I kicked it further away from him toward my door. "Kindly return my telephone," he said. He had audacity enough, you had to give him that.

"Yeah, shove it right up his arse sideways," Share said.

I swung the limo around at the next opportunity and tooled back toward the city. Balwyn seemed the place to be, since that's where the boys had taken the incontinent orca. I fished out Culpepper's phone, started to key in Mauricio's number with my thumb. Share was perched uncomfortably between the two seats; she plucked the phone out of my hand. There wasn't much I could do without relinquishing the steering wheel, not a good move on the Hume.

"Calling for take-out?"

She ignored me, and I heard her own voice tinnily telling her that she wasn't able to come to the phone just now and asking her to leave a message. This was a bit worrying; Mauricio shouldn't have had any trouble entering the place and settling Cookie, he had Dago with him for the lock and Chook's heft at a pinch.

"Rodolph, if you get home before me, call back at this mobile." She peered at the envelope where she'd written Culpepper's number down earlier, then repeated it. "We shouldn't be more than half an hour. If there's a van full of thugs trying to get into the house, invite them in. They've got poor Jonquil with them, and she'll need a bath and something to eat. Love you."

"The pool boy?"

"I'm expecting my husband back from Kuala Lumpur within the hour. He'll have something to say to Mr. Culpepper."

"You misunderstand my motives," our kidnapper explained in an aggrieved tone. "We share a common interest. I would prefer to be let off near my club, these clothes reek of your daughter."

Share was still holding the phone. Her vicious backhander caught him on the cheek. Blood flowed. He made no cry, which impressed me a bit.

"If you've quite finished with the instrument—" He held out his hand, ignoring the gash in his face which leaked slowly down, I saw in a quick glance, into his impeccable collar.

"Call Mauricio for me, Share." I gave her the number. Princes Park had a few joggers doing their circuit in the cooling night. I turned left at Cemetery Road West, heading past the university colleges, my ruined accommodation and offices not a dozen blocks behind me. Melbourne General Cemetery passed on the left behind its tall iron fence and its tall sentry trees, closed for the night. These days I was haunted by the dead.

At the Lygon Street lights Culpepper tried to open the centrally-locked door, but I reached behind Share and squeezed the back of his neck with my left hand. He yelped a bit. Share held the phone to my ear. "What the fuck, Mauricio?"

His voice was clear and crisp without the marble and steel to block it.

"Things aren't as neat as we'd hoped they might be, matey. Listen, why the fuck haven't you been answering your phone, anyway?"

"It's a long story. You didn't make it to the Lesser mansion, I take it?"

A heavy sigh. Mauricio Cimino was a man of sensitivity and you could sense his frustration and disappointment with the world. "Oh yeah, no trubs. Jonquil showed us where the key was hidden, but we didn't need it. The front door was wide open."

"Rodolph," I said. "But he isn't answering the phone."

"Rudolph's the husband?"

"So it seems."

"Little wonder he's not picking up, mate. Some bastard's blown half his head off."

We ripped lickety-split but just under the speed limit up the Eastern Freeway, through the green urban wilderness and sports grounds of Yarra Bend, and tooled along Harp and Belmore into Balwyn. I said nothing to Sharon Lesser about the death of her husband, because I knew it would make driving difficult and probably get Culpepper stirred up as well. I wondered who he'd been speaking with when I'd activated his call-waiting signal. Or was Rodolph Lesser's messy exit sheer coincidence? I don't like coincidences. I don't believe in them. It's bad *feng shui*.

I dislike the sight of blood, too, and not only my own. A man with a record like mine can't afford to be seen around blood, not the kind that's hard to explain at any rate. Blood bank contributions, that's fine, proof of redemption and community spirit—in Australia, at least, where you can't sell a quart for your next hit. A pint of claret from the flared nostrils of a bloke pummeling another beefy bloke in the ring, that's fine too. But the cops look askance when they come by and find you swanning around the living room of a Balwyn household with an emotional widow, an obese and shrieking daughter, and a brain-splattered and only freshly ex-husband.

Déjà vu set in with a thud as we approached the Lesser establishment down a street of mature trees and well watered lawns. The bourgeoisie keep themselves neat and tidy in the suburbs. But the crime scene tapes and the flashing lights reminded me of home. So did the detective who appeared to be in charge. I parked the hearse and got out.

"You again, Purdue," the cop said. It wasn't a question and this evening he seemed to have remembered my name. "You're a bit willing. And what the hell's that you're carrying? Think this is a party?"

"Willing? Rebeiro," I said with a nod, having no trouble at all remembering his. I swung the Esky negligently. Whatever it contained, I wasn't leaving it with bloody Culpepper.

"The fucking hearse. You appear to be carrying a coffin. Ambulance chasing's one thing, but this is macabre."

"A coincidence," I said.

Share climbed out of the driver's door. Culpepper stayed put, looking haughty. He had no wish to invite police attention.

"This is the widow," I said to Rebeiro.

Share sent me a look of disbelief and shrieked.

"How do you know she's a widow?" This was very definitely a question.

"My landlord told me."

"Fucking Cimino. I thought we'd got his phone off him." He glanced back at the house.

So Mauricio was still *in situ*, along with his relatives and thug Chook presumably. He would not be pleased with me. "That's the guy. Now if you'll excuse us…"

"This is a crime scene, Purdue. No one crosses the tape. Madam, would you please calm down and tell me your name."

Share, still shrieking, ignored the cop and lifted the tape. In a flash she was across the nature strip and through her front gate. Two uniformed cops grabbed her on the path and escorted her, kicking and screaming, back to the tape.

"Where's my husband? What have you done to poor Rodolph, you bastards?"

"Take it easy, missus…"

"Get your hands off me."

A woman cop with her hair in a bun joined the fray. Between them they managed to get Share into the back seat of a parked police Ford. The woman cop got in the back as well and could be seen talking to Share in a sensitive and caring fashion.

"Counseling," Rebeiro said. "Grief management."

"You all been on a course or something?"

"Shut up, Purdue."

I turned and looked at the hearse. Rebeiro did too. Culpepper had abandoned the passenger seat and was bumping himself across toward the driver's door. No, he wasn't, the bastard was slamming the limo into reverse and making a getaway. I checked my pockets with incredulous futility. No keys, you moron, Dago hotwired the fucker, you'd locked the keys in the crypt with the heavies. Obviously not; Culpepper had them tucked in his own expensive suit pocket, along with his cell phone. With a screech of burnt rubber the hearse went into a tight U-turn, mounting the nature strip with a violent shudder and broadsiding across the grass. A couple of seconds later the tail lights were disappearing towards the city. Rebeiro watched impassively.

"You're not planning to book him for speeding, then?"

"Who's that prick?"

"Felix Culpepper."

"Fucking Stonecraft," Rebeiro said.

"Who?" It rang a small bell, like a cow high on an alpine pasture on the next mountain over. I don't follow the social pages closely, though. Or even the law court stories, these days. A nag with an inside chance, a bottle of decent red and a bit of tucker a man can sink his teeth into, some well-heeled nitwits eager to pay good plastic money to learn about the forces of the ancients and the best geometries to placate them, a frustrating visit now and then to see my wife Juliet, that was enough.

"Frank Stonecraft, QC. Counsel for the defense. They keep him in a cage and feed him raw meat and let him out to defend Toorak scum like Culpepper. Ever been cross-examined in court, Purdue?"

"No," I lied.

"Just hope and pray you don't become a material witness to this can of worms. Go and sit in the back seat of that Fairlane, wait for me."

I did as I was told, there didn't seem anything better to do. As I walked across to the Fairlane I looked into the back of the marked police car. Share was sitting forward, her head in her hands. The cop had her arm around her shoulder. I wouldn't know, of course, but Share's shock and grief looked a bit ersatz to me. It's a good word, ersatz. If we used it more often we'd understand the world better.

I waited for some time in Reberio's Fairlane. It smelled of stale tobacco. I propped the Esky on my lap and thought about opening it and having a poke about but this didn't seem the propitious time. It'd be my luck to find it packed with cocaine in little baggies.

There was a lot of coming and going: cops, forensic, ace reporters. They kept the TV crews at bay somehow. I watched Mauricio and the boys troop out of the house and drive their van away. Apparently not under arrest. An ambulance arrived and a gurney was wheeled up the front path. It didn't return with the deceased. It returned with Cookie. Poor girl—first imprisoned in Culpepper's dungeon and then confronted with the mangled remains of her dad. It's a hard life, my heart went out to her. My heart returned fairly smartly to my chest. Cookie was lying back on the gurney laughing and wise cracking with the ambos, all ten tons of her. You'd think she was being taken for a hay ride at the village fair. The women in the late, lamented Rodolph Lesser's life were taking his demise with reasonable fortitude. Very reasonable fortitude indeed.

"Oh," I said to myself, three or four innocent little fragments falling together belatedly into a disgusting picture. I wondered if Share had made the same connections. She must have done. "Oh, fuck," I said, still out loud. "Poor kid." Nobody heard me, but then nobody was there to hear me. Not that it would have mattered. People never pay any attention, that's what's wrong with the world.

I dozed off. I'd had a hard day. Rebeiro and some mate of his jolted me awake by climbing into the front of the Fairlane and slamming both doors. I rubbed the side window where my snoozy breath had fogged the glass, looked at the scene of the crime. The tape had been rolled up. The house no longer blazed with light. Most of the cars had gone, including the one in which Share had been experiencing the first flush of widowhood. The cops said nothing to me, but started the car and drove us off with the unhurried casualness of men who are just doing their job.

Fifteen minutes later we were in an all-night truck stop on the Dandenong Road. Rebeiro and his mate favored straight black coffee and French fries with tomato sauce. I ordered up big, I was incredibly hungry. We sat in a booth in a far corner where there weren't many other customers and those that were either found reasons to move away fairly smartly or were too stoned to understand anything they might overhear. It was a clean well lighted place. And it wasn't a cop shop. Unless Rebeiro and his mate were wired, nothing would go down on the record.

"It's all in the distribution, is what I hear," Rebeiro said.

"Sorry?"

"If you don't get the exposure you might as well've not made the flick in the first place. Unless all you are going for is the negative gearing."

"You've lost me, Rebeiro," I said.

"I'm talking about your career as a film producer, Purdue. Remember? You make movies. You were making one this afternoon, outside a smut shop in Cooloroo."

"Dracula," I said. "Art. Any nudity will be artistically responsible. We have a panel of clergymen vetting..." I trailed off. Sometimes my mouth is its own worse enemy.

"There's a village bobby out Cooloroo way who became so

excited about his little burg being the location of a major movie that he reported the license number of your meat wagon to State Emergency. And then what happens, Purdue? What happens is that an hour and a half later this cinematic hearse of yours turns up at the scene of a major crime, complete with the widow of the deceased male person. And this happy event occurs a mere twenty four hours after the headquarters of your mystic bullshit scam is destroyed by a stolen semi-trailer. I think you'd better start telling us something convincing, Purdue. Forget the vampires and the art flicks."

I looked at the detective and his poor dumb sidekick. Ignorance shone from every pore of their hard, unshaven faces. What about the camel, I wanted to say. What about the mutilated ship of the desert by the side of the road? Don't you guys watch the news— does a helicopter crash mean nothing to you? But I'm a modest man, I didn't wise them up. I kept the story simple so they could understand it.

"It's that Culpepper bloke," I said. "I was investigating him on behalf of a client."

"Correct me if I'm wrong, Purdue, but wasn't your Private Investigator's license revoked rather suddenly some years ago?"

"I wasn't charging a fee," I said. "Anybody can ask questions. It's a free country."

"And this client? For whom you were working for nix?"

"My daughter."

"Christ, he's got a daughter. The poor tart. So what low rent 'investigation' was she employing you on."

"I told you—Culpepper."

"Interested in the life and times of the rich and infamous, was she?"

"More or less."

"Cut the crap, Purdue," the sidekick suddenly snarled, leaned forward, struggling to keep his hands away from my throat. "What the fuck are you playing at?"

"I don't think we've been introduced," I said amicably. "I'm Tom Purdue."

"Start fucking talking, Purdue."

I spoke to Rebeiro, "In your capacity as soft cop, do you think you could introduce me to hard cop here?"

"His name's Kirkpatrick," Rebeiro said evenly, "and if you don't start talking, he'll make sure you choke to death on your own quarter pounder."

It rose a little in my gullet. I sat back in the booth and told them all about Cookie's abduction and the valiant part Share and myself had played in her rescue. I figured Cookie would be telling a similar story wherever she was, presumably in a hospital bed. There was no point in complicating matters unduly. My companions listened politely enough, although Kirkpatrick snarled and grunted from time to time just for the form of the thing.

"And Lesser," Rebeiro finally asked. "Why was Lesser topped with a shotgun?"

I blinked. "Search me," I said. "I never met the guy."

"You seem pretty friendly with his wife. Widow."

"I only met her yesterday. She wasn't a widow then."

"You were seen with her on the day before yesterday."

"Forgive me, officer, I'd forgotten it is now after midnight."

"You're in deep shit," the hard cop snarled. His specialty, and I was getting used to it.

"Yeah, yeah," I said. "But if I help you with your enquiries…"

I looked at Rebeiro. I'd had mutually profitable dealings with Gabe Rebeiro before, I could have them again. Rebeiro didn't smile. He didn't say anything. But we understood each other well enough.

"We'll be in touch," he said. Without another word the two cops left the booth and then the truck stop. They hadn't paid, and nobody had brought us a check.

I looked at my watch. It was 3.48 am and I was alone somewhere on the Dandenong Road, my car was in a cemetery car park on the other side of town, assuming it hadn't been stolen, and I was in need of a slug of bourbon, a shower, a slug of bourbon, and a sleep. The taxi to Animal's would cost, but what the hell. I reached for my mobile. Cursed and went looking for a public phone that worked. I left the Esky behind me in the booth. When I remembered it after called Silver Top I went back. It was still there.

In the darkness of her doorway, Grime Grrl shoved a can of mustard gas or some other illegal male repellant in my face. I was too tired. I took it from her, pushed my way ungraciously inside, found the light switch, slammed the door behind me.

"Sorry," I said. "Didn't mean to scare you."

She looked on the edge of a nervous breakdown.

"Look, I'm not carrying a gun or a blackjack or a small nuclear weapon." To prove it I put down the Esky, turned out my pockets, threw my keys and billfold down on the table. If Annabelle wanted to pilfer a hundred bucks or so to top up her reserves, it was easier this way and would save me being woken up as she tried to sneak into the bedroom. Just to make the point absolutely clear I took off my watch and put it on the table as well. "Oh, and look—my Private Investigator's X-Ray Specs." I took my shades from my breast pocket and placed them on the table as well.

Animal's white face peered from their bedroom door, roused by my presence and my voice. Some more little pieces fell into place. I must have passed along my bad criminal genes, that's all I can say. Or the heritage of some noble foolish templar, some horseback righter of wrongs. Annabelle, Warrior Princess.

"I'll sleep in the orc— In Jonquil's room. Wake me at," I looked for my watch, "ten thirty at the earliest." Fuck. My skin was crinkling up, I wasn't as young as I'd been in the days when a couple of little white pills kept me raging all night but let me bounce back bright-eyed the next afternoon. Had that ever been the case? Maybe I was bullshitting myself, an occupational hazard. "We have a lot to discuss, Annabelle. I hope you got rid of the shotgun."

"We put it in Cookie's wardrobe wrapped up in canvas." Eyes as big as saucers, surrounded by Goth-dark makeup. She was shaking, I could see that. "Where's Cookie?"

"Private hospital, I assume. She looked all right. See you in the morning, love."

I shoved the Esky in the wardrobe without opening it, next to the shotgun. Some questions tease at the mind but are too trivial to compete with sleep. I lay down, woke up an instant later with perfume in my clogged nostrils. Cookie's pillows. I looked at my bare wrist.

"Eleven thirty, Dad." Animal held out a mug of black Nescafé. "You should just be able to make noon divine service at St. Paul's."

Sunday bloody Sunday, half gone. I took a swig of the filthy stuff and burnt the roof off my mouth. Microwave superheating. Ersatz every fucking where. Still, the caffeine kick-started my brain with a diffident, moccasin-clad suburban foot. I couldn't understand why the rozzers hadn't kicked down Animal's door by now.

"Got a paper?"

"Jesus, Tom, it's not a hotel." But she was back a moment later with the *Sunday Age*, folded open at page 3. Financier and art collector found shot dead in his Balwyn home, police suspect interrupted robbery. Not much in it, nothing about the sorrowing widow Sharon Lesser or the kidnapped daughter of the deceased, let alone a premature hearse and a batch of wog bovver boys loitering with unplumbable intent. Certainly no hint of the well-shod footprints of Felix Culpepper of Toorak, 3142.

I propped myself higher against Cookie's fragrant pillows and opened the paper to the front page. Splash shot of a downed, mangled, somewhat burned chopper in a field. This story was also light-on in details, played ever so faintly for smiles if not laughs. A camel had been apprehended fleeing the scene, but then sadly shot dead by an over-eager constabulary. Maybe Vinnie had been wrong about the bus crash. Maybe the Church was covering it up, like all those child sex cases. Unconfirmed rumors of mysterious wounds to its body, RSPCA officials promising an investigation. No names I recognized, luckily including my own, although a mysterious doctor of veterinary science was mentioned. The Sheikh of Araby was nowhere to be seen in the report.

I groaned a bit, and searched the pages for word on ravenous twin thugs found eating the bodies of the dead in an underground crypt at Fawkner Memorial Park, but that was missing too. You just can't rely on the media these days, and anyway Culpepper would have released them by now. On page 21, I did find a handsome photo of a noble visitor from an oil-rich realm and his lovely wives and daughters, masked in layers of silk and linen. Prince Abdul bin Sahal al Din, an honorable man, had been the honored guest with members of his family at a recent reception of honor hosted by the honorable governor of Victoria, the Right Honorable— No doubt Culpepper and his respectable Toorak wife would have been in attendance, too, Felix dodging the cameras.

I climbed out and pulled on my soiled and unironed clothes after I found them on the floor near the door. A larger portion of my wardrobe, or at least a selection from St. Vincent's Op Shop, lay beneath rubble in Parkville, along with a minimal selection of my personal effects, just enough to convince the insurance adjusters not to adjust Mauricio's policy into a hole in the ground, just enough to earn me a decent return from my own rather extravagant household policy. The rest had been moved piecemeal during the previous month into several Portable Self Storage Units now resident in a large warehouse in Melton, "Open 24/7, you have the key".

Thank god for night soil once more! No suspicious movement of furnishings in plain view of the neighbors a scant week prior to the terrible and unforeseeable Mack truck accident. Just a large storage unit or two delivered via the discretion of the cobbled lane to the rear entrance and all my earthlies minus a scam proportion spirited away to safety. In principle I could get the car from the cemetery, tool out to Melton, and grab a change of clothes, but it seemed easier to stay grubby for a while and borrow something from Chook. We were about the same size, and I could put up with the humiliation of wearing a crimplene shirt and a Suit from Sire's With Free Matching Extra Pair of Trousers for a couple of days.

The silence in the kitchen was unnerving. The young women were too shaken to fill the main room with awful noise from the surround sound system. I tossed the *Age* on the table, put my watch back on, retrieved my keys and billfold, stuck the shades on my nose, then quickly checked to see that my folding money and credit cards were intact. For a wonder, they were untouched. I nuked another horrible quasi-coffee, found a stale croissant and wolfed it down without a word, thinking gloomy thoughts. Then I said, "Vinnie around?"

"He goes out to see his dogs on Sundays," Animal said. Her borrowed grand dad owned the back end of a couple of greyhounds. I suppose an interest is a good thing for those moving out of the silver age and toward the old crock's home, but I was fairly sure he'd never got a penny back from the brace of them. They affected a Buddhist attitude of live and let live toward the fake rabbit on the rail. Vinnie craved the company of his old cronies, I suppose. As would I, if my old cronies hadn't been the likes of Mauricio Cimino.

I wondered how Share Lesser was getting on, in the depths of her grieving and abrupt widowhood. I wondered again whether she'd known about her husband and his younger daughter. Surely Share couldn't have known. Yet surely she couldn't have not known.

"How long had it been going on?" I asked, taking another appalled sip.

Animal looked at me, at Grime Grrl who tightened her lips and shook her head, back to me. She knew I knew. She didn't know how I knew I knew, and neither did I, but I've been around this shithole of a world longer than she has.

"After mum died. Cookie's and mine."

"He tried it with you?" Succeeded, is what I wanted to know.

"Only once. I said I'd cut his dick off."

"How old were you? Sorry, I have to ask."

"Twelve. Just getting tits."

"Shit. Sorry, Grime. And she's had trouble getting around since—"

Grime Grrl shook her head, lost in the void of the past.

"Years." Animal shuddered, and even in the dark of noon I could see two tears roll down her cheeks. "Stuck at home most of the time."

"And she loved him, too, in a way, I suppose," I said carefully, trying to avoid an ideological outburst from Grime. I could feel an outburst of my own coming on. The bastard. I'd have blown his fucking head off myself.

"He looked after her, see," Grime said in a flat, flat voice. "I didn't think he'd dare try it again. He bought her everything she wanted. Nothing was too much for dear old Rodolph. He'd even wash—" Her voice locked up, and she clutched at my daughter's hands.

"And when you saw the note you thought he'd had your sister abducted and murdered?"

They stared up at me, shocked.

"We would have *told* you," Animal said crossly. "Do you think we're *stupid?*"

"No, sorry." I rocked back on my heels, bum against the sink. "I know you're not stupid, so I know neither of you pulled the trigger. I just hope you've made sure there's no obvious trail back between you and whatever mad bloody vigilante vengeance sisterhood hit squad..." I shook my head. "Not that I blame you, or Cookie, for killing the evil shit. Not that I blame you for a moment."

Animal looked at me, streaks in her white and black makeup. "Well, good," she said, finally.

"The less I know the better," I told them. "Give me the key to downstairs, Annabelle, I need to make a phone call." Better not to let her know I had my own key.

I was halfway down the stairs when I remembered the Esky and the shotgun. I had to dispose of one or both before the cops or Culpepper, in cahoots or independently, came breaking down the door to my daughter's household. I trudged back up, marched past their dark sighs, reached into the wardrobe.

Not there.

I flung the doors open and rummaged harder. The gun was gone. And some bastard had nicked my stolen Esky.

My stomach turned over, a sort of imagined terror of retribution. Could Culpepper really have snuck into the room while I lay there snoring? No. Paranoia. Impossible. Well, someone had.

I marched out again. "Who's got them?"

"Got what? Aren't you going?"

"The bloody gun. The bloody Esky."

"*What* Esky? Jeez Dad, are you turning into an alkie or something?"

"He brought an Esky in with him last night," Grime told her.

"I put it in Cookie's wardrobe. There was also the shotgun you left there, wrapped up in canvas."

They carefully didn't look guiltily at each other.

"We've been out, see? For a couple of hours. At Grime's machine shop. Not that we were doing anything special, just hanging out. On a Sunday morning, it's boring, you know? Could have been anyone."

"Christ, who else comes in here? That's a god-damned murder weapon."

"Well, sound like it's gone now."

They'd had someone drop by to collect it. The vengeance grrls, presumably. I hoped the grrls weren't too disappointed to open the Esky and find half a dozen empty Foster's cans. I hoped, too, that they didn't find a few keys of prime heroin.

Mauricio was at Mass at St. Patrick's Cathedral in East Melbourne with his sainted mother, just up the road from the *Nippon Tuck*. Dago answered the phone. It broke his mother's heart that he was a declared unbeliever, but what can you do, these clever ones leap over the wall in their pride, like Juliet had done, the slut, you just have to pray and do novenas until the cows come home in the faith that the Virgin Mary will touch their hearts at the last moment, hopefully before a police bullet gets there first. I said I needed a cell phone and a lift out to collect my transport. He told me to fuckin go up the street and buy a new one from any of the hundred hole-in-wall shops in Sydney Road's Magic Mile of Mobiles, then catch a number 19 tram all the way to the terminus followed by a brisk stroll to the bone yard. I reminded him that it was Sunday, the day of rest, all the shops were shut. He made in rejoinder the same general point about the day of rest, and wondered where the fuck I'd been during the last decade and a half of market liberation from the binding constraints of No Sunday Trading superstition and restraint of trade? I said I'd spent a bit of it in an American jail surrounded by very large black dudes, exercising my civil rights and other muscles, and Dago agreed to come by in fifteen minutes with a spare Nokia that had fallen off a truck.

The Cobra was still in the cemetery car park, which was a wonder. The graf was a wonder too—four different colors with shadows. It ran all down the passenger side, from turning light to turning light. It took me three minutes to decipher it: I think it said SCRUBBER, but the letters were so deformed and intertwined that it might have read EAT AT JOE'S. It gave the crate a manly air, there was a touch of the freight train to it. One of the spray cans had been abandoned. It lay on the ground, perhaps the bearer of usable finger prints. Perhaps not, and anyway the police would not be sympathetic to my grievance. I left it where it was and drove away in the general direction of my stash of clean clothes. While I did so I keyed in Share's home number.

"Sharon Lesser," the widow said.

"Tom," I said.

"Who did it?"

"No idea," I said.

"The cops are useless. They won't tell me a thing."

"Take it easy."

"I want to know who did it, Purdue."

"Yeah, well, I cashed in my private dick's license years ago."

"Had it taken away for irregularities, is what I heard."

"Depends on your perspective," I said.

"They don't let jailbirds hold a license, isn't that right?"

"Jailbird"," I said. "Have you been watching old Edward G. Robinson flicks on the midday movie?"

"I know you did time in the States, and they won't let crims back in there. I doubt the Australian authorities allow old cons to get a P.I. ticket, either."

True enough. So I was obliged to pursue the *feng shui* trade and other novelties not paying anything like Yank bucks.

"That was Recherché D. T. Purdue," I told her. "Good plain Tom is a different bloke entirely."

"Really. Changed your fingerprints, eh?"

"Trickier now, admittedly, with the terrorism police on the job. Back then you just had to be very sincere. I can do sincere."

"I need to talk to you, Purdue."

"We're talking now."

"Not on the fucking phone, you idiot."

The widow was in fine fettle and abruptly very businesslike. It occurred to me that she might be about to offer me another job, one that paid better than camel doping.

"I'll call you later about a meet," I said and rang off.

As I drove to Melton, I pondered the pros and cons of gainful employ in the service of Sharon Lesser: I needed money, I didn't need any more excitement in my life. Mutually exclusive propositions as far as the widow was concerned. I deferred my decision.

The U Store It facility skulked in a square kilometer of dubious light industry: glaziers, crash repair specialists, spray painters, aluminum windows, spare parts all makes and models. You wouldn't want to ask too many questions, but the glaziers were known to drink with the cops who attended home break-ins and if the spare parts boyos didn't have what you needed, they knew someone who just happened to be wrecking the model in question. I stated my business to the ex-lifer on the gate and parked the Cobra outside my particular concrete box. I had the key all right. Nothing so sophisticated as a digital keyboard for U Store It—the clients wouldn't be able to remember their own names, half of them. They made up for it with their key. It was an elaborate thing with two parallel sets of irregular teeth—you could imagine a paleontologist unearthing it. You sure as hell couldn't get a spare one cut at your local hardware.

All my worldly possessions were present and correct. So were someone else's.

I walked back to the gate house and had a yarn with the ex-lifer. The guy might have been the terror of Pentridge H block back in the sixties, but age had withered him and the years condemned. He had few teeth and fewer neurons. He knew nothing, as he was slow to tell me.

"You're the only one who has the key, Mr. Purdue."

"I don't think so. Some other bugger has parked his stuff in my unit."

"Couldn't happen, Mr. Purdue. Could not happen."

"But it has. There's all this expensive gear in my unit."

"You must have loaned the key to a mate."

"I didn't."

"Yours is the only key, Mr. Purdue. Besides, the only person I've seen here today was an old lady with a couple of fishing rods wrapped up real good in canvas. Very quiet Sunday."

"Funny time of year to be fishing," I said.

He laughed, rolled his eyes. "Yeah, but she was hopeful. Had an Esky."

"For keeping her fish cool?"

"Yeah." He laughed some more. "I told her not to go storing any fish. Right on the nose quick smart, that'd be." He found this imagined prospect uproarious, and uproared.

"She did, though," I said. "She left it in my locker."

"Couldn't of, not without your key." It sobered him but not as much as it puzzled him.

"Management must have a key."

"It would be in a safe, Mr. Purdue, locked up tight."

"So anything in that unit must be mine?"

"Gotta be." I took out my wallet and consulted the contents. But the ex-lifer wasn't selling. "If I knew anything, I'd tell you, Mr. Purdue."

I gave up and walked back to the unit. The "fishing rods" in canvas was jammed up behind my own stuff. I didn't touch it. The last thing I wanted was my fingerprints on a murder weapon. I carefully popped the tabs on the top of the Esky. No drugs. No empty beer cans. White fumes boiled out. I pulled my face away. Nothing toxic, but cold. Dry ice, frozen carbon dioxide, cupping something large and blue-gray and repulsive. I slapped the lid on at once to keep the day's mild warmth out.

$\mathcal{My}$ new phone rang. Caller ID blocked. What was the point of having it, everyone did this shit now. I was about to announce myself when it occurred to me that no one knew the number of this borrowed phone from Dago. Probably a phone spammer. I disguised my voice and said, "Yo, bro, how dey hanging?"

"Don't get smart with me, sport."

"Who you be, boy?"

"I know who you are, scumbag."

"Who I be?"

"You're the arsehole who stole my fucking best mobile and I'm coming round to your place to rip your ears off your head."

"My place has been bulldozed."

"That dyke's den above Vinnie's shop."

"Jesus, Mauricio, your brother—"

"Bloody Dago, would he ask? Would he so much as say please? No. He needs a mobile to lend to some jerk who's smashed up his own, so he grabs the nearest... just grabs the bastard."

"You'll get your phone back, Mauricio."

"In one piece, Purdue."

"Yeah, yeah."

"We need to talk about things."

"We are talking about things."

"I'd rather not run up my fucking phone bill."

"Don't worry. I'll come round to your place later, Mauricio, we'll have a heart to heart. Face to face."

"You do that, Tom. And, Tom?"

"Yeah."

"If the phone rings again... don't answer it, you hear?"

"Outgoings only," I said.

"And not too many of them either."

"Be generous, Mauricio. Think family. My phone is your phone, that sort of thing."

"See you real soon, Purdue."

I wondered if Mauricio was about to offer me employment. Two possible opportunities in a single day. A man needs clients.

"*Girls* in, Vin?"

"Dunno. Poor Jonquil's having a lie-down in the best suite at the John Fawkner."

That gave me a start until I remembered that it was the big private hospital on Moreland Road hill, nothing to do with Fawkner Crematorium. Old Fawkner must have had his hand in a number of adjacent and lucrative pies, if it was the same man, in this case one hand shuffling its failures to the other. Enough to put you off visiting the quack. Vinnie, back from ministering to his greyhounds, was surrounded by a blizzard of paper: small slips in various hues, like a scene from some awful old ABC television serial about SP bookies, in disarray. He peered shortsightedly, scribbled a notation in a large ledger, groaned, put it aside, clutched his head. "You couldn't give a bloke a hand?"

"Computers down?"

"It's all a mystery to me, Tom. Leave it to the girl. I used to have two women in the back room handling the phones and the books, then young Jonquil went through like a... what do they say on that ad?"

"A dose of salts?"

"A white tornado. Automated the whole thing. What am I meant to do now?"

"Hire a 12 year old," I said. I looked over his shoulder at the desk. On the small TV set, small figures mouthed at each other. It was true, he'd lost his craft. Fall off, climb straight back on, you get it back, they say, but Vinnie hadn't been that successful of late, business had been dropping away with the rise and rise of Taberet and all the pokie machine in the pubs, it was wonder to me that Cookie had found enough to do. But here were the slips to prove that starting price gambling retained its lure. I couldn't see anything that looked like big money wagered on a camel.

"You still got that shotgun, Vinnie?"

He said nothing, but his mouth tightened.

"I suppose it's been cleaned and disposed of?"

"Dunno what you're talking about. Handed it in during the amnesty, I reckon. Cost me eight hundred fuckin bucks, shoulda sold it to your mate Mauricio."

"Yeah." I unkinked. "Going upstairs to wait for Annabelle, anyone asks."

"They don't like people messing about up there."

"I'll leave them a note and drive over to the hospital."

"Take her some flowers," Vinnie said. "Woulda gone myself, but I have all this—" He gestured in despair at the midden of betting slips.

Sappho the cat met me on the stairs, twining herself around my legs and making hungry sounds.

"I'm the last person to ask," I told the cat. "I assume the girls are still out, then?"

"*Mmmmrrp,*" Sappho said. After I opened the door with the key Animal didn't know I owned, I found a can of Cat-O-Meat and the cat opener, spooned a mound of the smelly stuff into her saucer. She set to, casting me a wary glance.

"Never eat it," I reassured her. "Well, there was that one week."

I went into Cookie's empty bedroom, clicked the desk lamp. The computer sat on the desk, lifeless without her authorizing codes. Inside her robe, where I'd left the Esky next to the shotgun before falling into the sleep of the damned, I found robes: commodious, ample, overflowing black Goth robes with embroidery in deep scarlet and deeper blue metallic thread, just the thing for the lifestyle challenged fattie. On the floor of the robe, a laptop computer lay in an inexpensive leather or *faux*-leather case. I took the computer to the bed and powered it up.

On my lap the laptop showed a desktop picture of Rembrandt's wife. Not only a powerfully decorated Goth, young Cookie, a culture freak as well. I ran my thumb over the pad and finally got the arrow onto the hard drive icon. I tapped the pad and Rembrandt's wife was half replaced by a list of the laptop's contents. The usual suspects: word processing, internet access, email, spreadsheet, executive games for long flights and a list of documents with little icons of keys next to them. I ran my eye down the list of sub-directories. PURDUE caught my eye. Just for the form of the thing I clicked on it. *Secure directory. Enter password.* No kidding. Same obstacle course as the machine on the desk. Unless I was greatly mistaken, it was Cookie's password I needed, and for that I'd have to pay a visit to my wife Juliet who was probably up to her elbows in molten metal.

I sighed, wondering what *quid pro quo* would be required to secure access to the laptop's secrets.

Or I could just ask Cookie, maybe she would like to employ me in some capacity as recompense for my Galahad rescue. If the poor cow was up to it. Probably she'd still be recuperating in the Fawkner hospital for a few days. I wondered if she and her sister had come into some money from the daughter-molester with no cranium, or if Share had bagged the lot. I sat on the bed and sighed. I didn't wish to impose myself on Jules. The move of choice, the obvious move really, was to pop up the road to the John Fawkner and have a word with the brutalized orca. Assuming the cops let me see her. Well, they had no cause not to. They could hardly intend to charge *her* with her father's death, or the death of a hyped-up, sugar-maddened and allegedly UFO-mutilated camel for that matter. Assuming UFO aliens carried Eskys on board.

I rubbed the bristles on my face. Good Christ, had that only been yesterday? It felt like a month. Sappho sashayed in and jumped up beside me, stropping the bedcovers with her claws and making concrete-churning sounds. I stroked her from the top of her head to her tail, and she settled down happily. When Mauricio's phone rang I thought twice, but answered it anyway. No caller ID on the screen.

"Yep."

"They let me in at Melton?" A pause. The woman was nervous. "Well, now what?"

"Eh."

"I put that piece of meat in with the gun?" I knew the voice from somewhere, fucked if I could pin it down. An older woman, querulous. Presumably she'd been ready to pass herself off as my mother or elderly aunt or something, better than offering money, but good old Thick-as-a-brick had just waved her through with no more than a snigger at her fishing exploits. Mauricio was the only one who knew about the U Store It hoard except for me. Thanks a fucking lot, pal. What was the madman up to?

The silence lengthened.

"Should I go up and see him?"

"Uh," I said.

"Oh dear, I don't know. I'm just across the street now, in Ivy's."

Good Christ, it was Maeve Murphy. "Nngg," I said, and disconnected.

Mauricio would stop at nothing, use anyone, family, friends, stray little old ladies. Mauricio, Mauricio, I swore to myself. Your machinations beggar the imagination of lesser men and Lesser women, and they will bring you undone one day, you little shit.

I rang Telstra, got put through to admissions at Fawkner. "I'm enquiring about a young woman who was brought in very early this morning, Jonquil Lesser's her name, is she still—"

The woman on the desk did her computer checking, while a man in the office told her or someone else gloatingly about the bundle he'd made yesterday on Brute Force.

"She was released at noon, sir."

"Someone picked her up? Jonquil has trouble getting around, you see."

"Oh yes, the very overweight— Um, a family member arranged her transport."

"Thanks."

I went out again to the car, nodding to Vinnie. The Cobra was parked in Sydney Road just up from the shop, probably illegally, although on a Sunday afternoon the rules of the clearway were too Byzantine for me to grasp. Leaning into the luggage hold, I retrieved the horrid thing in its white casing, then came back the round-about way along the alley to avoid running into Maeve and giving her a heart attack. I left the Esky and its gruesome contents once more in Cookie's room, inside the same wardrobe where the cat couldn't play with it, and took Sappho out to the kitchen for some milk, saw to it that her kitty litter tray was reasonably wholesome, then let myself out into the shop with a click. Vinnie was poring through his slips of paper with a certain resolute desperation, aided by Mrs. Murphy. If the powers of reincarnation could be brought to bear on his task, she was the woman to save his day.

"Hello, Maeve," I said. "Can I get you both a cuppa? I think the girls must be on their way back," I told Vinnie. "The hospital reckons Cookie's fighting fit."

"Needs to lose a few pounds," he said gloomily. "I'll take mine with milk and two, Mrs. Murphy the same."

"None for me, dearie," Maeve said. "I've just had a nice pot of tea and a Cambodian crumpet with the girl over the road. It's not really a crumpet?"

"In that case, Vinnie," I said, "I'll leave you to make your own swill. Top of the morning to you, Madam Cleopatra."

"I feel the Czarina upon me today," she said. "I can't say I approve of the decorations on your motor car."

"It's all the rage in Melton," I said. She flinched, developed an interest in sorting the betting tickets. I jotted down the borrowed cellphone number on the back of one, tucked it into Vinnie's top pocket. "Tell Animal she can reach me on that number."

Three or four barely teenaged hoons on BMX bikes, stack hats hanging from their handle bars, propped on the footpath admiring the artwork on the Cobra. Their well-heeled parents probably resided in affluent comfort in Pentridge bloody Village. One held an enamel paint can, perhaps to add a small contribution of his own, perhaps to elevate his mood with a snort. I took it away from him with the hand that wasn't holding the laptop and lobbed it into the back of a passing ute. When I pulled into the traffic, I couldn't be sure if their hoots were jeering catcalls or cries of admiration. I prefer to think it was the latter.

"Share," I said, driving one handed.

"I'm not going to discuss this over the phone." She sounded exasperated. "I've just got the child back from—"

"I'm coming over. I'm enthralled by the mysterious case of Nile

Fever's mutilation and would like an in-depth—"

"What the *fuck* do you know about that? Purdue, if this is one of your hare-brained scam—"

"Pure guesswork, sweetheart, and keen attention to trash television rumors and the tireless press. Strike that." A tram rumbled past backwards as I put my foot to the floor. "Sheer dogged detective work. Put some lunch on, would you, I'm starving."

"Lunch was two hours ago."

"Make it afternoon tea. A pot of Darjeeling, cucumber sandwiches. Mind you cut the crusts off of the sandwiches. And a meat pie or two. Lashings of tomato sauce."

"Why should I feed you, you bastard?"

That sounded genuinely indignant. Scratch one theory. "If Grime's there, put her on."

"You mean Animal."

"I mean your step-daughter, Share. Fetch her to the phone, it would be a kindness, and your karma will be adjusted by three points to offset what you did to that poor camel."

She hollered into the void. "Ruby!"

I waited, thinking hard. In the distance, I heard a whine. "Wha-a-a-t?"

"You have an admirer on the phone."

"Tell her to... Oh, fuck." Heavy Doc Maartens boots clumped along the polished floorboards. "What do you want now, Gracie? I told her it's over."

"I found the shotgun in the U Store It," I told her. Presumably Grime or Animal had coolly nicked my keys while I snored the sleep of the up-way-too-late-and-cop-pestered, and had them copied. Could you do that on a Sunday morning? Probably the clever little bitch had some laser cutting tool at work that did it in a trice. They must have been moving like greased pigs, though. And whose bright idea was that? Oh, I thought. Who else but Mauricio? "And the Esky, of course," I added.

"Bullshit," Ruby Lesser said hopefully.

"You and Mauricio placed your faith in a weak reed," I said. "Maeve's away with the pixies. One hard stare and she gave it up."

"Oh shit, you prick, if you've hurt that poor old lady—"

"You'll have the top of my head blown off? That would look

suspicious, Grime, don't you think?" A van load of Maori rugby players pulled past me in the wrong lane, jeering at the graffiti job, showing me their tattooed tongues. I saluted them with the mobile, put it back against my ear just in time to monitor the end of a stream of futile obscenity.

"Look, hold your tongue for once, Ruby." To my surprise that worked. In the grudging quiet, I said, "I need to know if Cookie's up to some conversation. I have her laptop with me."

"Don't you *dare* to—"

"For Christ's sake put a sock in it, Grime. Is she awake and lucid."

"No."

"Sleeping, or something the quacks gave her?"

"Some narcotic shit. Those bastards at the hospital—"

Good god, was I about to have a Just Say No tirade inflicted on me by a bolt-tongued Goth? The thought of a mutilated tongue made me shudder briefly.

"All right, Grime, my plans have changed. Tell your mother—"

"She's not my fucking mother!"

"Tell Sharon I'm taking a rain check on the tea and scones. I want her to call me at this number the moment Cookie wakes up. Have you got a pencil or pen or something?"

"I've got an eidetic memory."

"What?"

"I don't forget shit."

"Okay, good for you." I told her the number of Mauricio's mobile, and put it back in my pocket, concentrated on swinging around the next corner. Fairly soon I parked askew next to the smelly Dumpster, raced up the steps. It only took a minutes to retrieve the Esky, which was more likely not to disappear if I kept it close than if I left it there for the grrls to trip over again, assuming they ever went home, or for Maeve to reclaim. I groaned to myself. Life is just so damned complicated sometimes.

I gunned my streetwise artwork ride toward the Tullamarine toll road, then south over the Yarra river as it headed for freedom into Hobson's Bay, and looped onto the Westgate Freeway. The great bridge took me high into the air with the city's commerce all phallic mirrored glass and Victorian remnants to one side and low-slung industry on the other, with water glimpses like burnished steel between them. I ripped through the Sunday afternoon traffic headed for the insalubrious boundary of Laverton North and Sunshine West where my wife has her iron foundry and works her will upon the materials of the earth in ways that draw applause and large amounts of money from home renovators throughout the continent. And they call what *I* do a scam.

I met Juliet Cimino first and her siblings later, so she knew me initially as a grieving widower with a soulful gaze and only later as a scam artist with a modest criminal record, like her older brother Mauricio but rather less so.

In those days she was a high-powered and power-dressed publisher for Pen Inc, one of the black clad young band of superwomen who had remade the local book industry in the image of their sensitive but tough, laconic but knowing, tasteful but market-savvy feminist souls. Juliet went on to make heaps of money for the global conglomerate with fat novels about colonial criminals and their brutalized womenfolk, fat cookbooks promising the abolition of fat, slender improving rants in large typeface that showed fat to be a postfeminist issue, and an entire line of bogus but terrifying autobiographies by contemporary criminals who wished they were Chopper Read, the gunman who had his ears hacked off in jail to make a point. I met Chopper a few times, when I couldn't avoid it, and have gone out of my way to avoid the occasion since.

Juliet migrated out of publishing and into her current trade by an interesting chance. She was flying home from the biennial Adelaide Arts Festival, a sunny cultural gathering under large open tents beneath a grassy knoll not far from the center of the city of churches. The event is washed with fine wines of the region and excellent food if you're a publisher or one of the high fliers in the fat, fat-free or near-criminal genres.

Poor Juliet had sparkled relentlessly for five days, and was jaded. The beefy man in the narrow seat next to her explained that he was an important executive for one of the steel giants that undergirded the national economy for a time. He was fascinated to learn that she was in publishing, or perhaps by her beautiful breasts and delicately flavored Italian accent. She'd picked up more than art history at Deakin university. Mauricio had gone there, too, for a year of Economics and Law, before shifting gear and moving his accent in the other direction.

"So you're in publishing? Fascinating! Do you know," the businessman told her in a reflective tone, "I've always thought that when I retire from the steel business I might open a small publishing house."

Juliet gazed at him, I'm certain, with her ferocious Italian long-lashed gaze and said thoughtfully, "Now that's really an extraordinary coincidence."

"Oh?" The tycoon was baffled, and sipped at his Cabernet Sauvignon with a frown.

"Yes, I've always thought that when I retire from publishing I'd like to open a small iron foundry."

Sprayed red wine does not leave an especially visible mark on black, so it was lucky that Jules was a publisher at the time. But the jesting idea, whimsical and *ad hoc* as it was, stuck somehow in her mind. She fancied herself the distant daughter of Benvenuto Cellini and couldn't help noticing how real estate prices were rising dizzyingly and the demand for wrought iron lacework with them.

Lace iron had first come to Australia as ballast in the bottoms of cargo ships, and the supply had been pretty much exhausted by the 1980s. In the '90s you couldn't find any for love or money, so everyone wanted it. Aluminum was cheaper and lighter but it had a fatally ersatz lightness and cheapness. Iron struck from the soil of the land, that was the thing. Iron crushed and melted and poured bright white into moulds shaped with fleurs des lys and little doggies' faces and vine leaves and sunbursts and God knows what all. Noble iron lions standing atop pillars of iron, and gryphons wrapped in writhing snakes with iron scales and frozen flickering iron tongues. There was money in it, and art, of a sort. Juliet resigned from Pen with a nice bonus and bought up a failing foundry in a sunless portion of Sunshine, not all that far from where she'd grown up in Footscray when that was still a working class suburb. Her sainted mother was scandalized. Not as scandalized, it's true, as when Jules married me.

I pulled into the small parking space, next to Juliet's old Holden ute, tossed Mauricio's phone in the glove box, grabbed Cookie's laptop by the serviceable handle of its *faux*-leather case. I went through the decorative metal fence's more conventional chain link gate to the foundry's heavy sliding timber side door at the back, which stood half-open in its ancient worn runners. Hot white stuff spattered in the loud dimness. During the week the place rang with the shouts of her workers, often yelling in Sicilian. Today Juliet was working by herself. Seemed hazardous to me.

She wore a pair of wrap-around safety glasses, a baseball cap backwards to hold her long dark hair in place, and a shapeless blue overall almost black with iron dust. Large gloves, surely not asbestos but something developed by NASA, covered her delicate publisher's fingers as she wrestled runny metal into a frame. Those fingers had once danced nimbly on computer keyboards. Jules was no hacker, but she knew a damned sight more about programming and de-programming computers than I ever will. And I could trust her not to run to the cops, or to the bad guys for that matter.

She noticed me. "Hi, sweetie. With you in a mo."

I tilted my head in greeting, knowing better than to distract her. Liquid light cooled to red, to an orange glow, faded slowly to dullness as she carefully completed her madly dangerous if routine task. Couldn't be good for the skin, you'd think, but when she joined me and we walked side by side to the Cimino Iron Works office, it was far from obvious. The blush of youth still lay on her cheek, unless it was heat from the furnace. I clicked the door shut behind us and Juliet shucked her coverall and baseball hat.

"Art or commerce?" I asked.

"Nothing fancy this time," she told me. Her black hair, a touch moist from well-earned sweat, nuzzled her shoulders, and who could blame it? "A set of angels for a tomb in the Fawkner cemetery."

"Now there's a coincidence," I said, and we leaned toward each other, not embracing, and did that air kiss thing. My bristles scrapped her cheek.

"Hey!"

"Sorry, on a case. No time to shave this morning."

"It's afternoon, Tom." She rubbed her cheek lightly without knowing it. "I assume you're not here for a few meters of verandah iron? Not that it would go terribly convincingly with your porch."

"We'd have to throw it on the rubble heap. Your mad brother wrecked the place night before last."

She stared. "Mauricio wrecked your—Oh, yes, he owns that Parkville place doesn't he?" Juliet burst into appalled laughter, and moved behind her desk. I put the laptop on top of some bills, pulled up a wooden chair and sat down with my elbows propped and fists under my bristly chin. "An insurance scam, I take it?"

"Urban renewal," I said. "There's nothing déclassé about Mauricio. How have you been, love?"

"Bonzer, cobber. Have you seen the horrible child lately?"

They had not got on, Annabelle and her stepmother. What had Share called that sort of thing? *"Trophy wife syndrome"*. Unfair, of course. In those days I was wildly in love with Juliet and she with me, and she'd never treated my daughter like Cinderella, but there you are. The thuddingly recurrent Freudian mysteries of the family romance. Or so Juliet had explained to me once.

"Animal is why I'm here, Jules."

"I'm not going to give her a part-time job if that's what you're thinking. She'd have the whole place up in flames."

"A friend of hers was kidnapped."

"Oh." When she squeezed her eyes shut the lashes meshed like a dark Cloud of Unknowing, suitably enough given her religious background. They opened instantly on eyes dark as a computer monitor screen. "Hence the whiskers. Have you found the friend?"

"Yep. But she's still in danger, I think."

"Okay." Her computer monitor eyes flicked to the computer. "So there's a clue in the machine. She was getting threatening emails. You can't get in because it's password protected. And you can't just ask her for it because she's—"

"In hospital, and probably wouldn't tell me."

You can see why I fell in love with Jules, even while I was still grieving for Patty. She is simply dazzling, and then there's that black hair and eyelashes, too, and the eyes themselves, and the delightful breasts, and some more good stuff.

"Can you get it open, do you think?" I asked.

"Worth a burl, cobber. Push it over."

To my surprise, Juliet reached first into a drawer and drew out a pair of stylish narrow glasses and perched them on her nose as I opened the case and rotated the machine for her, flicking the power button. Surprisingly light, these current models. She started tapping immediately, thumb easy on the touch pad. "We're both getting older, Mr. Purdue," she said, and sent me a look over the top rim of the specs.

"We are indeed, Ms. Cimino."

"Okay, you're right, there's no simple way past the security." Juliet pushed the machine aside and steepled her fingers, which naturally bore no ring of marriage or other commitment. Well, you would hardly wear jewelry while pouring molten metal in any case. " It won't be her name or birthday or anything obvious, unless she's really stupid. I don't suppose she's really stupid?" she said hopefully.

"Smart as a whip, far as I can make out," I said. "The cat's called Sappho." I got up and went around the desk, hovered over her shoulder. Usually she gets very quiet and freezes up when I do that, but it made sense this time, I wasn't spying or being fond or invading her space. Fingers flashed: *SAPPHO*

Password error. Re-enter.

Juliet hummed. "She's a kid, right, same age as Annabelle?"

"Near enough."

SAPPH0

I looked at the screen, puzzled. "Oh, zero instead of Oh."

"Yeah. Leetspeak."

I didn't get it, but okay. However, when Jules pushed Enter she was told sternly to try again.

"Shit, these programs usually only allow three or four bloopers and then they lock up. Is this really critical?"

"Well, there's a guy with his head blown apart, and a girl who was buried in a lightless crypt for several days."

Another flashing glance. "The Fawkner cemetery coincidence. Good god, the poor child. Let's get this sucker *right*. I want something mnemonic, a household gag, maybe, a nickname hardly anyone knows, come on, use your *feng shui*, man."

So she knew about that, she'd been keeping up. I sat in silence, searching my memory. "Jonquil's a Goth who calls herself Cookie," I said. "Like Animal and Cookie's sister Grime Grrl." I suspected Juliet wanted to snigger, but the gravity of the moment and her intentness kept her quiet. "She's been involved with starting price bookies or whatever the computer age equivalent is. Peer to peer, I think Grime said. She's shockingly overweight, severely limited mobility. I think she's a lesbian like the other two, or going through a phase, but then again maybe she's never had a chance to try either side of the road. Or the motivation. Except for cybersex of some kind, which is how they trapped her, the bastards." I took a breath. "And her father fucked her when she was a kid."

"Jesus." Juliet eyes closed again behind glass. I was watching her face from the side. They stayed closed for a long moment. "I don't think she'd use the word 'incest' or one of its cognates, too raw and wounding. But something connected…"

I saw light in darkness. "They have a sign on the door of their squat, no punctuation: *Well cut your balls off.*"

Jules scribbled it on a sheet of paper, showed it to me.

"Yeah, that's it."

She considered it. "Worth a try." In it went with the words jammed together.

Password error. Re-enter.

"Shit! Hang on, she's definitely a hacker, you reckon? Not a n00b?"

A *noobie?* Good Christ, where does she get this stuff. "I suppose."

Juliet's fingers danced. *W311CUTURB@1150FF.* Her right pinky paused above the Enter key, and she backspaced two letters, retyped one.

W311CUTURB@1150V. Enter.

The screen opened with a thudding racket of hip-hop. A black grrl group was snarling, "We'll cut yo *balls* off, motherfucker, cut your *balls* off, your *balls* off, *balls* off." And above their posturing image the menu lay open for rifling.

"*How* the fuck did you know that?"

"Edited a book for Pen Inc on leetspeak. 'Elite' to you, you pitiful newbie. That's enn-zero-zero-bee. The contractions are quite witty, actually, in a puerile—"

"I'm sure they are, sweetie. Could you whack your cursor over to…" I stuck my finger on the screen, which deformed away from my fingernail. "Yep. Right, down and… PURDUE, as I expected."

Juliet opened the directory with a deft click, and four icons popped on to the screen. She opened the first, which was an image that loaded into some sort of graphics program. It was a rap sheet from the Seattle Police Department, dated 1989, scanned from paper presumably. I don't think they'd computerized their files that long ago. The picture was not fetching but by God I looked a damned sight fresher-faced in those days, not to say gaunt and long-haired and as poetical as Emily Dickinson.

"Darling! How charming!"

I was embarrassed. "Close the bloody thing and get on with the search, Madame Sherlock." Short of reaching over her shoulder and dashing the machine to death against the edge of her desk, which would be both rude and wasteful since it contained my only clues, I could only stand there and prevail upon my wife's better angels. Fat chance. She scrolled down, sniggering.

"Six foot two, well, I knew that, but good grief, Tom, a hundred and forty two pounds? I have no idea what that is in real metric weights and measures, but—"

"Sixty five kilos, give or take. Americans didn't use metric, still don't. Better than the celebrated 90 pound weakling, Juliet, you've got to give me that."

"The one who was always getting sand kicked in his face by the beach bully in the Charles... Charles what was it? Oh yes, Charles Atlas isometric projection ads."

"Not exactly," I said. I looked away from the mug shots. "I ate a lot in prison."

"And built up those big arms," she told me, batting her eyes. "My hero! While you were paying your debt to society or rather to the people of the State of Washington and of the United States for the shocking crime of—"

"Jeez, give a man a break, willyuh?" I reached over her shoulder and instead of smashing the computer I hit the Back button, then clicked down to the next file.

It was a list of the naughty goodies I had been smuggling into the USA, along with color photos of my right and left arms, then full and side shots of the way I'd been dressed when the Custom guys nobbled me.

"You *were* a spindly fellow."

"I had a late growth spurt."

"Not inside these garments, I trust," Juliet said, as her voice went up an octave or two. She clicked the mouse and the images doubled in size. By God I made an ugly girl. Even in flat heels and makeup, I looked like someone escaping from a circus of freaks. The silk blouse with its high neck, and long loose sleeves gathered tightly at the wrists to hide the contraband, the calf-length Mexican skirt in vivid hues hanging from my bony hips, the heavy bulges on my chest, the excruciatingly uncomfortable and smelly panty hose…

"How did you disguise your manly voice, Marilyn?" Jules gasped, falling about in her chair. "Oh, officer, I'm sure there's been a terrible mistake," she squeaked in falsetto.

"I coughed pitifully and pointed to my throat," I said, "and offered them a Strepsil cold lozenge."

"Twenty six jingle-jangle hollow plastic bangles," Juliet said admiringly. "Plugged with top grade super strength hash seeds from the bloody fields of Cambodia."

"Laos," I said. "Sepon. They upped their output of *cannabis sativa* that year."

"Very attractive," Juliet told me. "Bangles stretched from your skinny wrists to your bony elbows. Hey, and what's this?" She was hoarse with laughter. "More reefer madness tucked into your natty padded bra."

"Shut up."

"And for this disgraceful impersonation and attempted violation of your host nation's righteous import prohibitions," Juliet wheezed, slapping weakly at my reaching hands, "they sent you up to the big house, where I understand the principal currency is—"

"Narcotics. Yeah, yeah, I was a dope," I said, surly but starting to grin too, despite myself, at the bleak horrid absurdity of it all. "I was a stone criminal, man."

After she got control of herself again, Juliet squeezed past me and let me into her chair. I sank into its padding, feeling the burn of a man who has made truly stupid mistakes for love. The bitter comedy of a life ill-spent. It was supposed to be Patty who carried the premium dope seeds into Seattle, not me. But by the date of the run she was sick, tired to exhaustion, with what we thought was mononucleosis. Both of us knew with sweaty fright that the thugs who'd paid our mules' fee would not look kindly upon us if we failed to get the stuff into the States. I was barely 21, and not what anyone would call worldly, despite my swagger. What could we do?

Her passport got me through. They didn't care that much, back in those innocent days.

Innocent? Ignorant! If I'd known then that my 19 year old wife was pregnant, and not only carrying our daughter but slowly being eaten by carcinomas in her lymph glands, I'd have taken my chances with the drug-dealing bikers at the Croxton Bloodhouse. But you don't know these things, how can you? So I blundered into prison on the eager nostrils of a hash puppy in SeaTac's luggage carousel, attended by the raucous laughter and bruising thumps of the cops. I was dressed like a fool, on a fool's mission. By the time I got out and they extradited me home at the Australian Embassy's expense, my wife was two years from death. I didn't know that, either, until I stepped off the plane, because she'd refused to tell me in her twice-weekly letters, the stupid, beloved bitch. Of course she couldn't come to see me in the States because I'd been using her passport, which had been seized. And so I'd stayed in jail, of my own free will, pumping iron, eating protein and consolidating my bad boy education and contacts, for six fucking extra months. I could have been a good boy instead, God damn it to hell, and brown-nosed the system and gone home to nurse Patty and seen my daughter through her first years.

"Careful," Juliet said in a slightly alarmed tone. "You don't want to smash the keyboard."

"I do, but I won't." I closed the PURDUE directory and started trawling through the rest of the directories, sampling files. We were silent for a time, with keys clicking.

"Sorry," Juliet said. "Patty. I know. I just never realized—"

Through gritted teeth, I said on her behalf, in the new silence, "—how tawdry the whole fucking thing was."

I felt her hand touch my back softly, and a little jolt went through me. Equally softly she said, "No. You did it for love, you great lovable fool."

My throat felt swollen, suddenly. I cleared it. "Yeah, actually."

"Yeah, sweetie, I know. And shit happens."

I looked up at her. She was professorial in her reading glasses. I chose to be wry. "You've been studying philosophy with your brother."

Juliet threw her head back and laughed, that wonderful spontaneous peal of hers. "Mauricio *makes* shit happen. *Par example,* your house. Do you have anywhere to sleep?"

I shook my head, sighed. It came from deep inside me, and said more than I wanted it to. I shut down the machine, closed the lid, got out of her chair.

"Let's go for a swim, Jules. I need to stretch my legs. I'm turning into a wreck of a man. It's been days since I've got to the gym."

"Okay. Williamstown beach sounds good to me. Listen." She hesitated, switched off the office lights, closed the door. We made our way through the hot dimness of the foundry. "You can stay at my place for a couple of days if you need to."

"Jules, that's not— Okay, thank you."

We went out into the brighter daylight, and I rolled the great door shut with one arm while holding the laptop in my left hand, and Juliet keyed the electronic lock. She blinked at me in the sun.

"I trust you realize that—"

I shrugged, tried to smile. "Yeah, yeah, Juliet, I realize. A fuck's entirely out of the question."

My wife grinned up at me and took my arm in hers, companionably, and we went through the chain link gate to admire the paint job on the Cobra.

The phone was playing an Abba medley in the glove box.

"Aren't you going to answer it?"

"It's your brother's cell phone."

"What are you doing with Mauricio's phone? Won't he be rather... cross?"

"Long story. Here's my plan. You pick up your bikini, I'll saunter about the sand in my Speedos, we'll catch the day's last rays and then have a bite to eat at Pelicans Landing. Then back to John Street and you get your beauty sleep in perfect celibacy and I wrestle with the laptop."

The phone stopped ringing. Juliet opened the door of her Holden ute and hopped in. The interior was clean as a hound's tooth, no food wrappers, no Dr. Pepper cans rolling under foot, no half empty McDonald's Styrofoam packages. Certainly no evil polyurethane Esky of the kind hidden in the back of my Cobra. That's the kind of human my wife is. Pure in mind and body. Damn it. "No need for swimsuits," she said, starting the motor. "There's a nude beach at the top end of the Strand now. Free Willie, the wags call it." She grinned. "You really have had your head down."

"Such is the life of crime," I said ruefully. "Okay, last one there's a bare-arsed monkey's uncle."

Juliet gave a derisive snort and bounded backwards out of the parking lot with a shriek of burning rubber. Clean in mind and body, but a fiend behind the wheel. I was glad I had my own ride, even though the snooty *nouveaux riches* of Williamstown would look down their long noses at my graffed side panels.

I wondered if we should stop at the house anyway to pick up beach towels. I fished out the phone and thought of calling Juliet on her mobile, but couldn't remember the number. Since it was Mauricio's mobile phone he'd surely have her number in his directory, but I tried JUL and nothing came up. I spelled it out completely, thumb jumping; nothing. What the hell was his childhood pet name for her? Dolly? Dooly? Nothing worked. I threw the damned thing back in the glove box with the Split Enz' *Gold Collection* CD, mint fresheners and Kleenexes.

We veered left into the long, increasingly prosperous curve of The Strand. Speed bumps slowed us a bit. At the far end, past the fishing boats and Sunday strollers on the grass, her Holden swung off the road into a parking lot above Shelley Beach with a stand of discreet bushes and a pair of handsome pebble-encrusted public amenities. Not so much changing rooms as undressing rooms. Unlike my poor Cobra, the walls of the men's block were surprisingly free of graffiti.

We walked side by side past the rock pools and broken shells, and the handful of naturists reading fat blockbusters and the *Sunday Age* carefully failed to look at us. Nakedness was simply too ordinary to these jaded folks, you could tell. Well, except for one skinny teenager who blushed an improbable red all down his shoulders and chest when I stared fiercely at him for ogling Juliet. You couldn't blame him. I had to hold my shirt wadded in front of me as we crabbed down the crab grass to the crushed shells, cigarette butts and mild lapping waves. No surf here except when a storm whipped things up. I dropped the clothes and ran as fast as I could into the water, bellyflopping and getting salty water up my nose.

The thing in the portable cooler, resting in a Ziploc plastic baggie on fuming dry ice, was a severed tongue. A camel's tongue, I was fairly sure.

Someone had found the poor brute by the side of the road and hacked out its tongue. And then the prick had persuaded Maeve to hide the disgusting thing in my U Store It locker.

I spat salt water, fuming myself, and slammed butterfly through the low waves until my head rang with exertion and my blood pounded. When my anger ebbed, I turned and looked back a long way to the white and green shore. A condom floated past me, bobbing like some primitive life form. Anti-life form in fact. Ah well. I held my breath and swam back toward my beautiful naked childless wife.

I sipped at my martini, gazing west across water turned bloody and golden in alternating ripples. A cool breeze was rising over Port Phillip Bay, coming pretty much straight up from Antarctica and across the mass of Tasmania before being diverted left around the corner at Point Gellibrand. That was enough to take its chill off, but it was still a reminder that winter was not so many months away. In Seattle it was probably cooler and danker, even with summer up ahead hot on the heels of spring. But then my memories of Seattle were not that cheerful.

A polite waiter hovered. "Your table is ready, sir."

I offered Juliet my arm and we went inside, where lots of gleaming golden timber held intimate tables clad in clean white heavy tablecloths. Large wine glasses waited for us, also gleaming modestly. I could smell food, and the smell was good. So was the salty smell of my wife's sun-dried hair. I tried to ignore that.

A gilded youth brought us crusty warm bread and small bowls of dips. I absently shoveled dip into my face and opened the menu. "My god, this is the first proper thing I've eaten since last night."

"You're getting a bit tubby anyway," Juliet said.

I sucked in my gut, outraged. "Me? I can do fifty Turkish push-ups with one arm. I can hold a bridge for—"

"You're allowed," she told me placidly. "It's like my reading glasses. The long slow slide down mortality's hill has begun. Part of nature's order."

I muttered mutinously and gestured the waiter over. "For starters I'll have a dozen Coffin Bay oysters, and so will she. Kilpatrick. Then we'll share the mixed seafood plate, with the crab." Good Christ, what was I thinking? That was a hundred and fifty bucks for the main course. Oh well, what the fuck, it was just paper. Or plastic. A man had to eat.

"My husband may eat what he wishes," Juliet told the waiter. "I shall have the Barramundi fillet, and a green salad. And a bottle of chilled Perrier water."

The bumptious little prat said, "Sorry, sir, so for *your* main course that will be—?"

"Just bring me a bloody steak."

"A very rare steak, yes, sir."

"No, you nitwit. I'll have a bloody standard Australian medium-rare steak, with roast potatoes and beans and a bottle of tomato sauce."

The waiter blenched, wrote the order with a trembling hand, and stalked back to the kitchen.

"You're so beautiful when you're angry," Juliet told me. "You're not really going to eat it with ketchup are you?"

"Oh shut up." I stared at my clenched fists. "You're going to help me work this out, Jules. My kid's mixed up in something horrible, and bad bastards are fucking with my life from three different directions, someone mutilated a fucking innocent *camel* for Christ's sake, by the side of the highway, and, and—"

She nodded in an understanding way. "Your personal *feng shui* is shot to shit."

I took a deep breath, opened my mouth, choked deep at the back of my throat, and started to laugh. I couldn't stop. It rolled out of me in waves. Tears poured down my cheeks. After a second or two Juliet started up as well, her high peals ringing in the ceiling of Pelicans Landing. The other couples and small groups of patrons stared at us with evident mixed feelings, a few frowning, more smiling, a couple of contagious giggles. The waiter moved toward us. A fat jowly man in the far corner started to guffaw, watching Juliet with bright liquid blue eyes, face red with apoplectic laughter. He held his fork with its tined white fish tight in his grip, elbow propped on the tablecloth, and roared.

It subsided in fits and starts throughout the restaurant. After a while I blew my nose with a stertorous snort. Juliet went away to the women's room to repair her face. I beckoned the waiter.

"Sorry about that, old son. It's been a day."

"Not a worry, mate."

I decided on a larger tip than usual.

"Steak's on its way. Would you care to see the wine list?"

"You're a champion. Let's throw caution to the winds," I said, and ordered a bottle of chilled Wolf Blass Gold label chardonnay for the oysters and fillet, and to accompany my honest beef a nicely warmed and breathing bottle of 1920s' Block shiraz from Bailey of Glenrowan. Another hundred bucks, near enough, and well worth it.

As I sawed through my meat, late afternoon light fell through the red wine like... well, like the charged blood of a sugar-laden and doomed camel. Laughter exhausted, my mouth quirked in guilt, despite myself. I hadn't explained to Juliet about the camel. I hadn't told her about Share, either. Not that there was any reason to. Our marriage didn't work that way.

No. Be honest. Our marriage just plain didn't work.

"Glenrowan," I said, nodding at the shiraz. "Sure you won't have a glass?"

"Just half a glass of the white."

Was I meant to hang about for the waiter to do it? Bugger that. I glugged her glass to the three-quarters point. "I was headed out that way yesterday before I got diverted into a cemetery, as one does. Cheers, my dear."

We clinked our glasses.

"Good health and plenty of it. Kelly country?"

"Bushranger country. Makes me proud to be a criminal."

My pal the waiter came back after a time with the dessert card. "We'll have the Macadamia Nut Tart," I decided. "Lashings of ice cream *and* whipped cream. This red's damned good. My compliments to the *sommelier.*"

"He'll have that," Juliet said pleasantly. "None at all for me today, thank you."

"Certainly, ma'am."

She gave him a dazzling smile in recompense. "We poor womenfolk have to keep an eye on our figure, you know."

"You're doing very nicely at it."

My mood hardened again. Pushing your luck, chum, I thought but did not say. Juliet found me lovable but crass. She had always found me crass, even when I tried my damnedest to adopt the smooth bullshit and contrived claptrap her adopted class went in for. Apparently their rules had been handed down from God Almighty or someone similarly placed rather than, as you might think, from some clique of indolent wankers with nothing better to do. It was one reason we no longer lived together. Damn, damn, damn.

"Shall we take a turn along the foreshore," I asked her in my most debonair manner, signing a name on the check and adding a sizeable tip. When I was a kid that was still un-Australian, tipping. The custom seems to have spread here from the United States where the poor buggers are paid starvation wages and make up the difference in gratuities if they're lucky or pretty or deft at their job. Not that I knew this from experience. They'd grabbed me at the airport, I went to jail without passing go, and then got flown home a year and a half later pretty much the same way. The waiter beamed. In less friendly places he'd have curled his lip anyway and marched off in an attitude of lordly hauteur.

Juliet came downstairs at John Street in ravishing white silk pajamas and clip-clopping flip-flops. Those one-toed rubber items used to be called thongs in Australia, until the term acquired a naughtier meaning overnight. Movies. MTV. DVDs. It's a global village all right. I hear they're thinking of changing the name of this State from Victoria to *Victoria's Secret*.

I sat at the living room table where she'd jacked the laptop into a cable socket and fed a transformer power line from a wall point so I didn't run Cookie's battery down. I'd been jotting notes on the back of defaced paper from the fax machine that had been hijacked as usual by spam advertisers. Why do they bother, the dumb fucks? Don't they know it drives you mad with resentment? You wake up to find your in-tray full of their shit, printed on your paper with your ink at your expense. Meanwhile it leaves the machine useless for the one real message you've been waiting for. Yeah, right, I'll be sure to rush and buy my insurance and electronic wheel balancing from *you* jackasses.

I bit the end of the biro and nodded to my unattainable wife.

"Just going for a last glass of milk before I clean my teeth and get some shut-eye," she said brightly. "Can I bring you anything from the kitchen?"

"I'll make myself some coffee later, sweetie. Unless it's decaf."

"It's decaf."

"Damn. Do you want me to come up and tuck you in?"

She frowned just a little. "You're not going to be difficult."

"Certainly not." I flung up my hands, and the biro flew across the room over my shoulder. I let it lie on the polished floorboards where it fell. "A gentleman never forces his intentions."

"Attentions," she said. "I trust."

"That's what I meant."

The screen held three opened windows, none of them my rap sheets. Two were Excel spreadsheets Cookie had prepared for Vinnie, row upon rank of the names and starting prices of three-legged nags. Well, not all of them were spavined dogmeat waiting to be canned, some at least could canter across the finishing line in third, second or even first position. But those horses tended to be the favorites and would earn little more than the punters had laid out. So they were not greatly favored by Vinnie's sporting men and women, who preferred some edge in their investment. Linked to that tedious flood of data entries were the names and phone details of the sporting men and women foolish enough to have a flutter on their promise and dubious enough not to wish to place their bets with the official totalizator service at Taberet. Mostly it was the same few names, Vinnie's established and aging clientele. I had decided to work my way doggedly through them anyway, see if anything of a cluelike nature might be secreted away in the records.

So far no luck.

"What the hell's this thing doing here?"

"What thing?"

"The Esky in my kitchen. Have you got to the stage where you need to lug a dozen cold beer cans wherever you go?"

Was I putting her in danger, having it here? But who knew I was in Williamstown, other than Jules herself?

"It's not beer," I said. "Just shove it back under the bench for the moment, will you? Don't open it, there's dry ice in it."

The third window was more interesting. Betting on the camel races in Dubai and Jenadriyah is strictly forbidden by Islamic law, although Google told me there were ways around that for those attending the festivities. Door prizes, for one thing. You could drive home in a new BMW to go with your other BMWs and Hummers. The animals themselves were worth decent dough, a hundred kay wasn't unusual for a good racing camel, and they raced a whole lot of them at once on their twelve mile track. But of course, human nature being what it is, the blessed injunctions of the Prophet sometimes fell on deaf ears as long as the wicked could cover themselves with the anonymizing cloak of the global Internet.

Cookie had got herself into the black gambling scene in a big way. Nor was she the first.

I clicked through some more pages, winding my way into the maze. I hardly noticed Juliet pad by with her mug of warm milk and that's saying something for my concentration. I did notice when she paused, bent down, kissed me quickly on the cheek.

"Goodnight, Lochinvar. Try to get some sleep."

"The decaf should do the trick."

Amused, she hummed in my ear, withdrew. "I'm off first thing in the morning, I'll leave you the spare key. Don't forget to take your mysterious Esky away with you, it's lowering the tone."

I grunted and turned but she was away already and up the stairs. With a sigh I went back to the nest of snakes on the screen. Our friend Felix Culpepper and his associates were evidently in play, and in a big way, if you read between the lines. Probably I wouldn't have seen anything between the lines except bland white pixels if it hadn't been for Culpepper's ham-fisted kidnapping of his youthful and unwieldy new-technology rival. Anxiety and greed can make people do truly stupid things. Look at me and Seattle.

I went to the kitchen and drank two long glasses of water from the jug in the fridge. It tasted faintly of its floating slice of lemon. My head was whirring a little from the bottle and a half of excellent wine. Bottle and two thirds. Well, minus the half glass Juliet had sipped, two full bottles. But I have the constitution of a horse, and not the sort Vinnie's punters favor. I put my head under the sink faucet for a time. It washed the salt out of my hair and left it fresh and manageable. There was no hand towel handy so I scrubbed my skull with a Flopsy Bunny tea towel, and threw it in the corner. God damn. I badly needed help. I went upstairs and knocked on Jules' door.

"Oh Christ, Tom." She didn't open it, so I snicked it an inch. It was dark inside. "If you insist on acting the goat, you can bloody well just fuck off."

"Julie," I said through the crack, "it's not that. Scout's honor and hope to die."

After a long moment I heard her smother a laugh and sit up.

"Oh for God's sake, come in. You're such a child sometimes."

"I was deprived of childhood," I explained, and sat on the end of the bed chastely at a distance from my wife. "I was denied the breast."

"You're denied it now."

"I know, I know. Jules, I have to talk to somebody about this. It's beyond the power of my small and brain-damaged mind."

"How flattering." She flicked on the bedside lamp, hitched an embroidered pillow behind her. "If you'd been staying at Mum's place, I suppose you'd have crept into her room for a chinwag at midnight."

"Your sainted mother would not understand my problem," I said. "If she did understand, she would not approve."

"My sainted mother does not approve of anything, but you and bloody Mauricio and the other two morons don't make it easy for her to expand her mental horizons. Tell me about the camel."

"How did you know about the *camel?*"

"Well, Master Sherlock, I was listening to the news yesterday, and besides you mentioned the poor thing during your meltdown at dinner."

"Oh. Yes. All right." I told her about Sharon Lesser and loading up poor Nile Fever with sugar and the flying Saudi prince and his crashing machine. I told her about the kidnapping of Share's step-daughter and the threat to her life and limb—

"Oh, it's *Share*, is it?"

"That's what she calls herself, Jules. What am I, the name police?"

"Is she a good fuck?"

"I can't remember. Anyway, that's not your business any more, is it?" I was thrilled that she cared, and maintained an attitude of lofty indifference to throw her off the trail.

"You can't *remember*? Tom, you're such a romantic."

"Are you playing or not?"

"'You Be The Detective'? Or 'You Be The Race Doper'?"

"Either should do the trick. I do hope I'm not trampling on your ethics, Juliet."

"Shut up, you. Now." She settled back against the cushion, adopted a thoughtful expression. I knew she had the brain for it. The question was whether she had the stomach. I wasn't sure I had. "Let's work backwards. How did *Share,* that middle-class minx, know about your doping expertise? Answer: Annabelle told her."

"I certainly hope so. Either that or Vinnie, or Vinnie's squeeze Mrs. Murphy, who we can't rule out because Maeve's the one who carried the murder weap—"

"Slow down, Euclid. Step by step." She glanced at the clock and gritted her white perfect teeth. "I hope we can crack the case in time for me to get to sleep before one o'bloody clock."

"I didn't get to bed until after four this morning," I said.

"No need to inflict your underworld circadian rhythms on me, boyo. All right, it could have been any of them, but let's assume simplicity. Animal told her. Suppose they're thick as, you should forgive the expression, thieves."

"I don't think Share is a dyke, if that's what you mean." I bit my lower lip. There *had* been that fond embrace. No, Animal would never go for it, not someone that old, older than me for heaven's sake. It was a mother Annabelle craved, and Juliet hadn't been it. Sharon Lesser might make a suitable raffish surrogate. "Animal thinks of her as a step-Mum," I said hopefully.

"Of course, which has no bearing on whether *Share* is a dyke as well, or fucks camels for that matter."

I said in a suppressed tone, "Her husband fucked his daughters, according to one of them."

"Shit. Christ, sometimes I just want to throw up and leave the human race behind me." Her face screwed up, and she shook her head. "The now fortunately *dead* husband, I take it?"

"Grime Grrl and Animal arranged a vigilante hit from the sisterhood," I said. "Vagilantes."

"Well, good for them! I hope they haven't been fools enough to be stuck with the murder weapon. Oh. That's what you started to say. *You...*"

"Got stuck with it. Yes. Oy vey." I lay back on the bed, my throbbing head on her blanketed feet. "It was in my storage unit. Wrapped up to look like dismantled fishing rods."

She moved her feet away, perhaps with some irritation. "So the police don't yet know about this."

I thought of Rebeiro and Kirkpatrick, and our adventures in Balwyn and the all-night truck stop grill. No, I'd be undergoing a different sort of grilling if they knew about the shotgun. I shook my head.

"Well, that's something. So Sharon Lesser learns that you once doped a horse and decides that you could give her dud camel a shot in the arm."

"I don't think it's fair to the memory of Nile Fever to call her a *dud*," I said indignantly. "She was a perfectly nice camel. Certainly she didn't deserve to be shot to death by a policeman, or run into by a bus, or whatever it was. Opinions appear to be in conflict. And she *certainly* didn't ask to have her tongue cut out."

"You actually did mean that. Her *tongue* cut out!"

"I have it on ice," I said. "Dry ice. In an Esky."

Juliet looked at me, appalled. "In my kitchen."

I shrugged.

"Oh dear God give me strength," Jules said. Her Sicilian upbringing, I imagine, and her convent schooling. She lay back against her decorated pillow and closed her eyes. "An accessory before and after the mutilation of a *Camelus dromedarius*. Not to mention of a vengeance slaying. And you mentioned a kidnapping, I believe?"

"I had nothing to do with killing the scumbag," I said with dignity, propped on one elbow. "I'd happily have been involved, mind you, but the grrls failed to take me into their confidence. Their opinion of me can be summed up in one phrase."

"Well cut your balls off."

"Precisely."

"I think it was directed at the dead guy and those like him," Juliet said reassuringly. "I don't find your child especially pleasing as a human being, but I think your balls are safe."

The context of our merry quips caught up with both of us then, and we winced together.

"Jesus, what a rotten world," I said.

"Look, I'm getting up, this is unseemly, having my husband sprawled on my bed in the fastness of the night. Go downstairs and make some more coffee. You'll find some beans in the back of the fridge, and the electric grinder's in the top right cabinet. Yellow door. Ignore the Esky, I'm told it's unsavory."

"Not decaf?"

"We need something a damned sight stronger than decaf, Sherlock," she told me, and shooed me out the bedroom door.

I got the percolator perking and sat at the computer screen waiting for Juliet to get dressed again and heard music playing horribly from the driveway, through the side window. Was it the theme music from *Gone With the Wind*? One night when I'd had a bad cold I sat up and watched the damned dreary thing for about five hours on a television screen the size of a bread basket. "Tara's Theme", was that it? I went outside and took Mauricio's mobile out of the glove box.

"Why is that in your hand and not mine, you bloody ratbag? You were supposed to meet me."

"Sorry, got distracted," I said. "I'm at Juliet's."

I heard an uncouth whooping. "Oh, God be praised, Mama will be able to give up on the perpetual novenas. Got your leg over finally, have you?"

"This is your sister you're talking about, you pervert."

"I take it the answer's no." Mauricio sounded gloomy, and I shared the sentiment. "Listen, I've found a place for you to stay. It'll bring back happy memories of the good old days. Beautiful little unit not far from here in—"

"Culpepper," I said. Maybe I growled it. "Sheikh Abdul bin Sahal al Din."

A moment's silence.

"Don't fucking bother lying to me, Mauricio." Through the window and its pale drapes, I could see Juliet coming down the stairs. She was dressed for a night of action, jeans, boots, leather jacket, and her black hair was pulled back and cinched. I tapped on the window. She peered, sent me a sharp salute followed by coffee-drinking motions.

"Culpepper, Culpepper." Mauricio tried to place the name. "Aw yeah, the prat me and the boys dragged out of the crypt, right? I saw him drive away in your hearse last night. What a get-away!"

"You knew him the first time I mentioned his name," I said angrily. "Culpepper's Crypt, that famous gathering place."

"I think it was on *Burke's Back Yard.*"

"Don't bullshit a bullshitter. Culpepper's working with the Sheikh."

"Yeah, well, mate, these things are complicated." You could almost hear Mauricio shrug. I saw his sister fetch two steaming mugs of coffee and set them on mats on the table. I started back inside the house. "So anyway, where's the Esky?"

"You pissant little shitkicker," I said. "You set me up with the shotgun. You gave Maeve that poor animal's tongue." I heard what I was saying as I went through the front door, and stopped dead on the doorstep. "Son of a bitch, *you* were the one who cut Nile's tongue off!"

"Not me, mate. Sent Wozza back to take care of that task the moment I heard the animal was down. Bloody near missed his chance, the silly prick. Had to carve off a slice and bung it in with a cold slab of Fosters. Just got out with it before the cops rolled up with half the RSPCA and a troupe of TV cameramen."

"My brother?" mouthed Juliet. I nodded, beside myself with anger.

"Wozza called you from his van, I suppose."

"'Course. Was meant to pick up a skin sample for the sheikh but then silly bloody Muttonhead had to fall under a collapsing camel and get more bits busted. Couldn't very well let his old mate bleed to death or something, could he?"

"That lying cow!"

"Who? No, set your mind at ease, mate, your widowed lady friend had nothing to do with it. Innocent as the day is long. All Wozza's plan. Him and the Mutt, they're her associates in crime you know. No honor among scam merchants, matey, as you and I both know."

"*Wozza?* Wozza came up with this master plan?"

"He's got a degree in Information Technology from an accredited institution. So anyway, where's the Esky got to, mate? It's not in the U Store It any more, and Maeve swears black and blue she never went back for it."

I flung the damned phone into the stone fireplace, where it bounced from one of Juliet's artistic cast iron log-holding constructions and lay unhurt, flashing purple light. I followed it across the room and put it on the stone flags and raised my heel and smashed it into several useless pieces of plastic shell and solid state innards. I was breathing heavily, like a man who has run a mile uphill with a heavy backpack.

"That was careless," Jules told me. She held out one of the coffees. "You seem to have trodden on it by accident. I don't think we'll ever hear it sing *Money, Money, Money* again."

I drank the coffee and burned my mouth. Now Mauricio knew where I was.

"Shit," I said. I raised my voice. "Shit, shit, *shit!*"

Since she had no prospect of getting to sleep at this stage, and was dressed for night work, Juliet slid into the passenger seat of the Cobra. The day's warmth was gone, and I shivered at the breeze coming up from the water. With the house lights off, it seemed curiously dark outside. I looked up at clouds coming in from the south. One by one, without any fuss, the stars were going out as the clouds covered the sky. Typical mercurial Melbourne weather. It was going to be a dark and stormy night. Juliet ducked her head as I raised the roof on the Cobra. At least that still worked and was still graffiti-free.

I gunned it out of her drive, distressing the hard-working or hard-retired citizens of Willie, and ripped back up the Strand and onto the Freeway system. It can take half an hour or more to reach Brunswick from that corner of the Bay. I filled Jules in on the rest of the current madness, running red lights and worrying about the speed cameras later. We nearly collected one of the great lumbering trams returning toward Moreland depot for the night, but I spun off the slithery tram tracks and my Cobra made the noise a hundred hounds might have bayed before they banning fox hunting in England.

"Tallyho!" shouted Jules, thinking alike.

I was terrified for my kid's safety, but the merry shout made me grin. I glanced at the dash clock. Twenty minutes, good going.

"Try Vinnie again?"

"He's dead drunk somewhere," she said, but took out her own neat cell phone and clicked a couple of keys. God damn, I thought, she's still got the number in her on-board directory. A warm glow burned for a moment in my chest, up near the sternum, and I don't think it was indigestion. "Nope, sorry, still not answering. I don't have a number for his lady friend."

"Bloody Maeve," I said, and found that my teeth were gritted. "Bloody duplicitous Cleopatra."

"I beg your pardon?"

"She's the reborn soul of many of the great and near-great."

"Well, indeed," Juliet said, "and so are we all."

It caused my shoulders to twitch. That was the sort of gibberish Martin Kundalini Richardson and the old farts had taught us out in Eltham when I was an innocent, gullible young cigarette thief.

"In a manner of speaking," she added. "Mother Church has declared the doctrine of reincarnation anathema."

"The light's on," I said, wheeling into the free space as far away as possible from the jumbo Dumpster bin. It stank worse. Maybe they empty them on Mondays. Juliet followed me up the outside steps. You could just see a patch or two of light through the black curtains, probably from where I'd disturbed them.

"You don't have a gun," she whispered in my ear as I bent to peer at the doorknob and lock, "I suppose?"

"Hate the damned things. You're right, though, maybe I should go back down and grab a brick or a decomposing cheeseburger to menace them with."

"Better still—" Jules pressed something smooth and cool and phallic into my hand.

"Deodorant? That might unnerve Animal, but I don't think it'd—"

"Capsicum spray."

It was illegal for her to be carrying that, but then who was I to talk? I shook the container, found the press button, pointed it in the darkness away from us, I hoped. And went back to prodding at the door. I couldn't hear anyone moving around inside, and no baleful music playing.

The door was already unlocked, an ominous sign. The kitchen light being on was an ominous sign in itself, the grrls being the grrls they were. I cracked the door, pressed one eye to the gap.

Sappho made a *pweet* and tried to get one leg through the gap.

I nudged her back with my own, reached with a long arm and flipped the switch off.

Nobody cried out angrily in the new darkness. Nobody blundered blindly into the edge of a table. The cat made hungry sounds. I went in and Juliet followed, shining the narrow beam of a penlight ahead of us.

"Good god, woman, have you taken up cat burglary in your spare time?"

"'Be prepared' is my motto, Thomas. Why are we whispering?"

The beam went back and forth across the Gothic space, revealed nothing human. The room smelled of strange oils and incense. I turned on the kitchen light, dropped the sprayer in my pocket and grabbed a long knife from the sink drainer. Capsicum spray in a deodorant roller isn't as daunting as a brandished knife.

Sappho's water bowl had been overturned by someone's blundering foot, and her food bowl was empty.

"Would you mind feeding Sappho, sweetie? The cat opener is usually in the drawer."

"Let's check the other rooms first, shall we?" My delicate wife had picked up a heavy length of chain that some fetishists had left draped across an armchair. Or maybe Grime or Animal were working on repairing a Harley. She wrapped one end around her right hand after covering it with a black scarf and swung the chain speculatively.

"Try not to smack yourself in the chin," I said.

"Still the consummate sexist pig," she said, and walked into Animal's room. I shrugged, held the knife firmly at waist height, ready for an underarm blow, and entered Cookie's bedroom.

The doors of the robe of robes were wide open. Someone had been looking for the Esky with its portion of chilled camel. Or maybe just collecting some clothing for the recumbent Cookie.

"Fuck."

I sat down on the end of the unmade bed. I'd left it that way. I heard no girlish screams from the other room, and no thud of a body falling to the floor, so I started cleaning my nails with the tip of the carving knife and thinking the whole mess through again from the start.

Maeve might have come up to reclaim it. But she didn't know I'd found it in the U Store It. Somebody could have told her, though. Except that she was probably passed out drunk alongside my former father-in-law.

Culpepper or his thugs might have dropped by looking for a second try at Cookie.

My thoughts circled and circled through the same possibilities. Perhaps one or both of the grrls caught a cab back from Share's, from Cookie's bedside, to retrieve her favorite bathrobe or stuffed animal, or collect her laptop. They'd have been royally pissed to find the computer gone.

"Taking our ease, are we?"

"Nothing in the other rooms, I take it?"

"Correct, and the pussycat thanks you for your thoughts. That was the last can of Cat-O-Meat, by the way."

"The grrls will be back in time to prepare her next feast, I hope. Unless they've already been here and Culpepper nabbed them, the silly buggers."

"Good thing you relocated your gruesome trophy, although I'd rather you hadn't left it at my place. The thing seems to be a magnet for mayhem. On the other hand, given Sappho's enthusiasm for that foul-smelling muck, I think we can safely assume that if you'd left it here…" Juliet paused and struck an attitude. "…the cat would have got your tongue."

I stared at her. I narrowed my eyes. I waved the knife in the air.

"Just trying to lighten the mood, Sherlock."

"Oh dear oh dear," I said, deflated. "Come and sit beside me, my darling wife. Let us, as someone suggested to me the other day, reason together."

"That was Lyndon Baines Johnson, I think. But he's dead."

"So is Nile Fever," I said gloomily. "I just hope none of the grrls is likewise."

A clattering came up the inside steps from the shop, and a door was banged open loudly.

"Who the fuck's in there?" a voice shouted angrily from the kitchen. "Come out with your hands up, I've got a gun and I'm not afraid to use it."

I went to the bedroom door and looked out. "Animal," I told my daughter, "put that damned thing down. It's evidence in a murder case. Why do you think I left it in Melton? Now you've got your fingerprints all over it. Is that the way I raised you?"

"Dad?"

"And such a hopeless cliché," Juliet said, sauntering out with her chain.

"Oh. It's you."

"Don't sound so glum, Annabelle. I like your hair. What there is of it."

"What's she doing here, Dad? Don't tell me you've been fuckin *fucking* in poor Cookie's bed!"

"No such luck," I muttered under my breath. Juliet shot me a frowning glance.

"I fed your cat," she told my glowering daughter, putting the chain and scarf back where she found them and sitting carefully on a sagging velvet cushion covered in Sappho's hair. "You need some more cans."

Animal twitched a form of thanks and beetled her metallic brows at me some more. At least she wasn't pointing the shotgun at us. I took it carefully from her and broke it open. No rounds in the breech end of the barrels, luckily. I held it up to the light. Oh.

"This gun wasn't fired," I said. "You haven't cleaned it since the murder, I suppose?"

"What? Are you supposed to wash them or something? You think I've got nothing else to do with my time? Anyway, it wasn't murder, it was revenge. You know, an execution?"

"Please sit down, Annabelle," Juliet said. She looked relaxed. "You make a person nervous even without waving that shotgun around."

Animal opened her mouth. Light bounced off the embedded, spit-moistened metalwork. With a shrug, she sat down on a rickety bentwood chair at the table. Sappho magically appeared to jump up on her lap. She stroked the scruffy thing absently. "What?"

"You thought you were responsible for the death of Rodolph Lesser," Juliet said. "Morally."

"I woulda tortured the scumbag first."

"But you weren't there yourself, on the spot, right?"

I sat back in silence, watching the two. My daughter's hand moved to and fro on the cat's head and back. Sappho started to make a sound like a small industrial machine, but less noisy than a foundry.

"We're not stupid, Juliet. We knew the cops'd suspect us first off."

"By 'us' you mean you and, uh, Cookie, and um—"

"Ruby," I said.

"Grime Grrl," said Annabelle.

"Especially since Cookie had disappeared."

"Why was the sheriff looking for her the other day?" I said.

"Who told you that?"

"You did. Had she been making threats against Lesser?"

"Shit no! Evasion of jury duty or some bullshit. Failing to notify the court. Willful disregard. Blah blah. Can you imagine poor Cookie stuck on a narrow chair in a court room listing to some boring lawyers droning on?"

"She would have been excused from jury duty. All she had to do was—"

Annabelle shook her nearly bald head in confusion. I remembered her long hair and could have wept. "That fucking Culpepper! Why did he hafta choose now for his threats and demands?"

"Mere coincidence?" I said. "I think not."

"Ha ha," said Juliet.

"If the lady vigilantes didn't use this gun," I said, "how did Maeve get hold of it?"

"Uncle Morry gave it—"

"Uncle!" I said in outrage.

"*Morry?*" Juliet said, appalled.

Lights bounced at the edges of the blackout curtains. "Uh-oh, cool it, people," I said, and pointed the 12-gauge to one side of the door. It was unloaded but the intruder wouldn't know that. These things throw an ounce of lead shot with every shell. A rifle is far more accurate, but a rifle slug is only a quarter as heavy, and from one side of the kitchen to the other you didn't need accuracy. If I had any bullets, I could really put the fear of God into them. "You expecting Grime Grrl back?"

"She's staying with Cookie at home. I mean the Lesser house, with Share. The cops let them stay after the body was taken away and they dusted downstairs."

They *dusted?* I was too tired, my brain wasn't up to it. Finger-prints, obviously. And forensic photographs and all.

A car door banged in the night. Culpepper and his brutes, I thought.

"Go into Cookie's bedroom, okay?"

Both women looked disgusted but I made a shooing motion with the butt of the shotgun and they shooed.

Light clatter of feet on the outside steps, not brutish. A key went into the door and Share came in, pushing the key chain back into her pocket. Grimes' key, presumably. She saw me and jumped.

"For God's sake, man, don't point that thing at me! Really, you're little better than a thug."

"You're not much better yourself," I said. "Possibly you're worse. You've abused the trust of everyone you've had any deal-ings with, including Culpepper."

Points of red flared in her pale cheeks. "You're not going to shoot me, Purdue." She took a careful look at the shotgun. "In fact, I don't believe that's even loaded. Your daughter doesn't know one end of a weapon from the other." She started toward the bedroom and called out, "Annabelle, are you all right? Has this prick been threatening you?"

My daughter held her tongue, for a wonder. I said, "The Esky was in my storage unit, Share, but now it's gone."

She turned back. Sinews worked in her jaw. "Jesus Christ. What have you done with it?"

"It looked so tasty," I said, "I soaked it in brine for a couple of hours and ate it. With fava beans and a nice Chianti."

"Culpepper," she said. "That lying shit. That double-faced—"

"I don't think so," I said. "Sit down, Share. No, not on the one with the bike chain, it might tempt you into doing something reck-less and painful."

She placed her padded but quite nice buttocks on the cat-furred velvet cushions where Juliet's even nicer buttocks had rested a few minutes earlier. She sat forward, knees and heels pressed tightly together. Sappho kept her distance.

"Anyone waiting for you downstairs in the car?"

"No."

"You know, I'd have sworn Mauricio had totaled your car," I

said. "No, actually, I thought the *cops* had carelessly rolled the Mack truck back over the top of it. No, wait," I said, "how silly of me, the Lessers are bound to own more rides than one. I'm sure the dead child molester must have kept an attractive company vehicle in the Balwyn garage. A Mercedes? BMW?"

Tears spurted and started running down her eyes. It was entirely surprising, and quite shocking. Mascara smeared on her cheeks. "It's an imported Lincoln," she said in a choking voice. "He had it changed to right-hand drive. Jesus Christ, I didn't know. You can't really think I *knew* about it, Tom? It was when she was little. Both of them. Before I married the vile bastard."

Maybe so.

"They didn't tell me. They were ashamed. I think he threatened them."

"Until when?" I said. "When did they tell you?"

"Two weeks ago," Animal said, emerging from the bedroom with a hockey stick clutched in her hand. I think she'd forgotten she was holding it. How touching, I thought, that poor obese Jonquil should keep something so defiantly athletic in her room. Like posters of girl-group pop stars, maybe—something to aspire to, however hopelessly? I thought I heard the faintest clacking or tapping coming from the half-open door behind her. Juliet was lying low, and I didn't blame her.

"I don't want to talk about that," Sharon Lesser told me. "It's none of your business." She looked haggard.

"Suits me," I said. I found a chair myself and sat down, holding the shotgun by my side pointed at the floor. "Let us reason together, Share, as you suggested a while back."

"You've sold me out," she said bitterly. "Why should I—"

I stared at her. "We had no deal, Mrs. Lesser. You hornswoggled me into doping your poor camel and then left me high and dry when it was killed."

"Not just you," she said. "You and your sleazy pal Mauricio Cimino. Mafia son of a bitch."

"Hey!" yelled a voice from Cookie's bedroom.

For the second time in minutes, Share jumped. "Christ! What is this, a convention?"

"Never mind that," I said, and waved the business end of the shotgun vaguely at her. "Culpepper and his cronies have been dining and possibly wining the sheikh, it's been in all the social pages."

"Felix Culpepper works very hard to keep his name and picture *out* of the social pages," Share informed me.

"What are you talking about, his family crypt featured recently on *Burke's Back Yard.*"

"You spend your time watching *home improvement* shows?"

"Me and Mauricio, we put a lot of effort into home improvement. As you witnessed on Friday night."

"Oh, you've decided now that it wasn't Thursday after all?"

"Dad, what's all this crap? If you and her want to have a big lover's fight, how about fucking off out in the street and letting me get to sleep?"

"I'm not his lover," Share said furiously, just beating me to it. I imagined Juliet pausing in her computer searching with her ears pricked up. The only thing that would be pricked up if this kind of blather were allowed free rein.

"So Culpepper and his Melbourne Club mates," I said forcefully, "showed Sheikh Abdul bin Sahal al Din and his wives a good time, and discussed camel breeding, I surmise."

"Surmise all you like."

"Then he puts you up to a scam. He's not going to sell live camels to the Saudis, that's far too tedious. Import and export licenses, veterinary medical certification, checks for syphilis and ingrown toenails, expensive air charter arrangements, months of loitering in quarantine, Islamic *sharia* restrictions of an unpredictable kind, Christ knows what-all."

I heard tired footsteps on timber and the door from the shop downstairs creaked opened. My hair stood on end. Vinnie put his own bald head in. "Sorry, girls, thought I'd see if the pussycat had been fed. Ah, Tom, good, I see you've got my gun back."

Sharon lunged at me, and I felt the bite of her nails. I really hate to hit a woman, especially a woman I might just conceivably have screwed a few nights ago, but reflexes took over. I clocked her with the butt, and she staggered back a few steps. I'm a gentleman. Had it been a bloke coming at me, he'd have stayed stretched on the floor for a few hours. Share just shook her head in disbelieving indignation and touched the side of her head.

"You're not bleeding, Mrs. Lesser," I said. "There'll be a bit of a bruise though." Animal was shrieking in outrage, and Vinnie said hoarse things along the lines of I say, steady on, that's no way treat a—

"Shut up, Annabelle," I shouted very loudly. Vinnie withdrew his head. "This is serious." My fatherly advice astonished her into muteness. I wondered if I'd been too lax in her upbringing. "So Culpepper put you up to the whole thing, Share," I said. "The question on my mind is this."

I paused, searching through my jumbled head to see exactly what the question was. Or the answer.

"He did it, and do tell me if I'm right because it seems right and I love being right," I said, "he put you up to it because he wanted payback. Cookie was working the same side of the internet betting street as him. But she's just a kid, and you're Jonquil's mother, or that's what he assumes. Her flesh and blood. So the debt comes out of your flesh. As it turns out," I said glumly, "out of Nile Fever's flesh."

"Nobody wanted the animal to die," Share said in a flat, reluctant voice. "Stupid bastard went nuts and ran off, what was I meant to do?"

"Not have it shot to death."

"A cop did that. For the public safety."

Could be. In fact the whole thing could be a series of coincidences after all. Except for shithead Culpepper jamming Jonquil in a casket and burying her for a few threatening days in a lightless crypt, to teach her a lesson. Boundary patrol. Border restrictions in gamblers' nation. What a stupid prat. The business was global now, that was the whole point of the internet. If it wasn't a fat grrl in a Melbourne suburb today, it'd be a room of PhDs with a Triad operation in Macao tomorrow, if not yesterday. Or some *Nomenklatura* gang in Moscow, or the CIA. Felix Culpepper thought he was a world-class player because he could wear a Melbourne Club tie and swan around with Saudi princes. Malevolent little prick.

"Speaking of camels," said a light voice from the far bedroom.

"Who *is* that, Purdue? The last thing we need right now is someone else yapping away about all this." Share seemed to have put her guilty sorrow behind her. She followed me and Animal into Cookie's gothic den.

"Hey, what the hell are you doing with Cookie's computer?"

"Examining the scene of the crime," Juliet told my daughter coolly. She leaned back in the huge padded office chair with a look of satisfaction. A series of thumbprint images were hard to make out even on the big flat screen.

"How the fuck did you get into it? Cookie has that password protected!"

"Well cut your balls off," I said.

"Shit, you rotten sneak, Dad."

"Ah, and this is the lovely Sharon Lesser," Jules said. Her face was bland. "Camel scammer and hot screw, I take it."

"Tom and me are business associates, nothing more," Share said, affronted. "Who's *she*, Purdue?"

I gestured with the shotgun. "Share, meet my wife Juliet."

"I thought your wife was dead," Share said. Speaking sharply over the top of her, Juliet said, "For fuck's sake put that hogleg down!" And then, "Not this one."

"'Hogleg'? Good Christ, Jules, have you been editing bad crime fiction on your days off?"

"Must have been a movie I saw. Just don't point it at me."

"It never came up in your heart-to-hearts that you had an actual stepmother?" I said to Animal. I heard a certain resentment in my tone.

"Get her off the computer, dad. That's Cookie's private stuff." Animal's mouth and eyes widened in speculation, then narrowed at Juliet. "Shit! *You're* the stalker!"

"I *beg* your pardon?"

"Culpepper's the stalker, you idiot, or some nerd hireling of his," I said. "What are these pictures, Jules, your latest stamp collection?"

"Watch and learn." Her red-lit mouse clicked, moved, clicked, moved, clicked. A .jpg image expanded to fill the screen, flicked away, replaced by another, and another.

"I can't tell what I'm—Oh, good grief. What were these taken, from a bloody plane?"

"Resources survey satellite," Jules told me with satisfaction. She wasn't expressionless now, she was beaming. "Good, aren't they? Cookie the ace hacker at work. Not to mention your tax dollars. Somebody's dollars, anyway. Or Riyals."

Or what? I shrugged it away, agog at what I saw on the monitor.

You heard about things like this on the TV news. Those industrial surveillance satellites were a couple of hundred kilometers up, weren't they? Scanning the planet day and night. Searching for illegal crops and escaped terrorists when they weren't hunting mineral deposits and greenhouse gas emissions. Talk about a needle in a haystack. But then think of the shots those space probes send back from Mars and Saturn and Neptune. You could plan your holiday on Titan from some of those images, if Titan wasn't all frozen methane and a billion kilometers away.

A slight haze blurred the sharpness, looking down through a hundred klicks of atmosphere and wisps of cloud. Still, the machines had done some neat clean-up processing on the raw image, by the look of it. You could tell it was a camel, even gazing straight down from near-earth orbit. But then *we* already knew it was a camel. Maybe someone studying this frame without our prior and privileged knowledge would take it for a very sick horse, or an overstuffed sofa that had fallen off a removalist's truck.

"Oh, the poor thing," Animal cried. Under all the metal and black velvet, she was tender-hearted.

Had Cookie just now stumbled by accident upon these records, sitting propped in her Balwyn bed recovering from her visit to Culpepper's crypt? Impossible, the odds had to be millions, billions to one against. Had she taken control of the damned satellite and *steered* it in her search? That also struck me as impossible, or wildly improbably. The owners would fall on you like a commando raid. Anyway, no, hang on a moment, she'd been in a nasty dark place under the ground while this was going on. Maybe she and her scriptkiddie pals had scammed some black program code able to do any fast search you wanted, using the existing records. Had to be commercial rather than military, surely. It made me shudder. The whole planet under such detailed surveillance? Paranoiaville. Yet apparently so. Fuck.

The camel had clipped a bus and staggered off the road. In the next shot the bus was pulled over to the far side of the road and the camel was down. You could see its legs stuck out to one side. Ungainly creatures. A van was bearing down on the bus. Next shot: two human figures decamping from the van. Next: one distracting the driver of the bus, was my guess. The other—

"Can you blow that up a bit more?"

"Yeah, but it's going to degrade the image even more."

The crouched human was doing something to the head of the dead camel. At least I hoped it was dead.

"Aw, that's so nice," Annabelle said. "He's comforting the poor thing in its hour of death. Eee-*ew!*" Expanded another 50 percent, the next shot showed something gray-brown and indistinct but somehow *meaty* in the man's hand. The two men returned to their van and in the next shot it had gone, headed toward Melbourne.

"Wozza," I said. "Your personal secretary for behaving badly."

"And Muttonhead," said Share, white-lipped with betrayal. "Those dogs. All of you, no honor amongst any of you thieves and rogues."

I ignored her blithering. "You're a marvel, Juliet. How did you dig this out of Cookie's machine? You're not moonlighting for the National Security Agency?"

"I deserve no credit," she told me. The mouse clicked, and a message screen re-opened. "I've been chatting with Cookie and Ruby."

"Her name's Grime Grrl," Animal said sulkily. "Are you saying Cookie knows you're using her machine?"

"Of course she does, Annabelle. All her machines are wi-fi networked so she's got instant access to all her files."

I think that's what she said. Whatever it meant.

"Tell them to get the hell out of that house at once," I said, "and go to a hotel. One they've never stayed in before."

"Woz and Lamb wouldn't hurt those girls," Share said, but you could tell she was doubtful.

"Their charming associate Culpepper has already subjected Cookie to a premature burial," Juliet said. "I think Tom's right."

"Who cares what you—"

"You should get right back there yourself, Share, keep an eye on them," I said. "Those young women became your responsibility when you married Lesser."

She looked at me. I matched her angry, thwarted gaze until she dropped her eyes and shook her head.

"I'm going to be in deep shit with the prince," she said, and a moan came up from far down inside her well-stocked chest. "He advanced me a lot of money for the cell biopsy."

"He'll get it one way or another," I said, guessing. "Assuming any of us finds the Esky. I left it here a few hours ago." No need for anyone except Jules to know I still had it. I went to the wardrobe, flung the doors wide. Nothing but Goth garments and some old Cherry Ripe wrappers. "The place wasn't tossed. The door wasn't broken down."

"Vinnie, I suppose," Animal said. "Or Maeve. She's the one who gave the shotgun to Uncle Morry, and he gave it to me."

He'd been in my U Store It after I'd left. The prick! Maybe the stalwart fuckwit at the gate had tipped him off with a quick call. At least he hadn't got his paws on the Esky. I tried to remember exactly where I'd left it at Jules' place. He knew I'd been there. He'd called me on his borrowed phone, after all, before I put my heel on it.

"Mauricio," Juliet said through gritted teeth. "One of these days I'm going to—"

"You know that mad bastard too, do you?" Share said. "I suppose you're fucking him as well?"

Juliet hammered a few words, watched the reply come up on the screen, and closed the computer down with a series of clicks. She said in a cold voice, then, "I'm not fucking either of them."

"She's his sister," I said.

"Oh my god," Sharon Lesser said. She threw herself back heavily on Cookie's large bed and put both hands over her eyes. "Oh my god."

"They've decided to take their chances," Jules told me. "Cookie's not feeling well enough for a midnight dash. They'll be all right, there's a cop on patrol outside the house, evidently."

Something enormous was grinding its gears along the alley. Metal clashed on metal. For a moment I was frightened, but then I realized it was the trash collectors, come to collect the stinking garbage in the Dumpster.

"Bit early for council workers," I muttered. "Do the stores along here use contract cleaners, Animal?"

The wall rocked with a deep, awful thud, and the door to the outside steps sprang open of its own accord. Sappho the cat leapt from the place she'd been hiding and streaked into Animal's and Grime's bedroom.

"Fucking *Mauricio*," I yelled, and bounded to the door. The Mack truck, or another just like it, was jammed into the parking space behind Vinnie's shop. Its sides were stuck between the half-toppled Dumpster and Sharon Lesser's dead husband's premier imported and steering-adapted Lincoln. The Dumpster had spilled rubbish into the darkness, and its stench rose to choke our nostrils. Somehow he'd missed the Cobra. The Lincoln's passenger side was half stoved in, and when Share reached the door her scream rose to choke our ears.

"You fucking brain-damaged dago *bastard!*"

"What the hell are *you* doing up there, Share?" he hollered. "That *is* you isn't it?"

The big truck's headlights and running lights had the place lit up like Christmas, or a crime scene in the movies, and the diesel engine roared.

"I knew you had to be at the center of this, you lunatic," I yelled, standing back from the door. Maeve had thought she was talking to him on the borrowed phone when she'd reported in with news of the gun and the Esky. I stayed near the edge of the door out of sight. I didn't think he'd shoot his own brother-in-law, but you hear things about Sicilians.

"What? Who's there?

"It's Purdue, you fuckwit," I yelled. "What bullshit is this?"

"For Christ's sake, are you in there too? Get the fuck out right now, Purdue. If little Annabelle's there, take her with you."

"Bugger off, Mauricio, this is my father-in-law's shop, and my daughter's home. You have no right crashing in here on a Sunday night."

"Monday morning, Purdue. I had carefully laid plans, mate. I don't suppose you have the Esky with you, do you?"

"What Esky?"

He crashed his gears again, gunned the enormous diesel, pulled back a couple of inches, moved forward a couple of inches plus a bit. The side of the old brick shop's living quarters shook. A cup fell off the sink and broke.

"You have loyalties and obligations, Purdue," he shouted. Animal was shouting, too, Share was hollering, I was making some noise. "Which family is more important to you, Purdue?"

"I've only got a fake father left, your dad's long dead, and your mother's a religious nutter," I said, wondering how long I could keep the madman talking, wondering as well if there was some way to call the nearest psychiatric center. The borrowed phone was smashed in a fireplace back in Williamstown. Share probably had one in working order, and so did Jules. Wait a minute, didn't Share say she'd left hers in the Cobra? I was frantically gesturing the women toward the inside staircase, down through the shop and away to comparative safety in Sydney Road. They stared at me sullenly, angrily, and with crystalline intelligence. I nodded to the last of the three as Jules rounded up the other two and dragooned them through the door and downward into the darkness.

"Don't hurt him," she said urgently.

"*Me?* Hurt *him?* Jules, look what the maniac's *driving!*"

"We are very family-oriented, like he said," she insisted from the dimness. "I saved his life once, I won't have you hurting him."

"Sappho!" Annabelle shrieked belatedly, and tried to push past Share on the narrow stairs and return to rescue her pet. Her companion animal. I shoved her back.

"I'll bring the cat," I muttered. "I have no intention of hurting Uncle Morry. Just piss off and get hold of Vinnie and Maeve, I don't think they should be left alone either."

"What?"

"It's a simple enough request," Mauricio yelled, head out the driver's window. "Give us the bloody Esky and we'll get out of your hair." He floored the accelerator again, luckily with the clutch out.

"Go to that all nite IQ testing place the Scientologists run," I said in a whisper. "I'll get rid of this pest then come and pick you all up. Try not to sign up for anything while you're there."

"We won't all fit," Animal said obliquely, then she was gone. I flicked off the kitchen light and went out on to the landing.

I'd put the knife down much earlier and was feeling fairly naked and exposed. The capsicum spray was in my pocket, useless against a man in a Mack truck. Anyway, I didn't want to hurt Mauricio. Well, just a bit.

"So why are you working with that scumbag anyway?" I called down to him.

"What scumbag?"

"You know what scumbag, you scumbag. Felix fucking Culpepper. One minute you're smacking his thugs around the head, the next you're in bed with him."

The diesel engine roared, settled back. Mauricio was a bit toey.

"Bullshit, mate. Me, I'm doing a job for the towel head, no middlemen."

I frowned into the darkness, and took the spray from my pocket.

"You and Sheikh Abdul bin Sahal al Din. Thick as thieves, eh."

"Whatever his name is. He's got the best breeding program in Saudi."

"You're talking about his camels," I said, "not his wives?" Mauricio brought out the coarseness in me.

"Wouldn't mind getting the leg over them either, mate. I hear they're like animals under those hoods. Hey, speaking of animals—"

"She's not here, Mauricio. I'm all alone. Me and the cat. Look, turn that damned noisy thing off and come upstairs. I'll make you a cup of terrible coffee and we can discuss this like gentlemen. Like members of an extended family, if it comes to that."

The silence rang in my ears. He climbed down, slammed the door.

"You got my phone?"

I patted my pockets. "No, mate, must have left it somewhere. I'll get you anothery."

"You fucking *smashed* it, din't you, you clumsy shit." His boots beat a tattoo up the stairs and he pushed past me into the darkness of the kitchen. "What are you doing here with the lights off, you poofter? Having a wank or something?"

"I was taking a nap," I said with dignity, flipping the light switch. My eyes dazzled briefly. "I cannot tell a lie, I did break your phone."

He shook his head in despair. "Mate, you are the clumsiest—"

"But not before Mrs. Murphy and I had a little heart-to-heart."

He hesitated only for a moment. "Have they got anything to drink in this hell-hole except one percent milk and tap water?" He slammed the fridge door shut. "So Maeve mentioned her little cab trip out to Melton, then? Well, 'course she did, how else would you have known about the shotgun and the Esky?"

"I went out there for a change of clothes," I said. "You might recall knocking my house down."

"Christ, are you going to hold that against me forever? Anyway, it gave you a chance to fuck that Share Lesser bint, din't it? The thrill of falling masonry, the exciting escape, the drive through the night—"

I was getting tired of these unsupported speculations about my sex life, especially since I didn't currently have any. It seemed incredible. Here I was, a large strapping heterosexual bloke in the prime of life, money in my pocket, and nobody was up for a good healthy life-affirming fuck. Not even my lawful wedded wife.

Mauricio had found the whiskey and what looked like a lid of dope. He was rolling a joint and poking around in the cabinet for a couple of clean glasses. "The girls won't mind, will they. We can take them out to a lash-up dinner some time." He found matches, lit up, stopped talking for a bit, exhaled, handed me the roach. I took a quick hit, sipped some booze to be companionable and to give the girls as much time as possible to get as far from here as they could.

"Anyway, they owe me. I got rid of their shotgun, didn't I?"

I took another toke and tried to swallow my outrage. "By putting it in with my stored stuff, you mongrel!" But that was water well and truly under the bridge, and besides I was pretty convinced the murderers or avengers or what they were had used a different weapon. Someone was trying to frighten Animal, that was all—or maybe frighten Vinnie and Maeve. It made my head spin, thinking about it. Maybe that wasn't what was making my head spin.

"Yeah, and then I went and got it back. Good shit," Mauricio said. He didn't give his approval easily.

"Yeah. Hey."

"What."

"So you sent Wozza to cut out that tongue, right?"

"Wozz is a smart man, he knew what to do once I had a word in his ear." Mauricio gave an explosive laugh. "Don't think Muttonhead would have helped him much, but."

I laughed too. "No, but then he—" Something hit me in the hip and sent me spinning. "What the *fuck?*"

"Make sure he hasn't got a weapon," Culpepper's goon Bulldozer said, coming through the open doorway from the unlighted shop downstairs. The door vibrated where it had rebounded from my hip. I felt as if some major bone had broken. Mauricio was out the side door and headed down into the dark, judging from the clatter of boot heels. The second thug ignored the first, tearing off in pursuit. Well, I'd locked China and Bulldozer in Culpepper's crypt after biffing them around a little. They weren't likely to be well disposed to me. Action was called for. I took some. The capsicum spray shot out in a boiling jet that caught Bulldozer and splashed back on me. It's not recommended for indoor use, and now I understood why.

I wanted to throw up, and couldn't breathe, and my eyes were burning and watering and mostly blind. Coughing and hacking and spluttering and wiping at our faces, Bulldozer and I stumbled back and forth in Animal's kitchen and living room like antiwar demonstrators and cops writhing righteously in the street.

A little bubble of the toke swelled in my burning brain and broke into a giggle. I raised the spray canister, wondering if there was any left.

"This is going to hurt me more than it hurts you," I told him in a fatherly, regretful voice. I pressed the button, holding my breath, squeezing my eyes shut. More hissing. He vomited wetly. I peeled open one lacerated eyeball. Bulldozer had his head over the sink, face under the tap. "No, wait," I said. "Actually it's going to hurt you more." I drew back my right leg to kick him savagely in the nuts the moment he turned to face me.

Something ran between my legs, emitting an awful wailing. Oh shit. Poor Sappho. I took three fast steps after her through the door, paused at the top of the stairs, in the dark. I found my keys. Bulldozer turned, hair and face drenched, suit coat irreparable, and lunged at the edge of the closing door. I pulled it shut with a bang. I didn't trap his fingers with it, worse luck, but I did get the key in while I held the doorknob pulled against my chest, and snicked the lock. I heard banging and gnashing of teeth, but that diminished as I stumbled down into the shipwright bric-a-brac and followed the wailing cat through the jemmied front door and out into Sydney Road. Wind was blowing from the south, pushing discarded food wrappings this way and that, and light rain was beginning to fall.

Felix Culpepper opened the front passenger door of his parked limo. I banged into it, jerking blindly.

"No need to weep, Purdue," he told me. "Not just yet, anyway. Here, get in the back with your daughter." I clawed at him, and he shut his front door smartly. I made a grab and the top of his smoky window purred down to half mast. "Look at you," he said, "you're a disgrace to your ignoble profession. Step inside like a good fellow and we'll be on our way to Williamstown." His driver, brimmed hat and all, ignored us both.

The capsicum fumes had made me feel sick, and my hip still felt broken, but that really made me want to throw up. Nothing for it. I reached for the back door handle and climbed in next to Animal. Nobody else in the back. A heavy glass partition between the front seats and the rear compartment saved Culpepper from being immediately throttled.

"Sorry, daddy," she said.

"Please tell me you haven't signed up for a year of auditing."

Animal ignored that, perhaps because she didn't understand it. A lot of my attempts at gallows' humor get that reaction. "Ee-ew," she said. "You stink."

I shooshed her with one hand, showed her a glimpse of the capsicum spray canister in the other. "It's hot work," I said, "beating up Mr. Culpepper's henchmen." I probed my pockets, hauled out a dubious handkerchief, dabbed at my weeping eyes. It felt as if someone had jabbed hot pokers into the sockets. My only satisfaction was that Bulldozer surely felt much worse after copping a raw faceful of the noxious stuff. "Where's Juliet and Share?"

"This prick here was just parking his wankmobile outside Vinnie's as we came out," she said. "Some really big turd grabbed me and locked me in here."

"Mind your language, you ugly creature," said Culpepper's voice through an intercom. "Mr. Purdue, your stewardship of your daughter leaves a great deal to be desired."

I located the speaker, leaned back as far as I could in the leather upholstery, raised both knees, and kicked the shit out of it. Then I squirmed and squealed for a while and hugged my hip, which was obviously not broken after all but certainly still felt like it. The intercom was a state of the art Bose system, so my brutality didn't kill it, but you could tell from the chicken scratching sounds that it was badly maimed.

By this stage we were in fairly high-speed motion, ripping without a bump down the middle of empty early Monday morning

Sydney Road toward the city. I saw a flicking of blue light, heard the blessed muezzin of a cop car pulling over an errant driver. For a moment Culpepper's chauffer pressed his foot to the floor, but through the shatterproof glass I saw his master snap sharply at him. We slowed, smoothly, as if this had always been our intention, and pulled into the curb outside the Wonderland of Turkish Carpets showroom.

"Quick, where is she? Jules?"

"Got away. Kicked one of them in the knee, ran like fuck. *He* said to let her go, and to find you. Said he's got her address anyway."

"Shit." A uniformed policeman stood at the driver's window, heavy flashlight poised. With a show of reluctance and long-suffering, the chauffeur drew out his license and proffered it. Culpepper glanced back, showed me his eyes and his eye-teeth. Animal was banging at the door release, but the limo's central locking was in good order. The cloudy, rain-spattered outside glass protected the cop from the sight of Animal gesturing. Apparently his attention was firmly focused on the front seat, and the excellent insulation must have muffled her shrieks. The cop stood back, then, nodding, and the driver reached again for his keys. Culpepper treated us to one disdainful glance of triumph before the cop stood aside and Detective Rebeiro took his place.

"Oh, good," I told my noisy, foul-mouthed offspring. "We're saved!"

I heard a muted click, and my door sprang open. Another uniformed cop held it wide, then took me by the arm.

"Step out of the car." Two police Fords were stationed at angles to the nose and tail of the limo. The blue light rolled over us from both directions. It would have come in handy during our vampire movie.

"Hey, hang on—"

"Hands where I can see them. Put that fucking thing down."

I dropped the mace can in the gutter. It was empty anyway. "Annabelle," I called. I could see her bald, metal-glittering head across the top of the limo, struggling with a policewoman and swearing like one. "They're here to help us, take it easy, kiddo."

"Sorry for the inconvenience, Mr. Culpepper," Rebeiro was saying. I looked around, blinked. Shit, what? He turned to me, face hard. "As for you, Purdue, I'm placing you under arrest for the murder of Rodolph Charlton Lesser. Don't make any fuss and we'll let your kid go home. Give me the slightest—"

"You can't be fucking *serious!*" He was, though. The cop with his hand on my arm, grimacing and blinking at the capsicum residue I was giving off, pulled a plastic restrainer from his belt and clamped it on my crossed wrists, snugging it tightly.

Purring with automotive satisfaction, Culpepper's limousine drew away, carefully skirting the heavy rubber bumper of the front Ford Fairlane. Red tail lights glistened in the wet road. Jaw dropped, I watched it maintain the speed limit into the distance. I shook my aching head. Surly Animal was still pulling her own cop around, but she gave up abruptly with a half-hearted snarl when she saw that I was well and truly nicked. The woman cop led her briskly to the nice fancy inlaid brickwork that Sydney Road shoppers trod on these days.

"Get going," Rebeiro told her, and shooed her back toward Vinnie's open door and the shop's dark interior.

"Just a minute, Rebeiro, there's one of Culpepper's goddamned *heavies* in there," I said. "I hit him right in the face with pepper spray, he's probably still breathing but you can't send my daughter up to—"

"You better hope you haven't killed him too," Rebeiro said. Looking disgusted and irritated, he told my cop, "Go in there with her, Baxter. See the place is clear. Anyone gives you any trouble, shoot the bastard. You can carry on your patrol in Hudnik's car, I'll take this one."

"I've got to find my cat," Animal was shouting. "Here, Sappho, Sappho."

Rebeiro jostled me toward the Fairlane in front and shoved me in the back seat. I bleated a little as the door slammed on my hip, but the tears were from the residual capsicum. Tough guys don't cry.

I couldn't get the seat belt buckled as the law demands with my hands jammed behind me, and I couldn't sit back comfortably either. Rebeiro didn't bother heeding the speed limit, and the high performance cop car wasn't designed to smooth out the jolts of Sydney Road's traffic corrugations. I bounced around for a while, trying not to bite my tongue as I harangued him. He threw an abrupt right and pulled up next to a hydrant with a jerk that flung me into the head rest in front. It smelled of some rank hair gel. What was it with the police force these days? *Hair* gel. Give me strength.

Rebeiro came around to the side, got me out, released me without a word. He shoved the restrainer into his coat pocket.

"Oh, that was quick. You've just worked out that I couldn't possibly have killed this Lesser jerk, have you? Was it my honest face that convinced you? Or the superior odor of my hair gel, with its fragrant hint of capsicum?"

"I know you didn't do it," Rebeiro told me. "Get in the front with me."

"Of course I didn't fucking do it," I said. "I'm a *feng shui* master. We spiritual advisors just don't go around killing people. It's terrible karma." But my bluster was drying up, and my mouth with it. I had a headache, and that was bad enough, but deep inside my guts I cramped with a surge of fear. He'd found out about the Vagilantes. He'd been talking to Vinnie and that slack-arsed biddy of his, Mrs. Maeve Murphy. Who knows what those old farts might have leaked? Annabelle—

"I know you didn't do it," Rebeiro told me, starting the car and heading for the Freeway, "because we just arrested the bint who did."

"The... *bint*? Detective, is that any way for an officer of the law to speak about—"

"Oh shut up, Purdue," he said. "You're giving me a pain. You know what bint. Your squeeze of the moment. The widow, Mrs. Sharon Lesser."

Unless he was lying, that let my daughter and the grrls off the hook. Urgently, I said, "We have to go to Williamstown."

"We are going to Williamstown."

I looked sideways at Rebeiro. "Why are we going to Williamstown?"

"Are you completely insane? Are you on drugs, Purdue?"

"No, I know why *I* want to go to Williamstown. I just want to know why *you* want to—"

He took both hands off the wheel and slammed them back down again. The car leaped. "Jesus Christ! Just *shut up!*"

"Well, if you're going to be like that." I pulled my seat belt on as we dived down onto the tollway. "Listen, give me a lend of your mobile phone."

"You really *are* insane." But after a moment he leaned back, fished it off his belt and handed it to me. "No international calls or I put you back in those cuffs."

"My pal," I said, and made the ghastly face of a paranoid serial killer at him.

The first time I met Gabe Rebeiro, when he was still a uniformed cop on the way up—but amazingly not on the make—I *was* insane, or near enough. My wife Patty was only a few weeks from death. I saw her every day, trussed in tubes and machines that went *ping*, her face collapsing as if everything fluid and lifelike was being drawn away from its tissues and pissed into the waste bottles. I brought the baby every chance I could. She was a toddler then, running on her fat legs until she fell down and squalled.

I had Annabelle in a yellow jumper suit and soft red shoes with buckles. On our way in we stepped quickly into a room before Patty's, filched a bunch of bright sweet-smelling freesias from the unconscious bald old woman lying there, and carried it dripping to Patty's room.

"Come to Nana," said Harriet Gardner in a brittle voice, and my daughter waddled over with an uncertain look at me across her shoulder. Harriet clutched her up, displayed her to Patty. My wife smiled like a death's head. I could hardly see them both. I felt as though my throat and chest were ready to explode with grief. I groped for a vase, shoved the flowers in it, moved toward Patty.

Gavin Gardner's hand reached up and seized my shoulder. He was a head shorter than me, and had never spent time in a gym. His face was contorted, flushed red, lips white.

"You hulking brute," he said. "We don't want you coming here any more. Get out right now and leave the little girl with us."

I was agog. I shook my head, as you do when you've been clipped by a fist. I picked his hand off my upper arm and walked past him to Patty. Her eyes had closed again, and the machines clattered and hummed.

"Didn't you hear me? Just get the hell away from here. Haven't you got any respect?"

I turned on him, all my grief and rage cracking the cold chill of my heart.

"Be quiet, Gavin," I said. I was twenty four years old, and he was thirty years my senior, but I had experienced unpleasant things he probably couldn't imagine. Nothing so terrible as the slow murder of my wife by her own renegade cells and the poisons and rays used to fight them, but bad enough. Gavin Gardner did not frighten me. Somehow it did not occur to me, at the time, that I scared the hell out of Gavin.

"Don't you dare speak to him that way," Harriet told me in a thin voice. Her grip must have tightened on Annabelle's little hand, because my daughter suddenly started crying, trying to pull away. Her grandmother tightened her grip. "You guttersnipe. You coward. You let our daughter waste away while you lolled about in some filthy American holiday home for criminals and drug creatures..." The words spat out of her mouth with no attempt at logic. It was bile and hatred and terror for her dying child. I could see that much but I had no charity in my heart. Not at that moment. Not with my baby and my sick wife in the room hearing her bitter rant.

And I knew it was justified, which was killing me.

I crossed the room in two steps, took Annabelle away from her and popped the little girl up on the narrow hospital bed beside her scarecrow mother.

"I want you *both* out of this room right *now*," I told them in a clear, ringing tone. "We want to be alone with Annie's mother."

Harriet started to shriek. It was beyond words, a plaintive cry of woe and rebuke. Someone had to take the blame for her daughter's fatal illness, and I was there. I was the long-haired layabout who had taken her away from them to begin with. Then I was the drug criminal caught like a fool dressed as a preposterously ugly woman, imprisoned in a distant land, abandoning a pregnant woman. Now I was a thug looming like some reprisal from a folktale. I was everything hateful that a bad son-in-law can be, and worse. It came out of her throat in a wail of terror and detestation.

The baby picked up the terrible melody, and wound her piping screams into its racket.

A blue-clad nurse rushed to the opening of the room, hesitated, belted off for reinforcements. I stood mute and stupid holding the wailing child. Patty's eyes were appalled. Her monitor machines clattered and beeped their panic, and hers. Mute, with her captive arms she tried to reach for Annabelle and hug the child to her wasted breasts. Two hefty female nurses and a large red-headed white-clad male nurse swarmed into the room. One of the women took Harriet in hand, tried to calm her. The other, a sturdy, sensible creature who might have been a midwife of several decades' experience, plucked up Annabelle and held her to the comfort of her own large bosom. I turned away in despair from my wife's bed and Gavin Gardner slapped me hard across the face. Then again, cutting the corner of my mouth with his bony knuckles.

Harriet screamed more loudly, struggling. The baby hollered. I roared in awful wrath and whacked my father-in-law the hell across the room.

His backside hit a wheeled shiny tray of instruments that skittered away into the hall. He looked at me in disbelief and slid down on to the tiled floor.

By that time I was fighting the large male nurse. He had a hypodermic uncovered and came at me like a picador. I clocked him as well and started pushing people into the corridor. Everything would be all right if I could just sit here quietly with my daughter and my wife. All the screaming and panic would go away, and we'd be able to sit together and hold hands in the blessed silence.

The police arrived at that stage. I glared at constable Rebeiro like an ape raging in a cage. He stared calmly back at me, took one step sideways, and slapped me into unconsciousness with a Victoria Police-issue nightstick.

I punched in Juliet's number from memory. Some things stick, if they're important enough. It rang for a while, presumably a tinny rendition of "Bird on the Wire" or ""Famous Blue Raincoat". No doubt she was looking at the unfamiliar caller ID and wondering what the fuck.

"Who are you trying to reach?" she said finally.

"You, Jules. Listen, you've got to—"

"Tom, whose phone is *this?*"

"The property of the State. Detective-sergeant Gabriel Rebeiro, CIB, to be exact."

"Oh my God, have you gone and stolen the property of the Victoria Police force now?"

"Yeah, he arrested me—"

"You'll just have to sit this one out in the cell, bozo, I've got to get home to my computer."

"Shut up for a moment and listen to me, Juliet. Rebeiro arrested me years ago when I beat up my first father-in-law."

"I thought the beak let you off on that one. I'm not at all sure I would have done, it showed a want of feeling."

"He's driving me to Williamstown." I heard a growl. Rebeiro was not impressed by my putting it that way. "He's a very helpful chap, is Gabe Rebeiro. This phone, it's a loaner from him."

The detective reached across and tried to drag it away from my ear. "It's bloody well nothing of the sort," he told me.

"All right, calm down, you'll get it back. Jules, I take it you're not sitting around in Scientology's Brunswick test center." I sniggered. "Did you ever go clear?"

"Good grief, Purdue, you and I must be the only people under the age of forty who still listen to Lenny Cohen."

"Only just under forty, in my case."

"I'm in a Silver Top cab coming off the Westgate even as we speak. I think I know what this is all about, Tom, but I need my computer. I've been talking to Ruby."

"Ah. So much for my big news. You know Sharon Lesser's been arrested?"

"I saw them grab her as I was running for a cab. I never liked that bitch."

My heart leaped. "Are you going to the foundry or straight home?"

"Willie. It's quicker from here, and there are more solid citizens around to hear my screams. If it comes to that."

"It might. Culpepper is hot on your trail."

"My tail?"

"That too. And who can blame him?"

"Not a chance, Purdue, we've already been through that. Ten years of absolute purity committed to our Blessed Mother, that was the promise I made and the sacred vow I mean to keep."

I wanted to bury my face in my hands and snivel, but it wouldn't have been manly and Rebeiro would have laughed at me. I said, "Hide the Esky, sweetheart."

"Well, duh. I'll put it in the ute and park it near the beach. No chance anyone will find it. Do you know yet why they're all so eager to find Nile Fever's tongue?"

"Some sick reason. Identification, I guess, like when they cut off some stoolie's fingertips then deliver them to his gang as a warning. Maybe that's what happened to poor stupid Muttonhead with his nose. Christ. What a world."

"To who? Whom?"

The police radio said, "Whachinga hiss murmle con passerango blurt, carnine."

I glanced enquiringly at Rebeiro to see if he wanted his cell phone back. He'd already lifted a dinky little wireless headset off the rim of the steering wheel and fitted it in a slick motion over one ear, straightening the button mike near his blue-bristled chin. "In pursuit, entering King's. ETA Williamstown, seven minutes." I couldn't hear whatever garble HQ communications sent back to him. Obviously the headset overrode the crappy car speaker system. Rebeiro listened, slithering past a milk delivery behemoth and gunning the engine. I thought seven minutes was a bit hopeful, but maybe he could do it. He'd need to, bloody Culpepper had a decent lead on us.

"Look, can you give me Grime Grrl's home number?"

"Do you have any idea what time it is?" I heard Juliet yawn at the very thought.

"It's Cookie I want to speak with, and she's just been lying around for the last couple of days. Anyway, those hacker grrls keep American hours, don't they? So they can talk to their cracker web pals in real time?"

"A good point, Sherlock." She fiddled with her own phone, read me out a number. I did what I could to commit it to memory, muttering a mnemonic that brought a strange look from my police driver. "I'm just pulling up into John Street now," she said, "and there's nobody near the house that I can see. Oh, one last thing, just to reassure you. Annabelle is on her way to Balwyn in a cab. She has the cat."

"She called *you?*"

"Don't be absurd. She called Grime, who told me."

"Ah, so it's 'Grime' now, is it?"

"Thanks, driver. Keep the change. Wait here for a moment until I'm at the front door, would you? Thanks." A door slammed. "Okay, that's it from me. Give me your number."

I asked Rebeiro, who reluctantly gave it.

"Take care, honey," I said. "These are bad people."

"Luckily I'm not a camel or a child molester," she said.

"Even so."

She was gone, and I looked out the window. We were leaving the Westgate Bridge. Rain was falling harder, driven by the wind. I was glad I'd left the Cobra with its roof up. The Fairlane shook as we rushed past a large vehicle that was doing a pretty fair rate of knots itself. I glanced at it. Mack truck, burning bright. I lurched, peered through the rain. Was that my insane brother-in-law at the wheel, face illuminated by the dashboard lights?

Convulsively, I jabbed at the teeny keys on the phone, but of course no familiar name flared in blue letters when I poked in MAUR. I tried to recall his number. But that wouldn't help, because I'd broken his loaner phone. Or had he switched that number to his current phone? One thing was certain—Mauricio the scam artiste would never be without a phone. I punched in the old number. The machine told me the number I was trying to reach was out of range. Right, in small pieces on the flag stones. I tried to recall the mnemonic for the number for Cookie that Juliet had just given me. First four numerals, that was all I could retrieve. Shit.

"Am I ever going to get that back, you jerk-off?"

"One moment, detective," I told him soothingly. "I'm realigning its *feng shui.*"

"Don't you ever stop with the bullshit, Purdue?"

"I gave it up with my P.I. license, Rebeiro," I said. Offended, I slid the phone into my pocket. Rebeiro grabbed at it, and the wheel spun and the Fairlane with it. "Something you should remember well."

He'd been called to give testimony at my hearing. Obviously old jailbirds don't get licensed to carry guns and private detective credentials, but who was to know that Recherché Doubting Thomas Purdue, convicted felon in the former British colonies now known as the United States, was also honest Tom Purdue, antipodean widower and father? The Australian Federal Police computers, that's who, but back in 1998 they weren't too crash-hot, the Fed's computers. They were primitive. I wasn't sure they'd even heard of the Internet, the men and women in blue who keep our nation safe from the likes of me. But they were good enough to trip me up, match my prints, snatch back my P.I. license and threaten me with some more hard time. Rebeiro got me sprung, is my guess. The lawyer I used that time wasn't nearly as sharp as Sir Rupert Muldoon, Q.C., but then he only charged a tenth as much.

"That's the one," Rebeiro told the little solid-state nugget before his lips. "Keep an eye on it. We're coming up on Ferguson and Nelson. Wait for us at Cole and Nelson in case he takes fright and does a runner. No bloody sirens and flashers this time, either, Johnson."

The phone buzzed in my pocket. I snatched it out, had it against my ear before Rebeiro could claim it back.

"A big white car pulled into the driveway," Juliet told me. Her tone suggested that her blood was racing. "The limo, I take it."

"You inside or out?"

"Down the street behind a large pot plant."

"You got the ute parked elsewhere?"

"Do I look like an incompetent halfwit, you offensive fellow?"

"I love you too, Jules." I hesitated. "I really do, you know."

Another silence. Rebeiro shot me a glance, rolling his eyes. I ignored him, rolling down the window. Red lights ahead gleaming through the rain. We went through them without the siren.

"I know," she said.

"For Christ's sake stay out of this. I don't want you hurt."

"Listen, Cookie called. We have to—"

"No time," I said. "we're here." I snapped the phone shut and put it back in my pocket. Rebeiro went past the house with his lights off. The Fairlane was not obviously a cop car, unless you knew cop cars and had time to look at it. I was pretty sure Culpepper and his goon driver had more urgent matters on their mind, like a spot of breaking and entering. I wondered briefly why a distinguished practitioner of the facilitating and import-export industries and notable member of the haughty Melbourne Club would take such risks. Get his own lily-whites dirty. For the thrill, I decided. To show himself he was still a *mensch*.

And why not? It was my own motive, really.

"There they are," Rebeiro said. "Just getting out. I think we'll wait and catch them red-handed."

"Frozen-handed is what they have in mind," I told him, but he didn't know about the camel tongue on ice and I didn't feel this was the moment to explain my small perfidies. I opened the door and rain hit me in the face.

"We'll *stay* here, I said," the cop told me in a hard hissing command. I ignored him and started to walk toward Juliet's home. Mine, too, once.

I skeddadled across the road, then, getting drenched, as enormous lights boomed toward me around the angle of Nelson St. The Mack truck was doing sixty through the downpour. Mauricio knew exactly where he was headed, he'd been there plenty of times before, it was his sister's home after all.

In the rushing dazzle, Culpepper and his thug stared, and I saw them leap in panic from the verandah into shrubbery. The Mack twisted like Sappho ridding herself of a flea and slammed into the limo with a scream of metal upon metal. A light pole in the street shook and went out. The hood of the limo jerked forward into solid brick, shattering Juliet's favorite sandstone facings. The Mack truck mounted it from behind like some sex-mad steel dinosaur stupidly screwing an early mammal, or trying to. The long back of the limo, to the extent that I could see it as I ran along the street peering about in terror for Juliet, shrieked and collapsed into junk. I was kind of glad Annabelle and I were no longer sitting there.

Hatless in the rain, the chauffeur was belting away up the street when the other cop car spun around the corner and hit him with full bring-down lights and high head beams. He stumbled, slid in the water, went down on one knee. Cops piled out shouting, doors flung wide, approximations of human voices blaring from their speakers. Evidently the patrol cops were not favored with Rebeiro's snazzy technology. The thug got to his feet and put his hands on top of his wet hair.

Culpepper was still trying to disentangle his bespoke suit from the bushes. He stepped aside from his mangled car as Mauricio swarmed down out of the Mack truck cabin howling for his blood, then moved in a sprightly way toward the protection of law and order.

"Officer! I demand that you do something about this atrocious—"

The detective ignored him. He moved to block Mauricio.

"Mr. Cimino, isn't it? I want to have a word with you."

"I dunno who you are, mate, but get out of me way. I want a piece of that little shit."

"You shouldn't have any trouble recognizing me," Rebeiro said. He kept his hand by his sides. "You and your loutish brothers were found hanging around a murder scene. So was this arsehole." It took me a moment to realize he'd pointed with a jerk of his head to Culpepper rather than me.

"I won't have you speaking in that manner," Culpepper said, trying for his best manorial manner.

"I'm placing you under arrest as soon as I've seen this pest off, and his damned truck with him. Get out of here, Cimino. Next time—" He left the threat hanging but it was obviously not idle.

"Aargh," said Mauricio. He looked at me. "G'day, mate. Listen, I need to talk to you about a—"

"Off," said Rebeiro. "Now. And try not to break any more motor vehicles before dawn."

Grumbling and mutinous, Mauricio climbed back up into his truck and slowly, noisily, withdrew from the ruined limousine. Rebeiro was going through the motions with Culpepper. I heard blustering and threats, the name of Frank Stonecraft, Q.C., was deployed, Culpepper's close friendship with the chief of police. I tuned it out and went back across the street.

Juliet was huddled under a tee-tree, dripping in the dark night. I couldn't see the Holden.

"He made a mess of the pointings," I said.

"He hasn't got the McGuffin, that's the main thing," she said with a radiant smile that gleamed in the multihued lights from the cop vehicle where the chauffeur was helping police with their enquiries.

"By god, that's what I need right now," I told her. "An Egg Mc-Muffin. Where's the closest Big Mac joint?"

Juliet shuddered. "They wouldn't be open yet, thank heavens. Once this lot are gone we can take the Esky inside and have a good old chinwag. There are things you haven't been telling me, husband dear."

"I keep getting interrupted," I said. "What about a toasted

cheese sandwich and a glass of champers? You have some Moet et Chandon, I hope?"

"On ice," she said. "Like Nile Fever's tongue." Both the police cars were turning back toward town with a thrum and hiss of tires. I saw Culpepper sitting stiffly in the back of Rebeiro's Fairlane. The cop gave me a hard nod, and was gone in a slither of wet tail lights.

"Not quite that cold," I trust.

A car came around the angle of the road as we crossed to the house. Its headlights gleamed off the shiny fallen muffler of the crushed limo. We hurried to get across but the Porsche pulled in on the wrong side of the street. Something tugged downward inside my hungry gut.

"Fuck," I said. "Relentless."

"Come on now, matey," said Wozza O'Toole, baccalaureate in Information Technology and Sharon Lesser's right hand person. "You have something of ours. That's not very nice, is it."

Muttonhead Lamb got out the other side, pushing his noseless face at us. He really wasn't a pretty sight at three or four of a Monday morning. Neither of them looked at if they'd had any more sleep than Juliet and I. She gave me a look of submission and utter despair, walked with her hands extended to the Mutt's side, lifted her right booted foot and drove it into his crotch with a measure of force that took all of us by surprise. Muttonhead went down puking into the gutter, and she slapped him in the head with the edge of the Porsche door.

"Well, come on, man, do your stuff," she hollered at me. I was already in action. I jumped at Wozza, took his gun hand by the wrist and broke it across my knee. Christ! That hurt. So did my damaged hip. But it's true that you don't feel pain as acutely when you're in danger. I reached into the Porsche, tugged the keys from the dash, flung them into the gutter. They glistened for a moment in the rush of rain water, fell away into the drain inlet at the corner of the street. I whacked Wozz one across the back of the neck as he leaned over to nestle his wrist, and let him fall on the concrete.

"The Holden's this way," Jules said. She was already running across the street.

The Holden one-tonner was getting on a bit, but serviceable, with twin bucket seats that were worn and smelled of metal dust. I found the Esky under a folded blanket in the storage space behind the seats. It hadn't been tampered with.

"Get me the keyboard, will you?"

"What?" I said.

"I can't type on a mobile in the car. I need the QWERTY board."

"For fuck's sake, Jules, I'm not going to sit here while you simultaneously drive and msm your internet pals."

"Of course you're not." She spun into a side street, pulled into the kerb, jumped out. "Scoot over, big man. You're driving. Here, let me." She was delving behind me for the keyboard as I unplugged the seatbelt and heaved my bulk into the driver's seat. Normally I'm the spirit of sleek agility but my hip really was killing me. She ran lightly around behind the load tray, strapped in, found her Palm Pilot in the glove box and plugged the keyboard in, balancing it on her lap. It lit up like the lights on a cop car as she put on her reading specs.

"Good Christ, you can talk to the internet with that thing? No wires?"

"You're a real master of 21st century technology, aren't you, Tom? Yes, Virginia, there *is* a telecommunications revolution."

"Yeah? How come I can't read my favorite Robert Parker novel on some downloadable sheet of paper that I can roll up and stick in my back pocket, and it'll run for days without a recharge, and—"

"Any day now," my wife promised me. "Now don't distract me for a moment, dear. Do you have any idea where we should go, by the way?"

"If Share is in jail, and the girls are in Balwyn," I said, "s'pose that's the obvious destination."

"Okay."

Rain was easing a little, but the wipers still strobed droplets into the night. It was too early for the first dawn light. Not many other cars were on the road yet, but huge container trucks hurtled along the highway, exciting explosions of white light and crimson ringed with rain haloes. They were being driven by junkies insane with chronic speed. It cripples your brain, amphetamine does, something I learned by observation in the joint. It eats holes inside the parts of your head that are supposed to give you pleasure, something I learned on the Discovery Channel. What a pisser, eh. You throw the white pills down your throat year after year in the line of duty and profit until you're a crazed zombie, moving cargo for the men in neat shirts in bright large offices overlooking a kingdom of glass and steel. You drive hard for sixteen or twenty hours a day, you tear up and down vast endless lines of white in the bright sun and the dark of night, and all you get for it in the end is a pile of money you can't gain any value from because the soul's been eaten out of the middle of your head.

I shuddered. Drugs was something I'd never done, not much. Thank fuck for that, at least. I really needed to have a little talk to Animal before too long. Before it was entirely too late. If I could find some way to broach the topic without being a hideous old fart.

"Camel, camels," Juliet crooned. I glanced across at her intent face, lit by the pixels of the small handheld screen. There was a smile on her lovely unattainable face. "They wasted that poor camel, you know."

"Well, it was an accident, I heard. A bus load of nuns—"

"No, no, I mean the cops or the animal protection authorities or whoever it was. They just hauled the carcass off into quarantine and then buried it. Let it rot."

"Well, really, love, what do you suppose they should have done? Raffled it off in the local pub?"

"They could have cooked it."

I jerked back. "What, cut off its steaks and chops?"

"No, silly. Baked the animal. I have a recipe here."

"For a *whole camel?*"

"Yep. It's an old Saudi delicacy."

"You're shitting me."

"True dinks. Listen. It's in the *International Cuisine Cookbook.* Published by no less an authority than California's Home Economics Teachers."

"If you can't trust them, you can't trust anyone. This is some lunatic Intelligent Design outfit, right?"

"Certainly not." She was tapping and scrolling and chortling to herself. "Pay attention, Purdue. Keep this in mind for next time. You'll need to get in a bit more than your basic camel."

"Well, there's the stuffing," I surmised. We were bypassing the central city now, and light rose into the sky from hundreds of empty buildings. The sheer waste of electricity was staggering.

"Correct, M. Giradet. One lamb, large, cleaned, to shove inside the gutted camel. Twenty chickens, medium sized, featherless, to deposit within the lambkins. Sixty eggs, possibly from the same chickens."

"Great Scott. The mind reels. This is a feast fit for a... a..."

"A caliph," my bookish wife said. "The Saudis swear by it."

"It sounds rather weighted toward the protein end of the menu. Didn't Dr. Atkins die, though?"

"It's not really." Her thumb stroked the cursor. "There's the twelve kilos of rice and a couple of kilos each of almonds and pistachios. A well-full of pure water. Five pounds of black pepper." She burst out laughing suddenly.

"What."

"Salt," she said, eyes dancing at me in the mirror, "to taste."

I sniggered, although my attention was mostly on the road as we headed back into the suburbs. "You'd be eating leftovers for months."

"Well, it serves eighty to a hundred guests."

"I don't think I know that many people, Jules. Not well enough to invite them round for a lash-up baked camel."

"Poor boy." She patted my hand on the steering wheel. "See, if you'd stop hitting people and breaking their arms, you might have more friends."

I was gloomy, thinking about it. "I don't hit *that* many people. And they usually deserve it."

She fell silent, but I felt that she didn't really disagree. But then Juliet has a deep distaste for violence. Mauricio was stabbed next to the heart when she was twenty years old, before we met. She found him late at night after a drunken country dance on the raw soil outside their phoneless holiday shack, stretched out in a widening puddle of blood. Being the person she is, Jules failed to scream and faint and fall to the floor like the idiot women in movies, even though she's pretty enough to play one of those roles. Instead she plugged his wound with her scarf and ran half a mile to the nearest homestead, beat on the door until the old farmer opened up, tore through the house to the phone and called an air ambulance. They got her brother into emergency about ten minutes before his heart stopped. I'd heard the story more than once. It was a Cimino family favorite. Juliet had watched through a small observation window as they tried hopelessly to bring Mauricio back to life. Weeping, contained, she made a pact with God: let him live, and I will take a vow of celibacy. Her faith was powerful but not totally beyond reason. A moment later, she appended a codicil to her prayer: let him live, dear sweet Virgin Mary, and I will forego the joys of sex and parenthood for ten full years.

Through the glass, then, she'd heard a gurgling gasp from the table, a grunt from the doctor. Mauricio was back. God and his Mother had done their bit. Grimacing, she set about doing hers.

I met her a year later, when Mauricio was well and truly on his feet and up to his old tricks. Her beauty and intelligence dazzled me, sent my reason tottering. She revealed her quaint vow and I didn't care, not at the time, not for a time. There must have been something about me, and maybe my adorable little motherless girl, that appealed to Juliet as well. We married within the year, and slept celibate in separate beds until I couldn't stand it for one day more and moved away.

Something nibbled at my brain, and elsewhere.

I looked down furtively. I had an erection. I hunched deeper in the bucket seat and frowned at the road. Juliet, oblivious, hammered at the keyboard on her lap and peered through her glasses at the small Palm screen.

Something buzzed in my pocket.

"Yes, detective-sergeant?"

"You stole my phone, you light-fingered prick!"

I put on an aggrieved Cockney accent, while one sorrowful part of my mind tried not to imagine Juliet lightly fingering my prick. "It weren't me, guv. Guv'nor, I never done it!"

"Shut up, you retard. Division has reported a GBH at your last known location."

"No! Grievous bodily harm, that's terrible. Not at all the sort of thing you expect in a nice up and coming suburb like Williamstown. Oh, and I take it, therefore, that you're not totally bereft of phone links back to headquarters." I heard a strangled noise, like a walrus surfacing. "You should count yourself lucky, Rebeiro. No man should covet more than one telephone, it says so plainly there in the Ten Commandments and I speak as an authorized *feng shui* authority."

"A fractured wrist, Purdue. And a man with no nose—"

"I tell ya, I din't *do* that!"

"I know you didn't, you incorrigible arsehole. Muttonhead Lamb had his nose bitten off by a horse named Long and Cool at Flemington three years ago."

"'Incorrigible'? Have they sent you on a course recently?"

"A man without a nose who might end up without his balls. That was one brutal assault, Purdue."

"He rudely attacked a wife of mine. She defended her honor, and I applaud her initiative."

"You're not taking the fall for her? What happened to chivalry and good manners?"

Beside me, Juliet gasped.

"What?"

"Get off the phone, Tom. Cookie's sent me something extraordinary."

"The badinage is charming, Detective Rebeiro, but duty calls. Don't hesitate to contact us at a later date."

"My fucking *phone*—"

I clacked it shut, dropped it back in my pocket. "I intended to call Cookie earlier," I said, "but I forgot the number."

"You really have a deplorable memory, Tom. You should consider a course in Pelmanism."

"In *what?*"

"Damned if I know, it was one of the books I shepherded through Pen Inc but I wasn't going to waste my time *reading* it, was I?"

"Quite right. You mentioned Cookie. At this rate we'll be at the Lesser residence before I find out."

"She's weaseled out the source of the satellite images."

"I thought they scanned the whole planet."

"Don't be absurd, Sherlock. Those things are moving fast, they go around the whole planet in an hour and a half. Besides, they only capture a narrow swathe. No, some human operator was directing the lens. Cookie thinks she knows who."

"Maybe it was a coincidence. Maybe Google or something found those frames because she lucked out with the right search terms."

I was gratified by Juliet's glance of guarded approval.

"Not bad for a defrocked gumshoe. Nope. She managed to use much more powerful search engines to pull up the whole set. She and her pals in a great and powerful friendly nation."

"Shit, speak English, Mrs. Sherlock, wouldcha?"

"The opening frames show a paddock somewhere in the Dandenongs, judging from the positioning coordinate data. Stables, gravel drive apparently."

"Shangri-La," I said.

"Well, hardly that, but—"

"No, that's what it's called. What Share called it, anyway."

"Used for ajistment of horses, Cookie tells me."

"A home away from home for tired nags. Hence the stables."

"Just so. It's owned by House of Saud Investments, Ltd."

I was tooling fast up Doncaster, about to swing left along Bulleen Road. The Holden bounced a bit on the tram tracks but otherwise clung admirably to the road surface. Australia's own car, I thought with pride. Or was it made by the Japs now? Were they a great and powerful friendly nation? I couldn't remember the answer to either question. Really I'm not that patriotic. They didn't do a hell of a lot for me when I was stuck in Seattle shooting human growth hormone and lifting God's own pallet of weights each interminable day. They didn't even bother telling me my wife was pregnant.

I waited at the lights, and took the opportunity to stare at the small but perfectly formed Palm Pilot screen. Squinting, I saw a sequence of shots of something quadruped coming out from under a roof, a little thing mounting it, the animal moving into the paddock. Apparently it bolted, judging from its varied positions and attitudes in the next shots. A chopper descending into one corner of the frame. Then in the street. Along the highway, I guessed. A tragic incident with a bus. The rest I'd seen already.

The lights went green and I went with them, my mind dazed. I put my foot down and surged through the last of the failing rain. At this rate, Monday could turn out to be gorgeous. Melbourne weather, four seasons in a day.

A few cars were creeping onto the thoroughfare now, but the tram tracks were empty. I was dying for a McMuffin, and fries with that.

I turned into Sharon Lesser's street. No sign of a police car, but that just meant the cop on patrol was lying low. Either that or off slaking his hunger and thirst with an Egg McMuffin and Giant sized Coke. I pulled up a few houses short of the house.

"Not the Prince," I said speculatively. "Not the Sheikh himself, he wouldn't bother owning it. Culpepper. Wheeler & Dealer to the great and the potentially murderous."

"Now, now," my wife said, hammering away at the keyboard. "No need to tar a whole nation with the misdeeds of a few dozen well-heeled terrorists and a thousand richly funded madrasses teaching a vile and violent ideology and condemning any woman who dares to drive a car or speak to a man she's not married to or—"

"I see we're of one mind," I agreed. "But who was watching Culpepper's *pied á terre*, and why should the watchers care one hoot or sparrow fart in hell about a camel trotting around in the Dandenong mountains, for Christ's sake, or Allah's, or whatever the fuck?"

"Federal police." Juliet sat back from her keyboard looking pleased as punch, as happy as if she'd dug out the info herself. "And not just the usual lads in Canberra, it looks like the local equivalent of the NSA."

"The National Security Agency? In Maryland, right?"

"Spies to the world, yes. Or rather, on the world. The details were encrypted, of course, but Cookie turns out to be an ace when it comes to encryption."

"Should we get out and continue this conversation with our..." I trailed off, and found myself laughing. "The encrypted orca," I spluttered. "The orca in the crypt. My lord, I wonder if Culpepper has a sense of humor after all?"

"Sorry, Sherlock, I have no idea what you're babbling about." She turned to a look at her window. A tired cop in uniform was rapping at it. She ran down the glass. "Yes, officer?"

"I'll have to ask you what you're doing here?"

"Having a conversation with my husband. I believe that's still legal?"

"He's just keeping an eye on the grrls," I said soothingly to Jules, "and it's bloody late."

"Of course he is, and I shouldn't tease. Thank you, constable. I'm Juliet Cimino and this is my lawfully wedded, Recherché Purdue. You can check on the radio with HQ if you like, or ask Cookie if it's okay for us to come in. Jonquil Lesser, that is. The poor girl who was kidnapped."

The cop consulted a notebook, shielding it with a raincoated arm from the last of the drizzle. The pale sheets fluttered in the torch light. "That'll be fine, Madame, we have you listed here. Go ahead, please. Do you know you have a broken front right indicator lamp?"

Juliet squeezed her eyes together for a moment, but opened them brightly almost at once. "Thank you for that information, constable. I'll have it seen to the moment my local service station opens. And thank you for your consideration. Tom, let's not stand on ceremony."

The cop peered with renewed suspicion. "Hoy, you just told me his name was—"

"It's a long and tedious tale, officer," Jules said with an edge in her voice. "Sometimes he calls me Puss in Boots, sometimes I call him Recherché or Dangle Dick or—"

The cop drew back, face reddened even in the first dim light of dawn. Perhaps it was just the pink edge of sky on his youthful cheeks. "Good morning, then, Mrs. Purdue. Have a nice day."

Gnashing her teeth in a minimal way, Juliet went ahead of me into the enclosed porch where two days earlier a man had been shot to death by his wife while I slept in her bed. I followed docilely, not wanting to give Jules any ideas along the same lines. I had the Esky firmly in my left hand. I wasn't going to let the damned thing out of my sight.

"No ferocious guard dogs, I hope?"

I searched my memory for scraps of drunken conversation. "She used to have a pair of pitbulls."

My tremendously brave wife drew back, looked alarmed. "*Used to have?*"

"Yeah, fear not, they were put down on council instructions after the filthy things burrowed out and savaged a passer-by."

"Lovely family," Juliet said. She stepped into the porch and rang the doorbell.

It was odd, actually. As a kid in Eltham I always had dogs. The place was more like a farm than a twentieth century suburban sub-division, although a rather inefficient and stupidly designed one, organized around the principles of cosmical energy and cow horns filled with pig shit and baked in the earth by the light of the moon. After I left home there never seemed to be time or space for the kind of big dog I wanted, a Border Collie or German Pointer. A Spotted Dick appealed to me, a Dalmation, but they were complete fools in a domestic setting. Well, so were the others. Maybe it was the same for Jules, I'd never seen her with either a cat or a dog. She'd slaked her companion needs upon her Sicilian family, upon me for a while, and Annabelle. Until Annabelle turned on her in adolescence. On all of us.

"You bastard," Animal said to me, looking over Juliet's shoulder from the opened door. It was a different Animal from the one in Culpepper's limo. Short attention span, these kids. "You let Sappho run away. Into Sydney Road. I had to chase her."

"I know it's late, sweetheart, but if your attitude doesn't improve I'm going to have to... to..."

"Smack me around a bit?"

I'd never touched the child in her life, not once.

"...To cut back on your allowance," I said feebly.

But I was talking to her black-clad back. We went into the brightly lighted tasteful hallway, followed her around a corner into an abruptly gloomy part of the Lesser household I'd never seen before. The décor came straight from *Suicide Girl* magazine.

Two other young women in whiteface and vampire attire perched on elegant steel and leather chairs against one wall. They stared at us from mascara-rimmed eyes then looked at each other.

"Where's Ruby?"

"Grime's with Share," Animal said. She twisted her hands. "It wasn't her fault. And she did kill the prick."

"We haven't really been introduced," I said to Cookie.

Jonquil Lesser sprawled in a giant bed, propped by ergonomic pillows. A large flat screen monitor was cantilevered in front of her out from the wall, and she tapped with her small fat hands at a keyboard that seemed to have had its back broken. When I looked closer it made better sense. The plastic and metal formed a shallow V pointing at her navel, so each pudgy arm came at its half of the alphabet at a right angle. I wondered why she hadn't acquired one for her Brunswick bedroom. Still settling in there, maybe. To her left a tall, wide rustic nightstand was crammed with treats: giant-sized Cherry Ripes in their crimson foil covers, a packet of Tim Tam chocolate biscuits and some Iced Vovos in a plastic bowl, the empty box from a big burger, a Mr. Coffee machine and a large mug with an elongated smiley face with huge UFO eyes.

She looked up and her smile was wonderfully, surprisingly sweet.

"Thanks for getting me away from that bastard," she said. "Sorry I was such a shit."

"Well, the coffin didn't look all that comfortable," I said, and held out my hand. That made her blink, but she took it as if she were unfamiliar with the custom of shaking hands, and held it for a moment.

"You're Animal's Mum, right," she said past me. "Congratulations on cracking my password."

"She is bloody *not*," my daughter said. "Me Mum's dead. *She's* some Mafia moll."

Juliet had been through a long, trying day and half the night. While I've never touched my child, I understood perfectly when Juliet turned on her heel and slapped Animal once, hard. Echoes jumped back from the deep purple walls. I understood, but I squeezed my eyes shut for a moment.

When I opened them, Animal was standing stock-still holding one hand to her cheek, looking utterly astonished. The two vampires watched in bloodless silence.

"Well, shit," she said. "Okay." She turned and left the room.

"Don't mind her," Cookie said. "Animal's having her period. She's always a bitch then."

I blinked again. Wasn't that the vilest sexist remark anyone could make these days? Was there *no* sacred violation these Goth grrls would leave unspoken? Well, maybe one.

"You'll be from the Vagilantes, I assume," I said to the vampires. "Incest Vengeance R Us, right?"

They slitted their eyes.

"That's Rommie and Immie," Cookie said from her high blanketed perch. "They're experiencers too. This is Mr. Animal and his wife," she told the vampires.

"Tom," I said, "and actually that's Purdue. And this is Juliet. But that's not Purdue."

"G'day," said Rommie.

Incest *experiencers*, I thought. Not *victims*, that was too demeaning and disempowering. Drains the agency away from the child and hands it to the brutalizer. It made sense. But some unyielding Eltham runaway part of me that can't stand PC claptrap thought that it was powerlessness that was exactly the vilest crime of incest, that it does suck away the kid's agency and sense of self. "So you're both... *living with incest*," I said.

I regretted it the moment the gibe was out of my mouth, but the grrls just gazed at me with unmodulated loathing. I got a sharp stormy look of warning from Jules. "Okay," I said, shaking my head. "Rodolph Lesser absolutely deserved what he got, but I'm glad as hell that you young women had nothing to do with it. They still can't lock you up for what you're *thinking*, at least in Australia. Going to jail for years isn't recommended, trust me."

"You can get Share off, right?" Cookie gazed at me doubtfully. "You can prove she didn't do it?"

"The cops are pretty sure she did do it," I said. "Me too. Sorry."

"Has she got good legal representation?" Juliet asked. "We'll arrange an excellent lawyer for her if she hasn't—"

"Guy called Muldoon."

"He'll do," I said. I'd heard he was drinking with a higher grade of cop than the vice squad these days. I hoped Sharon Lesser's funds wouldn't be attached by the court until after the disposition of the trial. For sure Rudolph's insurance policies would all be voided the moment the beneficiary was convicted of murdering the client. They hate that. "Cookie—Do you mind if we call you Cookie?"

"It's my name, I loathe Jonquil, always did."

"Okay." I hoisted the Esky off the floor, propped it on the edge of the bed. "You know what this is?" I popped the clamps. White fumes rushed from it, freezing cold in the conditioned air of the bedroom. I fished out my handkerchief and Rebeiro's phone fell on the carpeted floor. I left it there, wrapped my fingers in the handkerchief, dragged out the ziploc with its solid slab of flesh, held it high. "I hope you're not a vegetarian."

"I am, but I'm not planning to eat that thing. Yeah, it's the tongue they cut off Nile Fever."

"And it's so important why? People have been badly hurt to get hold of this gruesome thing. Makes no sense. Nile Fever was a burned out nag your foster-mother bought from the knacker's yard and tried to pass off as a sprinter."

"No she wasn't."

"Yes she was, Cookie. Sorry, I was there. You can't see it in those digital pics from the satellite because we were under the stable roof, but I fitted up that poor animal with a sugar drip. Sharon paid me to do it. Nile was a worthless piece of catfood without her boost."

Cookie gazed back at me with satisfaction. Queen of the hacker grrls. Couldn't blame her.

"Nile Fever was worth millions, Mr. Purdue. She was one of a kind. Still is."

"She's dead and buried, and you're not going to get her back from this slab of gristle."

In a sort of sigh, touched by sudden insight and understanding, Juliet said, "Oh my dear god. Yes they will."

The vampire grrls smirked. They knew already.

I sure as shit didn't.

"The Saudis wanted to clone her," Cookie told me in a forgiving tone. Her fingers clattered on the keyboard and stringy images of multi-colored sausages opened on the big screen. "So do some people from the UAE. That's the United Arab Emirates."

"They still do," Animal said. I hadn't noticed her return to the room. "She's a super-camel."

"Was," Immie said from her steel chair, shaking her head. "Was. They always kill the thing they love."

We all stared at her for a moment, considering this absurd piece of poetical wisdom. Rommie nodded, she'd heard that too. I cleared my throat.

"Share imported a super-camel, whatever that is, from the middle of a war zone, yes, that makes a lot of sense. Then she got me to dope it with a crude race track technique, so she could sell it back to some prince of the desert?"

"They're chromosomes, aren't they?" Juliet said, ignoring me. On the screen, the sausages squirmed. Alongside them, a window opened up with endless lists of letters pouring down it at high speed. Just four letters, stuck together every possible way. UUAC-GGTCTTCAAGTCA. On and on. "Ah yes, Genome Project," my wife said happily.

"They've been mapping lots of animals now the Human Genome is completed," Cookie said. "The rat and the dog were done a while back."

"And now the Saudis have done the camel," I said.

"Yes, but that's not where I found this dataset. There's a department of CSIRO that's cloning endangered species. They've been working on camels."

The Aussie science research heavies? Shit. "You mean the camel was nicked from a *government research center?*"

"I think it's a sort of corporation these days, Tom," Juliet told me. "Has a Minister of the Commonwealth in charge, though. What they used to call a quango."

"Isn't that an endangered species from Rottnest Island?"

"That's a quocka, you fool. A quasi-non-governmental something or other. Nominally independent."

"Oh." I do like having my mind improved.

"Let's say 'borrowed' rather than 'nicked'," Cookie said, after waiting for us to finish our loveplay. I felt she might have a future in diplomacy. She'd need to shed a few kilos, though, or air travel was out. "Rudolph's dear friend Culpepper has his ways and means." She was snarling. "Pity she didn't blow *his* head off while she was at it."

"He's on his way to the lock-up even as we speak," I told her with considerable satisfaction. "Of course the bastard will be sprung the moment his Q.C. arrives. Or one of the legal minions, more likely. At least that won't be until noon."

"He'll get a rude shock next time he looks for his gambling software." A kind of contained rage flushed Cookie's slabs of chubby cheeks. I had a mournful image of her lying in the blackness amid her own stinking wastes. Culpepper must have thought it was his perfect opportunity—scare off Cookie and make a point to Sharon Lesser in one blow. What a damned fool. "I've deleted the lot. Then I've hunted down his backup codes and poisoned them. Prick. Fucking prick."

"Sharon didn't choose her men wisely," Juliet said.

"Don't look at me that way," I said. "There was nothing between us."

"Not even a sheet," Juliet hissed. The vampires watched this adult badinage in disgust.

"Jesus, Jules, I was pissed as a newt. I mean, I didn't even hear the gun go off." Except, I realized, as a nightmare memory of Mauricio smashing his bloody enormous truck through my front door. Fuck, I still didn't even have a place to lie my head down. And I badly needed to. I was grainy with exhaustion.

"I'm sure the court will listen to your explanation with the greatest interest," Juliet said. "But Cookie, why would anyone want to *clone* the creature? Why not put it out to the stud or whatever they call it in the racing game? Breed from it?"

"That's the long and tedious way," Cookie told her. "Nobody does that any more, especially in Saudi. No one wants to tie up their prime racing animals for a few years having babies. They harvest the ova."

"Ah. *In vitro* fertilization."

"Test tube camels," Immie said in a high silly voice, and started giggling.

"Carried in the womb by more contented camel cows, yes, I get that. But," I said loudly, to show that I'd caught up and even jumped ahead a move or two with my brilliant detective *feng shui* mind, "nobody from the Commonwealth Scientific and Bloody Industrial Organization was planning to *race* Nile Fever, were they? Here or abroad."

"Wouldn't work, *in vitro* from her ova. She was a mule," Juliet said. "Right?"

"Sterile, yep." The images on the screen jumped back and forth, and the cursor highlighted stretches of colored sausage. It was all just an abstract display of the butcher's red-lit meat tray to me. "See? They've used knock-in genes at these loci." Cookie sent me a long-suffering glance for the slow of thinking and the terminally ignorant. "Knock-in's the opposite of knock-out, see?"

"You can't knock Nile up because someone knocked her in," I said, and smiled modestly.

"Knocked her extra genes in, anyway." I looked across the room in surprise. That had been Animal. She was sulky still but her eyes showed some life for a change. "It's real interesting, dad. You get these genes for fast muscles and big lungs and blood, and that, and you glue them in. Once in a blue moon it works and you've got a super-camel."

"But chances are it's sterile."

"They love screwing around with female bodies," Rommie said. "Humans, animals, it doesn't matter."

It seemed like a fair point, although I've heard that most of the lab techs are women themselves. I stretched and took a step back, treading with a crunch on Rebeiro's phone. I bent and picked it up. It was made of sterner stuff than any I'd seen recently, and only a small portion of plastic was snapped off. The machine blinked at me in a deep blue request for attention. I put it back in my pocket. "So Nile can't—couldn't—have any little baby camels. And you reckon they're up to speed enough with cloning to make a duplicate or two?"

"Maybe not yet," Cookie said. "but any day now."

"Nobody bothered telling Share," I said.

"Rodolph the bastard and Culpepper knew," Animal said. "Lesser thought it up, I reckon. Share probably thought it was just an ordinary camel brought in from Central Australia. That's what she told me, anyway. Dunno if Wozza and Mutt knew."

"Woz must have known something," I said, "or he wouldn't have hacked the creature's tongue out. I hope Nile was dead already."

"If he already knew, why didn't he just take a buccal swab from its mouth?"

"A what?"

Juliet glanced at the Esky. "You don't need a bloody great lump of meat to make a clone. A scrap of DNA is all you want. You can get it by running a cotton bud inside someone's cheek." She met my disbelieving gaze. "I edited that Scottish guy's book, Tom. The Dolly the Sheep man?"

"Oh, all right. Maybe Wozza didn't fancy sticking his hand inside a camel's gob. She'd take it off at the wrist with one chomp."

"A blood sample would do as well."

"Uh oh." A mental movie slotted into my head, running in fast forward. Wozza and Muttonhead messing with the bloody sugar-drip needle. Mutt slipping something into his pocket and clambering up behind the hump. Racket of chopper. Thrown to the ground. I could almost hear the crackle of broken plastic. So some of the blood on his tattered riding silks wasn't human. Simple thugs that they were, taking off after to the runaway animal with boxcutters probably seemed a really smart salvaging move once Mauricio put them on the trail. The dry ice surprised me though. Probably Culpepper's superior suggestion, after they'd got it home with their cold beer. "Never mind. Why did the idiots put the thing in my storage unit?"

"They didn't," Animal said. "They gave it to Mauricio, and he gave it to Maeve and Vinnie to hold for him, and me and Grime needed your key anyway to hide the shotgun—"

"Which had never been fired."

"He was already fuckin *dead* when we got here," Rommie said, aggrieved and defensive. "We *woulda* done it."

"So Maeve took the Esky along at the same time, I guess, for safe keeping, the dear silly old thing," Animal suggested. "She probably thinks there's fish in it."

"No," I said, remembering the few words I'd trolled out of her on Mauricio's borrowed phone, "no, she knew something all right. She knew it was a tongue." But there was no telling how *much* she knew of what that meant. Not much. Not very much at all. About anything, really. I sighed. "I'm about to fall over and go to sleep on the carpet," I started to say.

"You can't sleep here," Animal told me, in a strong return to form.

"I have no intention of doing so." I went to the heavily-curtained window, pulled back the drape. A sickly gray light crawled in. It looked as drab as I felt. I watched the cop walking by, miserable in his rain-proof coat but at least the rain had stopped. Maybe that was his relief in the car pulling up across the street. "You grrls will be okay," I said. "Mr. Plod is just outside if you run into any more trouble."

"Mr. who?" said Immie.

Animal looked at her in surprise. "Mr. Plod. From Enid Blyton?"

Then her pale face blushed all the way up to her shaved awful scalp. Tough vampire grrls aren't supposed to retain fond memories of their daddy reading them gaudy old books about Noddy and Mr. Plod and especially, her favorite, the Magic Far-Away Tree.

"That's all right, Annabelle," I told her reassuringly, and kissed her on one metal-knobbed cheek as she cringed away. "I'll never tell."

The clouds were gone. I yawned, my shoulders cracking. I was still walking with a limp, lugging the piece of dead camel. It was starting to feel like an albatross. Daylight brightened perceptibly. The air smelled fresh.

"You reckon you'll be sleeping at my place, do you?" Juliet said. Her tone seemed odd. We leaned on either side of the ute's tray. More large heavy cars stood parked across from the Holden ute than I remembered. You couldn't see through their tinted windows. Oh well, it was only a matter of time before we were picked up. I ignored them and so did Juliet.

"Well, it's that or at the People's Palace." God bless the Salvation Army, I thought. "Wait a minute, Mauricio said he had something lined up for me." I found Rebeiro's phone and flicked it to life. Surprisingly, it was still active. What a gentleman. I'd have had the connection cancelled. Maybe there were too many other things on his mind, not least Francis Stonecraft, Q.C., and the brute's entire high-octane law chambers. "What's Uncle Morry's number, Jules?"

"*Uncle Morry?*"

"That's what my daughter with the engaging hair style calls him."

"That's all right, then." She gave it to me and I punched it in. "You do know it's six in the morning."

"Bastard sleeps too much any way. Oh, it's you, Mauricio. This is Roderick from Fit as a Fiddle. How are you today?"

"You rotten knob, Purdue. I just got to sleep. What cunt gave you this number?"

"Please don't refer to your sister that way. Her prayers saved your worthless hide once."

"Yeah, right, sorry." That actually gave him pause. He brightened. "Hey, fuck-knuckle, did I tell you I've found that great

place for you, come by sometime and you can have the key. For a
month, mate, the owner's... away, you know?"

"Yeah, I have a parking spot with a man in the same holiday
destination. Where's the pad, my man?"

"You'll love it, I was trying to tell you earlier, right near your
place, it'll bring back memories."

I started to laugh and couldn't stop until a gob of spit caught in
my throat. Juliet watched me, puzzled but starting to grin from the
contagion of it. "You bastard! You've got me a unit in..."

"Pentridge Village, mate. Between Governor's Road and Quarry
Circuit. It's right across from the Father Brosnon Community
Park."

I wheezed for a while and wiped tears from my eyes. "Okay,
mate, you're a prince," I said. I put the pilfered phone back in my
pocket, found my wife's car keys and threw them across the top of
the cabin to her, and put my hand to the passenger door.

A large heavy man in a boring suit climbed out of the car in
front and marched toward the Lesser driveway, followed by two
other large heavy men in boring suits from the back seat. A large
heavy hand grabbed my wrist from behind and a second plucked
the Esky away. Christ, they were everywhere.

"It's the Invasion of the Body Snatchers," I shouted to Juliet.
"Run for your life. They'll steal your very soul!" I spun around
with my spare fist pulled back but instantly thought better of it. I
could have decked one of them but where was the percentage? No
point in an extra charge of resisting arrest. Besides, my hip was
giving me hell. I leaned back against the tray of the ute.

"That's private property," I said. "Give it back."

"It's property of the Government of Australia," the federale
told me. He kept his grip on my wrist and marched me back to his
car. Another of the drab fellows was inviting my wife to assist the
Federal Police with their enquiries. She was coming quietly. Very
sensible.

From the corner of one eye, I saw the Lesser door being cracked
open by a large heavy shoulder, and a distant hoarse voice from
the porch calling, "Seize *all* the computers, software, ancillaries,
peripherals and phone equipment. CDs. Floppies. Paper. Don't
forget the Palm PAs." I paused, jerking my custodian's arm, and
watched in admiration as this crack team vanished through the

front door and three dark ninja Goth grrls squirted out the back way and over the side fence like drops of oily sweat from a bad conscience.

"Poor Cookie," I called to Juliet. "On a hiding to nothing."

"Life's a gamble," Juliet said.

The Federal Police didn't read us any rights, because this was the land of the only nominally free, not the United States of America where on Australian TV every night of the week they do things differently and according to the Constitution. We both were herded into the same back seat from opposite doors and sat comfortably together. I heard the boot slam as the last vital, if cryogenic, portion of Nile Fever was locked away. Unless they had samples stored in the lab. Well, of course they did, I realized. The idea wasn't to recover Nile's pacy being from this particular scrap of tongue but to stop anyone else trying and maybe succeeding. Sheikh Abdul bin Sahal al Din, for example. The tongue would be in a furnace before noon.

May her cells revive, I thought sentimentally. May a hundred sprightly young camels burst forth from a hundred homely camel host wombs, bearing her likeness from their twisted and infertile but athletically gifted DNA. I wouldn't have laid odds that they'd be champions, though. There's more to a man or a camel than their genes. Look at Mauricio and Juliet, for example. Same parents, I assumed—a safe assumption unless the sainted mother had conceived miraculously, and they weren't doing *in vitro* when Mauricio was a fetus. Same upbringing, more or less, allowing for gender. And look at them now. Not so much chalk and cheese as rough red rotgut and Penfold Grange Hermitage 1955.

"I was hoping to meet the Sheikh and his wives," Juliet told me. "His wives, anyway. An odd way to live. Horrible, really."

"Well, at least they'd get some sex occasionally."

"None of that filth in my authorized vehicle, mate," the federale said, accelerating smartly toward the city. An early morning tram was just nosing toward us in the brightening light. We passed a pair of golden arches, and my stomach cried out for an Egg Mc-Muffin.

"And children," Juliet said wistfully.

"Unlike poor old sterile Nile Fever," I said. I watched the morning's first joggers and rebuked myself for a lazy slackarse. It'd been days since I'd had a decent workout. Aside from the dip at the nude beach. I tried to sniff at my armpit without being obvious.

"Musky," Juliet said.

"I was afraid 'stinky' was the word."

"Musky," she said, and somehow she was a little closer, even with our seat belts and her vow of celibacy holding us apart. "I think it's nice."

"Jesus, you two, knock it off," the cop said.

"We're man and wife," I said frostily. "And the two shall cleave together and be one flesh, it's in the Bible."

"Never read it," he said. "I'm a Buddhist." It's a multicultural force, and good on it, I say.

"Yeah, poor old Nile," I said, leaning a bit further toward the center of the seat. I could smell her now as well. "I suppose a fuck was always out of the question for her."

"For her," Juliet agreed. Her lips looked oddly damp, and in the morning daylight her eyes were darker than usual and glistened in a way I hadn't seen for years. "Not necessarily for everyone."

"Steady *on*, I say," the cop said.

"Jesus, Jules," I said. We were coming out of the suburbs and headed fast toward Latrobe Street in the city proper, where the Federal cops hang their hats. In fact they rarely wear hats these days, but you'd never mistake them for a businessman or a lawyer, not even the lawyers among their number. "What about the sacred vow? How about your promise to God and the Virgin Mary."

"You incredible fuckwit," she said. "You really have no idea of the passage of time, do you?"

I blinked. Something troubled me but I couldn't put my finger on it. Then again I've had a few blows to the head in my time. "Ten years," I said. "Good Christ, your Mauricio miracle happened ten years ago."

"Nine years, eleven months, and twenty three days," my wife said lasciviously. "Can you wait eight more days?"

"My bloody oath," I said, and squeezed her hand for all I was worth.

LaVergne, TN USA
21 September 2010
197886LV00001B/81/P